# Riddle Me A Fish

Joan K. Wallis

PublishAmerica
Baltimore

This is a work of fiction. All the characters and most of the places are fictitious. Any actual places are used fictitiously.

First printing

ISBN: 1-4137-0312-7
PUBLISHED BY PUBLISHAMERICA, LLLP
www.publishamerica.com
Baltimore

Printed in the United States of America

To Doug, who makes it all possible.

# Acknowledgements

To Barb, Sandy, Rhian, Nancy and Rosemary,
for their encouragement and laughter

# RIDDLE - ME - REE

*Riddle me a secret, a fish for a locket.*
*What is the meaning? Nothing in my pocket.*
*Riddle me an insect, amber sealed stigma.*
*Bloodline? Lifeline? Spiracle enigma.*
*Riddle me a fish with a golden fetter.*
*What is the meaning? What is in the letter?*
*Riddle me a secret, one or the other,*
*I know where they found me, but where is Mother?*

# CHAPTER 1

It was an unlikely setting for intrigue and mystery. Certainly, neither of the two women in the small office had any idea of the strange new element about to enter their lives. Business that Tuesday morning had been like any other day in early May, which is to say not very brisk. A high-pressure system, straight from Hudson's Bay, leaned heavily on Nova Scotia, sending all the clouds scurrying to empty themselves over Newfoundland. The sky was clear, bright with a brittle sunshine. Here in the sheltered streets of the little town of Calderford there was a promising early warmth, foretelling the warmer days to come, but there was nothing to suggest what else might come with those warm summer days. The two women, one irritable, the other wary, were locked in a dialogue only too familiar to both of them. Spring sunlight filtering patchily through the cluttered window, cast dappled shadows over the quiet room.

"It won't do, Mattie! It just won't do! I have to ask myself whether you are at all suited to the work. I've seen your diplomas, and you say you are interested in houses, but really! You seem to frighten all your clients away. None of them ever come back. I mean, you've been here three months now. I was better off on my own!"

"I know I haven't sold any property yet, Mrs. Oxner, but I am more than willing to learn and I do all the office work."

"Pooh! I could do that with one hand! I always have. No, my dear, you're just too soft, that's all there is to it, a pushover." Her expression was a blend of contempt and exasperated affection. "I expected more fight in someone with your background. I was in foster care too, don't forget. I know what it's like. You must learn to *exert* yourself. Keep your elbows out."

Beth Oxner pumped her arms back and forth, as though she could literally drive her message home, like a busy little steam engine.

"See what can be done with a little effort?"

Looking round her office in self-congratulation, Beth adjusted the underpinning of her magnificent bosom, with which she liked to gesticulate to emphasise a point. Her dark, silver-streaked hair was immaculate, as was her purple wool suit. Her predilection for diamonds shone on her plump, managing hands, their sparkle giving her a sorely needed sense of worth and self-esteem. Indeed her continual criticism of Mattie stemming from her own ingrained uncertainties and deficiencies often drove her to extremes that she seemed unable to control. She lived, crustacean-like, within a shell of bravado.

"I am," said her outfit, "a successful business woman. Don't mess with me."

Very few people had even tried, as she worked and schemed to turn the small real-estate agency that she had run with her late husband, into a successful one-woman business. Remembering how she and Alec had struggled for all those years, she stood quietly, pretending to study the listings.

*Poor Alec,* she thought, her expression softening with love and regret. *He didn't live long enough to enjoy it.*

Her eyes turned back to her assistant, sitting disconsolately at the computer.

*She is so like Alec!* Beth marvelled, not for the first time. *I'm too hard on her.* Compassionately she studied the downcast face.

"Never mind," she said consolingly. "It's early days yet, you know. You'll soon get the hang of it." Then, annoyed with herself at this change of tone, she added severely. "Just buck your ideas up though, Miss Peters."

Mattie Peters, general dogsbody and aspiring saleswoman, fully appreciated the chance being given to her by Mrs. Oxner, all the more so because she knew herself to be lacking in drive. Never having had a home or family of her own made her all the more determined to find the perfect house for each home owner, quite overlooking the fact that people always want more than they can possibly afford. Inability to suggest a suitable compromise always led to dissatisfaction, both for the customer and for herself. Now, seeing Beth Oxner's expression, she smiled apologetically, promising to "try harder." Knowing that her new employer was ignorant of all her qualifications made her both uncomfortable and self-conscious, but it was sometimes better not to appear too clever. Mattie had learned this a long time ago.

*It's probably her colouring that reminds me of Alec,* reflected Beth. *Or maybe her gentle manner. Poor Alec! I do miss his common sense.* Covertly over a file she continued to study her assistant, busy now with the listings. *She looks like a sepia print, or one of those old photographs.*

Quite unaware of the scrutiny, Mattie moved between the filing cabinet and the computer, which she was updating. Two or three inches over middle height, her movements were graceful and unstudied, her whole appearance one of moderation and understatement but with the promise of a lamp yet to be lit. Only her smile, warm and generous, held any real attraction. Unfortunately Mattie had very little to smile about.

An uncomfortable silence fell on the little office. Dust motes danced in the sunlight, struggling through the photographs in the window. Every small sound, exaggerated by the quietness, escalated the feeling of tension.

*Why do I do it?* Beth asked herself. *I always speak so sharply, I'm becoming a real Mrs. Know-it-all. She has to learn, just as I did, and* I *had Alec to help me.*

It was with relief that she saw the hands of the clock creep round to mid-day and the escape that lunch hour provided. Rising to leave, she changed her mind on seeing Mattie's hang dog appearance.

"I know, why don't you take first lunch?" Her voice was friendly and gracious until she promptly spoiled it by adding briskly. "Mind you are back by one, and *eat* something, for goodness sake!"

This last, in a raised voice, caused Mattie to scurry self-consciously out of the door. Beth sagged back in her chair.

*That didn't come out as I meant it, at all! I'm getting to be a cranky old woman. I don't know what to do for the best. I really don't want to let Mattie go.* She sighed as she checked her accounts for the last quarter. *It doesn't help that Emily Hiltz owes me two months rent, either. I doubt that she has more than three or four customers a week.*

Emily Hiltz, a fluttering and vapourish fifty-seven, ran Busy Hands, the dispirited little craft shop adjoining Oxner's Real Estate. The tired and dusty window display was quite enough to discourage customers, the Christmas crafts being by now almost four months out of date.

*I believe she just hangs on so that she can keep an eye on things. She certainly loves to gossip, poor old thing.*

She sighed again, more deeply, remembering Emily's face watching her from behind a violently coloured crocheted throw. "Just the thing for Granny's Christmas," the tag proclaimed, though obviously no one had agreed.

Mattie, knowing nothing of Beth's troubles, thankfully left the office behind, crossed Main Street, and went up The Snicket to her apartment over the bookstore, Once Read Books. Horatio Bean, the owner, known familiarly as "Bookie' Bean, had his nose buried in a book as usual, so she managed to slip upstairs without disturbing him, her thoughts running in a familiar groove.

*I wonder whether the whole thing is a wild goose chase? How likely is it I could possibly trace my family if the authorities can't?*

The last six months had been full of disappointment, and Mattie's mood was despondent. Slathering peanut butter on a piece of whole wheat bread, spreading it meagrely with grape jelly, and grabbing a banana, she slumped into her one comfortable chair.

*I'm probably wasting my time. After all, next February I shall be twenty-four. Perhaps I should give up the whole idea. It's just as likely that they are in Ontario somewhere, or anywhere in the world, for that matter.*

Chomping stolidly on the unwanted sandwich, Mattie stared bleakly out of the window looking out on the car park of the Save Easy, the local supermarket.

*Maybe I should go back to Ontario and start over again. But even that seems pointless! No one in Atterbury knew anything, not even the vicar.*

Her eyes filled briefly with tears at the thought of Kendrick Gibson's kindness and generosity. *He is – was – the nearest thing to family after all. Why go back, now he is dead? No, I will stay a little longer, but my funds are getting dangerously low.No one can live for ever on peanut butter!*

Usually heedless of her appearance, she happened to glance in the bathroom mirror, as she freshened up for work.

*Just look at me! My hair is like old rope! I really must do something about it. Even brushing would help! Oh Lord, now I'm going to be late.*

Hurrying downstairs, she waved shyly at Horatio Bean as she left, arriving back in the office with ten minutes to spare, looking pale, anxious, and out of breath.

"You needn't have hurried after all!" Beth cried. "I grabbed a take-away at Tim Horton's. Want a 'Tim-Bit'?"

She was offering a box of the delicious and disastrously fattening little doughnuts, each not much bigger than a large walnut, but promising a moment or two of delight. Mattie took a couple from the carton, her face flushing with pleasure at the friendly gesture.

"Why, thank you, Mrs. Oxner! They are good, aren't they? I think I still like the plain ones best."

It was like a breaking of bread, a peace offering, and they munched away contentedly

*So I haven't quite forgotten how*, Beth reflected, tidying away the crumbs and opening a window to freshen the air. As though her gesture of good will had produced immediate results, she saw someone inspecting the photograph display, then heading for the office door.

"Here comes a client now! Look lively!"

She surged forward hopefully, bosom out-thrust as though in welcome, assessing the unpromising woman coming through the door, bringing with her a sudden chill, and this in spite of the warm sunshine outside. The shadow cast by the light behind her gave an illusion of filling the whole office with darkness, making her expression unreadable.

"May I help you?" asked Beth, acquisitive instincts disguised by an engaging cock of the head. As the newcomer's shuttered, bespectacled gaze turned towards her, Beth fell back a step, hands clammy, hair prickling in the nape of her neck, overwhelmed by a sudden cold feeling of loss, almost of fear. Recovering shakily, retreating behind her desk, she fixed a stiff smile on her face, gathering herself together.

"My assistant here will be happy to answer any inquiries. She has just re-organised our lists, and I am busy, very busy."

To prove her point she shuffled some papers about, furtively mopping her hands on her slacks, turning as ever to Alec's ghost for comfort.

*My God, Alec, what now? I'm babbling! Is my reason going, or is it my heart?*

Alas! Alec was silent.

Bewildered, Mattie looked up at the benignly smiling prospective client coming towards her, and taking a chair by the desk. Never had Beth passed a client over to her before.

*She must suspect that there isn't much hope of a sale,* Mattie thought, with an unaccustomed cynicism, as if the chill in the room had given a bite to her tongue, then adding more charitably. *Maybe she isn't feeling well. She certainly doesn't look it.*

Giving the client several listings to consider, she went over to Beth.

"Do you want a coffee, Mrs. Oxner? I am just about to take one to the customer."

"*Client*, Miss Peters, *client,* not customer! This isn't a shop," Beth admonished her.

There, that felt better! She was regaining her old form. "Yes, a coffee would be just the thing. Now, see what you can do with her. I feel she isn't my type of client." Repressing a shudder, she added brusquely, "Don't forget, 'pushover'."

"Oh! I am sure the young lady will do just fine," said a voice over her shoulder. Beth, not intending to be overheard, stood up flushing with embarrassment, annoyance, and an overwhelming need to escape.

"If you would be so good as to excuse me, I must leave at once," she said, rising abruptly. "A client, you know – yes, a client." Groping for a good reason, she grasped Emily Hiltz. "I need to see my tenant next door! I'll leave you to it."

Blindly looking at her watch and snatching up a jacket and brief case, she hurried out of the door, only to walk aimlessly towards the Save Easy, confused and angry, before she felt able to confront Emily Hiltz about the rent. As Beth fled, the elderly woman watched her with satisfaction, amused that she had been given such a wide berth, then followed Mattie to her desk,

"Let me introduce myself. My name is Miss Anahita Waters."

As she gave her name, she looked closely at Mattie, gauging her reaction. Indeed 'Anahita' is an unusual name for anyone, but particularly for this stooped and elderly woman. It was difficult to judge her size, enveloped as she was in a loose grey woollen coat against the weather of an uncertain Nova Scotian Spring. Removing her headscarf, she smoothed back her wavy white hair, coiled loosely in the nape of her neck. Her eyes, screened by large tinted glasses, studied Mattie carefully as though looking for signs of recognition. On the whole, she had more the appearance of an applicant for assistance than a house purchaser.

*Someone's elderly aunt, poor old soul,* thought Mattie, noting the fine lines etched on the customer's delicate skin. These, combined with her drab outfit and stooped shoulders, gave an impression of dependence, of being in need of help. Anna Waters's smile changed from benign to guarded, as she peered at the card on Mattie's desk.

"Miss Peters? Your name is Miss Peters? Well, Miss Peters, I like the look of this property, 'The Old Mill'. It looks very pretty, and secluded."

"Oh! That's been empty for ages!" Mattie said, astonished that anyone should want it, adding hurriedly as she suddenly remembered 'pushover', "It is very lovely though, a very lovely place. I would be happy to take you over to see it."

Once outside, Miss Waters looked doubtfully at Mattie's old car, the venerable Toyota in which Mattie had driven across from Ontario the previous fall.

"We'll take mine," she decided, heading for a smart red Subaru Outback. "Four-wheel drive, you see, for the country roads."

"Are you returning to the office, Miss Waters, or shall I follow you in my car?"

"Oh! you'll come with me, of course. I'll see you home safely, never worry." The tone was authoritative.

Mattie surprised herself by feeling resentful. *Another managing woman like Beth,* she thought, fastening her seat belt and starting to give directions. *Mrs. Oxner is right, I let myself be pushed about these days. I can't think what has come over me.*

"We're in The Snicket now, Miss Waters. Turn left on to School Street, then right on to River Road. Now, turn sharp left at St. James Church and take the bridge on your left, over the Calder River. Then go up the Hestler Road and straight ahead to the Gravel Pit Road. It's simple really. Calderford is only a small town, you see. What brings you here, Miss Waters? It's such a quiet place and so out of the way."

"Oh! I enjoy travelling and seeing new places," was the vague reply, there was no enthusiasm in her tone. "I especially like to be near rivers or lakes, and Calderford looks like a pleasant enough place to stay for a while, gathering my resources."

"Here's Gravel Pit Road. Turn right, go ahead over Kingfisher Creek. Now bear left. We're on Mill Road now, running beside the creek. Lovely, isn't it?"

All the rivers and creeks were in full spate after the spring thaw, and the creek chuckled and bubbled over the rocks, some twenty feet below them to their left. The road, no longer hardtop, was well gravelled and the side ditches in good condition. Anahita took note of all of it.

"Take a left fork here and you will soon see the Mill. The head pond has been partially restored and the wheel is still there, but all the machinery has gone long since. Pull over into the yard. There's plenty of room for parking and the gravel driveway is in good condition."

Mattie got out of the car, hurrying round to open the door for Miss Waters, anxious to make a good impression.

Anahita Waters looked around. "Now, tell me Miss Peters, why has this property remained so long unsold?"

"There are several reasons," Mattie began slowly, seeing one more sale escaping her. "For one thing, the owner, on taking advice, I believe from his uncle, has rejected one or two offers, preferring to wait for what he terms 'the right buyer'."

Noticing her client's sceptical smile, she pressed doggedly on.

"Then, for many years the place was thought to be haunted. Of course, that was before the restoration. But the rumour lingers on. Something to do with the property's isolation, I suppose. Also, the owner recommends that the head pond could do with further reinforcement, should the new owner be nervous of exceptionally bad weather."

"The man must be afraid of water!" she said derisively.

Nevertheless, she scrutinised the dam carefully.

"More than adequate!" she declared. "Well, this difficult man has met his match. I like being lonely, my dear. And I like to be near water. I always have. Perhaps it is because of my name."

Once more she studied Mattie's face as she spoke.

"You say he is waiting for the right purchaser?"

Mattie nodded.

They stood silently, side by side, looking at the scene before them. The Old Mill appeared to have grown out of the ground, the warm brown clapboard walls merging in complete harmony with the trees behind and with the mast of the forest floor below. The millstream ran softly through the old wheel, fluting into a cascade of chattering bubbles, sparkling in the Spring sunshine. At the end of the driveway stood a sturdy barn, with a loft and woodshed. Double doors at the front indicated a garage.

"I love this old place. I only wish I could afford to live here!" Mattie said dreamily. "The water has so much to say." Colouring with embarrassment, she took out the key. "Be careful. It's rather slick underfoot, Miss Waters."

"Miss Waters this, Miss waters that! Why don't you call me Anna? Anahita is rather a mouthful. And your name is?"

"Mattie," said Mattie firmly. Only the vicar of St.Peters, the church that had provided her second name, knew it to be anything else.

"Short for…?"

"Just plain Mattie, plain and simple."

*No,* thought Anna Waters. *She has no idea! How could she have? I have been far too clever.*

"This place looks in very good shape," she said. "I'm surprised. Why! There's even electricity!"

"They took a line from the gravel pit office, over the creek. It must have cost a bomb at the time, but electricity is needed for the water, and there is a heat pump too. Let's go inside, shall we?" suggested Mattie, putting the key in the lock. "This is a dead-bolt lock, Anna, and we have had no trouble with people trying to get in. Truth to tell, many people are afraid to come here," she said honestly. "I don't know what happened, but those round about stay well away."

"That's all to the good then, isn't it?" Anna replied, thoughtfully. "Who did all the work?"

"Oh, a come-from-away! That's what local people call those of us who come from out-of-province. His name is unusual, Kurma Watson, on the deed it is Kurma Enterprises. I am told he was interested in the fishing. There was some special fish he was after, as I understand it, but he didn't stay very long, just a year or two, after all this work! Mrs. Oxner says he was expecting someone to join him, but no one showed up."

A faint look of alarm disturbed Anna's bland expression. Like a whisper of wind over water, her calm was fleetingly full of uncertainty, a suggestion of agitation and dismay followed by scorn.

"This place was not meant for him, it was meant for me." This she said with great emphasis. "He spent his money on it, so it is good he came." The laugh she gave was short and angry. "It was even better that he should go."

Puzzled, Mattie made a vague, non-committal murmur.

"I think I should warn you, Miss Waters, that this place does not come cheap. It is on a 'select property' list in spite of the location, or perhaps because of it."

The heavy oak door opened easily on well-oiled hinges, and swung heavily to one side. They stepped into a porch-cum-mudroom, set with a red tile floor and a roomy pine hanging closet. A pine boot shelf along the right wall was wide enough for comfortable seating, offset with pads covered in an attractive blue denim. A mirror and shelf ran along the panelled wall above. The woodwork was solid, with a dull sheen, the porch filled with the spicy smell of cut wood. A second, lighter door opened on to a living room, which amply lived up to the promise of the entrance way. It was large and comfortable, with a recently re-set flag floor and inner walls lined with silky grey old barn siding.

"You will see from the deep-set windows, Anna, that there is plenty of insulation, R20 in the walls and up to R30 in the roof."

But Anna was giving all her attention to the wide stone fireplace, a fireplace that promised a warm welcome even without a fire in the fire basket. Going straight to it, spreading her hands as though to warm them, or in supplication, she started to speak, her voice low.

"Oh Ahuro Mazdao, it is I, Anahita, Anaista, Daeva of Water! Hear me, Ahuro Mazdao, Ormazd, I am here!"

As she stood, silent now, in front of the hearth, Mattie was transfixed, both fascinated and repelled by the urgency and vibrancy of Anna's voice. Suddenly aware of Mattie's startled expression, Anna stopped, and dropped her hands, smiling crookedly.

"An ancient prayer to the hearth stone, Mattie! A poem, nothing more."

Mattie, discomfited, cleared her throat, turning to practicalities, indicating a door by the fireplace, 'Through that door there is a kitchen, storeroom, and a useful powder room. A door beyond leads outside to the wood shed. There is plenty of split, dry maple in readiness. You notice the gallery upstairs? It leads to three bedrooms and a bathroom." She looked around wistfully. "It really is a lovely home, isn't it? But no one wants it! Aren't people strange?

"How much?" Anna was now all business.

"It's classed as a 'rural gem', you see, and I'm afraid he's asking $200,000," said Mattie despondently, turning to leave. "I know it's a lot of money."

"Yes, well, he won't get it from me! No, no, don't look so worried! I intend to buy it, if we can come to terms. I believe that man was sent to prepare this place for me!" She turned again to the fireplace. Was she whispering her poem again?

"I will offer $180,000, cash, as long as the taxes are reasonable and I can see the documents about water, heating costs and septic system. Better $180,000 now rather than $200,000 never. Don't you agree? I'm sure that I must be the right purchaser."

"Oh, thank you! How marvellous! Beth will be so pleased with me! I'm sure Mr. Watson will agree to it. He has waited so long for the right buyer."

"Well, *I* am pleased with you, and that is even more important, isn't it? Better brush up your sales pitch, my girl. The customer always comes first."

Mentally correcting 'customer' to 'client', Mattie flushed. "There I go again!" she said awkwardly. "There's no wonder I lose sales."

"I wouldn't worry about it. We'll soon be good friends, I can tell." The purring note of contentment in Anna's voice was surprising. "This is turning out very well. I must set about transferring funds, at once. I like to travel, you see, and my money is in Switzerland. Yes, things are going very well indeed."

Once in the car, Anna looked around at The Old Mill; then taking off her spectacles, without them she turned to look Mattie full in the face. The luminosity of her large dark-fringed eyes was electrifying. Their colour and intensity shifted from aqua blue to deep sea green, as though reflecting every emotion, like sun on water.

"You thanked me, but I should be thanking you. This place is perfect for me, and all that I must do."

She sat quietly for a moment, as if about to speak again, then shrugging, resumed the anonymity of her spectacles, driving out of The Old Mill yard with a spurt of gravel, heading back to town,

Mattie, transfixed by the intensity of that gaze, continued to stare, dazzled and unnerved. The compelling authority of those brilliant eyes, so much at variance with the elderly face and nondescript clothes, threw her off balance.

*I wonder what it is that she must do?* She wondered, now believing this surprising woman capable of anything. *She is a very forceful woman.*

Each for her own reason, they remained silent and thoughtful throughout the journey back to Calderford.

# CHAPTER 2

Back in the office, Beth fidgeted about, unable to sit still. She made phone calls, peered out of the windows, changed the display board, changed it back, made one or two appointments, and at last sat nervously looking at the time. Physically recovered, she remained shaken and deeply distrustful of this new client.

Such was her anxiety, the practical red Subaru Outback might have been a magic carpet, whirling young women away to an unknown fate. Perhaps it was the unsettling influence of their new client. Beth shivered.

*I have no reason to suspect that Miss Waters wishes me ill, but nevertheless, I do wish they would come back! It's after five thirty! Mattie is with her in that car. I hope the woman can drive! But she doesn't know our roads. I'm being foolish, but there's something about her I just don't trust.*

Knowing that she had chosen her assistant impulsively, she felt a growing responsibility for her, and she watched her struggles to get ahead with an empathy bordering on possessiveness.

*And I know what that's like,* she thought grimly. *And I know I hired her because she is so like Alec to look at! But of course, she isn't Alec and there is no going back to those days.* She gave a deep sigh. *Still, I think I can make something of her.* Glancing at the clock again, she fidgeted restlessly with some papers. *They certainly have been gone a long time. On those country roads, it's like driving on marbles.*

So she fretted and waited, watching the lengthening shadows. It was just after six o'clock when the Subaru Outback drove at last into the parking lot and Beth, watching anxiously through the window, felt enormously relieved. One look at Mattie's face showed no shadow of Beth's own foreboding. The tilt of her head, the set of her shoulders, all promised well. Mattie appeared to be on excellent terms with the client.

*She's smiling!* marvelled Beth. *What a difference that makes to her!*

Hurriedly she busied herself at her desk, affecting surprise when the door opened. Now to regain her lost confidence! Negotiating with this unnerving client might allay her earlier feelings of loss and dismay. However, it was soon obvious that there would be no negotiations after all.

"I have been convinced to buy The Old Mill," began Anna. "And we have agreed on terms." Turning dismissively from Beth, she gave Mattie a conniving smile. "This young woman drives a hard bargain, doesn't she? I eventually agreed to pay $180,000, cash, no mortgage, pending the paperwork being satisfactory."

The look she gave Beth as she spoke was one of triumph, as though in some way she had outwitted her. Beth was silenced. She had been prepared to settle for $180,000 herself, but now felt that if Mattie reached $180,000, she might have gone to $185,000. Still, 7% exclusive listing would be–

"I congratulate you on your astute saleswoman, Mrs. Oxner! She certainly had the better of me! But there, what could I do?"

Anna opened her hands in a gesture of rueful resignation. "I was putty in her hands."

"Miss Peters is certainly very persuasive," Beth prevaricated glibly. "Now, if you will come to my desk, I will get the papers ready."

She smiled benevolently at Mattie, not wholly insincerely, trying to regain her ascendancy and take things in hand. Her judgement in hiring her assistant had not been wrong after all.

*Alec would sometimes surprise me by his tenacity too*, she thought. *The quiet ones often do.*

Mattie was equally amused and disconcerted by Anna's dishonest manipulations of a flustered Mrs. Oxner, it never occurring to her that she might just as easily be falling victim herself. Nor did she recognise, as such, the unfamiliar seed of malice, now sown in her mind.

*I'm enjoying this!* she thought, watching Beth's discomfiture. *Anyone who can out-manoeuvre Mrs. Oxner has a lot to teach me.*

All her earlier thoughts of gratitude and appreciation had vanished, nor did she consider that some lessons were far better left unlearnt.

"It's easy when you know how," whispered a voice over her shoulder. "You can learn a great deal from me."

Embarrassed on finding her thoughts echoed so closely, Mattie turned to her desk. Had she spoken aloud? She was uncomfortably aware of Anna following her, as though shepherding her into place.

"I have put my offer in writing, Mattie, and now it is all in the hands of an agent, Mr. Watson having left the country. Of course he will agree, after all this time. It's lucky for him that I came along."

*Of course,* echoed Mattie's thoughts. *Nothing could stop this woman! Now I know I didn't speak aloud that time.*

Nevertheless, she shot a fearful look at Anna, who smiled blandly back.

Beth, catching the changing expressions, admiration, excitement, fear, flickering over Mattie's usually composed face, was alarmed, jolted out of her normal preoccupation with business into a wary protectiveness.

*What shall I do?* she worried. *Mattie's far too young and inexperienced to deal with the likes of Anna Waters, who, to my mind, is a devious and possibly dangerous woman. It would be better if we could steer clear of her! I know that I have been cheated in some way, and I don't trust her intentions.*

Such thoughts running through her head, based more on intuition than on valid judgement, were nevertheless convincing. Mattie needed – what? Advice? Protection?

*Friendship*, decided Beth. *She needs friendship, and that I can give her.*

Accordingly, as soon as Mattie, with uncharacteristic effusiveness, had seen Anna to the door, Beth called over cheerily.

"We shall celebrate, together, you and I. Your first big sale! And because it's your first, I am waiving the 70/30 agreement, and we'll go halves, 50% each." Cutting short Mattie's incredulous thank-you, she held up her hand.

"No more to be said about it! Tell you what, I'll go over to the Save Easy and buy a broiled chicken and a salad. Here, take this money and go over to the liquor store and buy a bottle of Jost's Comtessa white wine. Better take your own car and follow me to my place, so you can get back home under your own steam. I'll meet you in the Save Easy car park in twenty minutes."

Astonished, Mattie took the money. One more wonder in a day of wonders. Dropping her briefcase in her apartment over Once Read Books, she hurried back in time to follow Beth to her house. This should be interesting! Viewing the familiar out of context usually is.

*Beth at home, domesticated – it boggles the mind!* thought Mattie gleefully.

Taking a left turn on to River Road, Mattie's old Toyota followed Beth's new Elantra down Lower River Road, following the Calder River to Beth's home, a restored Cape Cod. At the office it would be listed as a "Historic Gem". The walls were of weathered grey cedar shakes, offset by cream trim and a dark red panelled door. The six-over-six windows, protected unobtrusively by new storms and screens, gave promise of warmth and shelter. An old-fashioned garden led to a comfortable barn, where they left the cars. The informal garden, set about with shrubs and evergreens, was well established. The house looked lived in, welcoming, inviting.

"Why, it's beautiful," exclaimed Mattie in surprise. She had imagined Mrs. Oxner's home would reflect her taste for vivid clothes and shiny rings. "Have you always lived here, Mrs. Oxner?"

"My name is Beth, you know that. Why not use it? Yes, Alec and I bought it twenty-two years ago. You should have seen it then! One of our

'Handyman Specials'. But the structure was sound, and we worked hard restoring it. It took a long time, I can tell you, and now Alec is not here to enjoy it...." She turned away. "Well, come on in and I'll just slip upstairs and get out of my war paint. Mustn't get chicken fat on it! Here," she said, kicking over a pair of slippers. "See if those fit you."

As Mattie went into the low-ceilinged living room, she felt her nerves untangling, the edgy feeling of the afternoon slipping away, until she began to feel comfortable again in her own skin. She could hear Beth upstairs, singing and humming softly as she showered and changed.

*Everyone should have a home they love*, thought Mattie dreamily. *Why do people make fun of real-estate offices? What could be more worthwhile? And I have completely underestimated Beth. I'm not very good at summing people up. It makes me wonder what Anna Waters is really like. Now there's an enigma.*

One conclusion she might have drawn, had she been older and wiser, is that all three women were quite different from each other, she, Beth and the unsettling woman they had encountered that day. And where was Anna Waters at that minute?

Like Beth, but driven by different needs, Anna had also been acting a part. Now, chafing both at the decisions she had made, and the constraints on her to make them, she was striding imperiously along the beach outside White Pines Lodge. Preferring to be solitary, she had taken a cabin and now was unrecognisable as the insignificant woman who had purchased a house earlier in the day. Drawing herself up to her full height, she made an impressive figure in dark blue slacks and sweater, swathed in a hooded cloak of sea green, lined with a flash of flame. She had the pre-Raphaelite look of a storybook figure, hair streaming over her shoulders, invincible, mysterious. Whereas Beth, to face her world, wore bright war paint, Anna's vivid arrogance had lurked dangerously camouflaged by a stoop, non-descript clothes, prim hair and tinted spectacles. In contrast to them both, Mattie remained, however insecurely, herself. It was the very thing that Anna intended to exploit.

*A vessel*, she promised herself, *waiting to be filled. A tool to be shaped to my needs.*

Staring over the water at the dark sky and the scudding clouds, her impatience suddenly drove her to pack.

*I will not fret my time away here. Far better to travel far away for the next month or so, until The Old Mill is mine, and I can get to work. I'll go to Egypt, to Switzerland, spend time at the lakes, visit the bank. I shall buy trinkets for Mattie, to tempt, to persuade. Nothing too rich or ornate. I will choose well. Modern pendants with simple necklets, but in gold, red gold, unique, different, hers alone. They must be simple stones to match her personality. There shall be amethyst, amber and peridot, for her colouring – opal for sorrow. I will bespeak a signet ring for her in obsidian.*

Her eyes narrowed, envisioning the future, seeing what she would do. Flinging clothes into her case, with an abandon typical of her, by next day she had gone. Five days later she called the real-estate office.

"No, not you, Mrs. Oxner," the accenting of the 'Mrs.' was noticeable, "I wish to speak to Mattie." The tone, dismissive, almost hostile, chilled Beth, who struggled to keep her voice even. "For you," she said, covering the mouthpiece. "It's your client, Miss Waters. Watch yourself with her, Mattie. I'm warning you, she's a really demanding customer."

"Client," Mattie corrected her, smiling.

Beth laughed.

To Mattie, charm oozing from her every intonation, Anna gave various instructions about hiring a cleaner, a gardener, airing the house, buying supplies.

"Excuse me, Miss Waters, but I do feel that would be a little premature. We have still to hear from the agent. He has yet to contact Mr. Watson."

"Then call him! Insist! He is only stalling for more money! Well, I told you he won't get it from me." Anna slammed the phone down angrily.

"I'd better try to hurry things up," Mattie said to an inquisitive Beth. "Miss Waters certainly has an erratic temper! I wouldn't want to give her cause to take offence, and maybe lose the sale."

"Mattie, my dear, she is a very strange woman, and very persuasive. Be on your guard!"

"Oh Beth, she's just an irritable old woman, poor old soul! I'm sure she's quite harmless!" Mattie smiled forgivingly.

It is always the Matties of this world who good-naturedly, and maybe inadvisedly, smooth the way for the temperamental and unreasonable, if only to keep the peace. However that may be, by the end of the week the deal was closed, and Anna Waters would be able to take possession on June 1st. Mattie was to go with her to help in the opening of the house.

"You're so clever!" Anna's honeyed tones assured her over the 'phone. "I know you can help me. There is very little furniture in the house, isn't there? And I shall need a new bed – oh, a great many things! I shall be relying on you, when I get back to Nova Scotia."

"Be warned, Mattie. She has no right! You have done your job, you know. She's just exploiting you! Look. You've found your feet, selling that other house in Hestler's Settlement proves it. You should do well now. The first sale is always the hardest."

"Don't worry so, Beth. What can she possibly do to me?"

What indeed?

"Well, just you be careful. I know the type."

But even Beth, with all her experience, knew nothing at all about Anna Waters' "type".

# CHAPTER 3

Spring in Nova Scotia is full of blossom as field, orchard and woodland celebrate the dismissal of winter with an orchestration of colour. The reclusive pink May flower, Nova Scotia's provincial flower, hides itself in secret places. More assertive, the wild pink azalea, 'Lamb-Kill', strides knee-high through the brush. Flowering trees of every size gaily tempt the spring pollen seekers. Forsythia is an early entrant, flaunting its pale gold blossom from slender branches, followed by the fruiting trees, some wild, some cultivated. This riot of promise is later echoed by opulent squash, plump root crops, fat cabbages, red and green, and luscious tomatoes. Before the silence of winter falls again, there will be plums, cherries, strawberries, raspberries, apples, pears, peaches, cranberries, blueberries, gooseberries – who could name them all? – filling larders with their bounty.

On June 1st, when Mattie and Anna drove over to open The Old Mill, it was the turn of the apple trees. Wild apples, self-sown among the saplings by the woods' fringe, spilled their fragile pink and white blossoms, like a lacy cuff on the dark mantle of evergreens behind. The water, riffling over the wheel of The Old Mill, catching the sunlight, lovelier by far than Beth's diamonds, gathered and fell in a cascade of light into the peat-brown water of Kingfisher Creek. It was a homecoming to delight anyone's heart. Or so it would have been, but for the blackfly. Breeding in the running water, eager for blood, they soon began to settle around eyes, ears, any bare flesh. Anna's volatile temperament was immediately outraged. Not for Anna the concept that perfection, without the black flies of life, would be self-defined and static.

"I'm afraid this is the very worst time of the year," Mattie apologised, as though accepting full responsibility. "They are just reaching their peak. I try to remember how much the birds enjoy them, and–"

"They are intolerable! I will not have them on this stretch of water! This was not so the last time I stayed here!"

Mattie looked at her in astonishment. When had Anna ever stayed here before for more than a hour or two? And where had the sober old lady gone? This voice was a voice vibrant with a terrible energy. Moreover, Anna, standing with arms upraised, was crying out imperiously.

"Begone! It is I Anahita, Anaista! Begone from me."

To Mattie, laughing nervously, it was as if everything suddenly became still and quiet, no trees rustling, no birds singing, no sound of water. It was as though even the stream itself had ceased to flow. Blinking her eyes in disbelief, Mattie was relieved to see everything return to normal.

*It must have been the dazzle of the sun on water,* she thought. *maybe it made me dizzy. I couldn't even hear, let alone see.*

There was Anna, once more a sedate elderly woman, standing quietly by her red Outback, smoothing back her hair and watching as Mattie struggled to brush the flies away from her face and hair,

*I'm getting fanciful,* Mattie thought. *Maybe Beth is right. I am trying to do too much.*

Together they unloaded the car, taking the luggage inside. Anna went straight to the hearth, repeating the old words she had used before. Mattie waited patiently, becoming accustomed to the oddities of this unusual client. Together they surveyed the old furniture, going at last upstairs to the bedroom, accompanied by Anna's exclamations of amazement as they went from room to room.

"Who could ever sleep on anything like this?" she said disdainfully, poking at the thin mattress on the bed.

"I believe Mr. Watson has very simple tastes," explained Mattie. "He preferred simplicity and old things, you see."

The aversion on Anna's face at the mention of Kurma Watson's name was very noticeable.

"Well, there is no way that *I* could sleep in his bed," she said firmly. "Until I can replace it I will spend a week at the Wayside Motel outside Calderford. Meanwhile, may I impose upon your time still further? Will you help me to find the things I need?"

"I could come tomorrow morning for two or three hours, but I have other obligations, Anna. Mrs. Oxner relies on me too, you know."

"Oh, Mrs. Oxner," said Anna dismissively. "Surely she can manage alone, a capable little woman like that? You could work for me! I will pay you of course. That would be much better for both of us."

Mattie shook her head, thankful that she had insisted on using her own car, and thus to be free to leave in her own time.

"I can spare some time for you, Anna, but I have commitments already made."

"You'll soon come round to my way of thinking!" Anna replied blandly. "It would be pleasant for both of us. Meet me here tomorrow morning at ten o'clock. For now, just bring out my overnight bag, and put it back in my Subaru."

Annoyed and frustrated by this peremptory demand, Mattie nevertheless did as she was told, and it was with a sigh of relief that she followed the Outback to Calderford. More and more she appreciated Beth's kindly common sense. Nevertheless, she felt some attraction to her client's eccentricities and changeability.

*Imagine telling the blackfly to "begone"!* she thought, giggling foolishly. *I'm afraid she may be a nickel short of a dollar! It is, at least, entertaining.*

No longer sure whether she had imagined the whole thing or not, she decided not to tell Beth about the blackfly incident, but to stay another couple of hours at the office, to make up for lost time. Next day, making her way to The Old Mill, Mattie was thoughtful, turning Anna's proposition over in her mind.

*I don't really want to be paid for helping out in this way. I don't want to be obligated to her. Who knows how long Anna will stay, or this whim last? But it could be very interesting, even exciting. She certainly is a different sort of person.*

How interesting and exciting it might be, she had no way of knowing. As she drove into the driveway of The Old Mill, Anna was already waiting, leaning against the Subaru, looking impatiently towards the road.

"I'm early," said Mattie, defensively, "and isn't it nice that the wind has blown away the blackfly for now? It must have been during the night though." She gave a puzzled look at the clear blue sky and the calm trees. There certainly was no sign of any wind at that moment.

"They have gone and will never be back." Anna's tone was flat and positive. "Now, here is what we must do. First we must go and buy a bed. Using the one already here is impossible."

"I have been thinking about that, Anna. If there is much you need, you could use a catalogue, then you could order from the catalogue and do all your shopping at once." At Anna's dismissive gesture, she added, "Then you should go into Lower Calder, the local market town. There are some very good stores there. I can show you around and we could arrange delivery. I know you will be able to find a good bed, at least."

Anna's shrug spoke of her impatience at the delay in being settled at The Old Mill.

*Had she expected me to bring a bed with me?* fumed Mattie. *What's her rush?* Aloud, she asked, "Are you likely to need much? Will you be staying here long? Is this only temporary ?"

"Great Heavens, child, all these questions!" Anna interrupted. "How do

I know how long it will take? I must be comfortable no matter how long it may be."

*Whatever it is that she must do, she's certainly impatient to get started,* Mattie mused, looking speculatively at Anna, who was irritably drumming her fingers on the car door, as she gave some consideration to the matter of where best to shop.

"Very well then, first we will go to Lower Calder to buy the essentials. I do not like new furniture, so we must go round the antique and secondhand stores for everything else. You shall show me where they are."

Mattie quailed inwardly, equally unwilling either to agree or to refuse this demand.

*Why am I so intimidated by this woman?* she wondered angrily. *What she does is no concern of mine.*

Then why did she partially assent?

"I will certainly show you where the stores are, Miss Waters," she said with deliberate formality, "but then I must attend to my other business."

"But I will pay you for your services! Handsomely. Better, I'm sure, than that little woman at the real-estate office.

"But I would rather not be paid for such little help as I shall be able to give, for I will only be able to come now and then. As I said before, I have other commitments."

Mattie's usually amiable face looked determined, even though she smiled to avoid giving offence. It was as well she couldn't see the expression behind Anna's spectacles, as anger, frustration and spite chased each other across the expressive eyes.

"I wouldn't dream of interfering with your so very *interesting* life, my dear. That would be most thoughtless and selfish of me, just because I value your opinion so highly."

Even Mattie's tolerant ear detected the note of falsity in those honeyed tones. Far from feeling flattered, she felt patronised and belittled. Noting this, Anna hurriedly changed her tactics.

"But there! I can see flattery such as that will not cut any ice with a clever girl like you, so let's get on with it. You could follow me as far as Calderford, park your car there, and I will take you back after shopping and an early lunch in Lower Calder. I must be back here later, for an important delivery, at four o'clock."

To this, at least, Mattie felt safe in agreeing. After parking her car at the office, and checking with Beth, she set off with Anna down the River Road, following the Calder to Lower Calder. After shopping and an early lunch, Anna dropped her off at Calderford as promised, but only after extracting an agreement that they would meet at The Old Mill on the following Saturday afternoon.

Relieved to be back in the office at last, Mattie sank gratefully into the seat at her office desk, happy to have escaped from Anna's caprices and demands.

Beth looked at her inquisitively.

"So?" she asked.

"All right, Beth. You win. She expects far too much attention, as you said. No! Please don't say I told you so! She keeps hinting that she has some important project on hand. But there is no telling what that might be, or how long it will take, or what she will do with The Old Mill when it is done."

"Whatever it is, it won't be to anyone's good but hers," said Beth darkly. "I'll stake my bottom dollar on that."

The rest of the day passed peacefully in the mundane business of selling real estate. *Quite an exciting enough occupation for anyone, especially me,* thought Mattie, picking up the phone to call another client. *Please let these people be nice, ordinary people, just looking for a house!*

Time enough for more complications on Saturday. For her part, Anna was full of restless energy, pacing up and down, muttering to herself.

*This will be more difficult than I expected! Who would have thought that such a little mouse could be so intractable? But my trunks will soon be here! My robes, my ancient things! And then we shall see. Yes, then we shall see.*

She looked irritably down Mill Road, awaiting delivery of her trunks and boxes. When at last they arrived, all but one large chest were carried up to her bedroom. They had been through Customs, and how difficult that had been! Grudgingly, they had at last been passed as "Theatrical Supplies". Theatrical indeed! Brushing aside the delivery man's inquisitive probings, ("Putting a play on? There's enough stuff here! In the theatre, are you, then? You going to perform here?") sending him on his way with a lavish tip, she turned at last to gloat over the large, dark chest, eyes glistening with anticipation and joy.

*But I must wait! I must wait until all is in place, and this is truly my home. Friday, by Friday! And then, Mattie, on Saturday I will begin!*

Thrusting aside the loose protective wrapping, she opened her arms in a gesture of welcome and pride. Then, taking a long, slender key out of her purse, she ran her hand over the smoothly carved surface of the chest. Intricately carved in mystifying designs, it had the heavy aroma of ancient cedar of Lebanon and exotic spices. A gilded latch at the front of the lid lifted to reveal a curiously wrought lock, a lock that claimed attention, inviting a key to open it. Anna ran a yearning hand over the chest's surface.

Hand and key moved slowly towards the lock, then drew back.

*Soon!* she crooned. *Soon! Then nothing can stop me.*

Regretfully returning the key to her purse, she lingered once more to caress the satiny surface of the old wood. Checking carefully that the dead bolt was in place, she locked The Old Mill once more and drove back to the motel.

As she drove away, through the darkened windows of the old building, came a faint glow, as of a dying fire, briefly flaring with its last embers. Then everything became still and dark, but in readiness, waiting.

# CHAPTER 4

Horatio Bean waited impatiently in Once Read Books for a delivery. The bookstore occupied what had once been the old food store, facing on to The Snicket, opposite Tim Horton's. Above the store was the apartment currently rented out to Mattie Peters. The property, some one hundred and twenty years old, was as sturdy as only those old Maritime buildings could be, built of first growth local pine. Constructed by skilled local carpenters, it had once been the heart of the town, and now, although replaced by the Save Easy, it still retained storage space. Horatio Bean vacillated between generous offers for its redevelopment, refusing to allow demolition. He liked to wander around, admiring the wide floorboards, and the carpenter-made windows and mouldings. He loved and respected all old things, buildings, furniture, and of course books.

*They knew how to make things in those days,* he would say, dreamily. *I should have lived then.*

Horatio's kindly but misguided parents had christened him "Horatio", hoping to instil in him an heroic spirit. He would be "Horatio Bean, heir to Nelson!" The Army would do, or, at a pinch, even the Air Force. Alas, Horatio turned out to be like his father, slender, unassuming and, to top it all off, shortsighted

"Nelson was quite slight," said Audrey Bean, his doting mother, defensively, "*and* he only had one eye."

"Now, now, Audrey. I'm afraid Horatio will be just like me. I'm all right, aren't I?"

"Of course, George," Audrey answered him, looking her husband doubtfully up and down. "But Horatio will excel at *something,* though. I mean, look at him!" she said proudly.

And he did. He excelled at reading, and by grade three had earned the nickname "Bookie". It was as 'Bookie Bean' that at eighteen, he had tied his hair back with a bootlace and taken to the road, in the great North American puberty rite of the sixties. Now fifty-five, an ageing hippie, his grey hair tied back with string (to save on bootlaces), he ran Once Read Books, the secondhand bookstore in the little town of Calderford. In spite of himself, he had become a businessman, a "capitalist", a property owner. Mum and Dad had done very well, in a quiet way, and Bookie had culled the fruits of their labours. His little economies were now just a matter of habit and principle. Respecting the hard-earned money left to him by George and Audrey, he determined not to squander it, nor had he. The books he now awaited were a different matter.

*An investment,* he reasoned, *that's what they are.* He was peering anxiously through the window.

"I can't wait!" he said, positively dancing with impatience. "Sid should be here by now! Just think what I may find! These old reverend gentlemen have such odd books! I never know what treasures may be among them! Oh, do hurry, Sid!" He jigged his feet restlessly. "The only trouble is, I have to sell them."

All around him was evidence that he kept a good many for himself. He stroked their spines lovingly, equally as fond of them as his mother had been of him.

"Certainly books from a vicarage are full of obscure mysteries, which interest no one but me, thank goodness! However would I bring myself to part with them?"

At that moment, seeing the delivery truck draw up, he ran to the door, rubbing his hands with satisfaction.

Sid Heddle the deliveryman came through the door, whistling cheerily. Looking around, he asked himself why on earth Bookie needed any more books to read, when he could be watching TV. Large and easygoing, a night with a bottle of Keith's beer, TV, and the company of his family spelled all the stimulation Sid asked of life.

"Here you are then, Bookie. More dust traps for you! Sign here."

As Bookie, all aflutter, signed, he half heard Sid going on about the theatre. His mind snapped to attention. It was an unlikely topic for Sid to choose, and the word 'theatre' held so much promise. He jerked to full attention.

"Here? In Calderford? A theatre? What are you on about?"

"Head in the clouds as usual, Bookie! Not a theatre exactly, but theatrical supplies, that's what the labels said. That new woman, who bought The Old Mill. Some old bird she is! A 'Miss A. Waters'. Boxes of stuff she had! Even the boxes were fancy! And heavy! Holy Ole Holy! I couldn't hardly lift them! House was sold by that Beth Oxner. Doesn't your tenant work there? Better ask her. Well, I'm off." Sid left, whistling cheerily.

This is why Mattie came to think of Anna as a performer of some kind, for she had not yet seen Anna's "things" for herself. Bookie had burst out with all this excitement as soon as he saw her.

"Did you say she was an *actress*, Bookie?" she asked when he gleefully told her his news.

"She has all her things with her! In big trunks! Theatrical! Of the theatre! Oh my! Oh my! Isn't it exciting? Whoever heard the like in Calderford? Will she perform, do you think?" Bookie's thin face glowed with enthusiasm.

"I shouldn't think it is likely. She is quite old, and says she prefers to live quietly, and be on her own. That's why she bought The Old Mill." Seeing poor Bookie's face fall, she added kindly, "I will certainly tell you, Bookie, if she is considering it-- not, of course, that older people can't act," she added, seeing his crestfallen face.

Mattie went slowly up to her apartment, full of speculation. This would explain a great deal about Anna, especially her power to impose her personality in spite of her insignificant appearance. She gave the impression of drawing strength from other people. Perhaps she needed an audience.

*As an actress would,* thought Mattie. *Is this what she plans to do? To start a theatre? Here? In Calderford? Oh, that's just silly! But she does travel a lot, and apparently has plenty of money.* Mattie began to look forward to Saturday, and the chance of finding out more about this intriguing new client.

*But I won't change my mind. I'm sticking with Beth Oxner. She's been very good to me, and my work there is my bread and butter.*

Mattie, in fact, looked as though something or someone was being very good to her. Perhaps it was Mattie herself. With Beth's outspoken encouragement, she had begun to take more interest in her appearance. Her well-brushed hair, no longer dull, shone with bronze highlights; her face glowed with animation at her small successes, and a cheerful smile, reflecting her growing confidence, lit up her face. Life was full of interest and surprises these days for Mattie.

On Saturday morning, well before the appointed time of ten o'clock, she drove up to The Old Mill, full of innocent curiosity. It was a changed Anna who met Mattie at the door. Her stoop gone, she was vigorous and vibrant, belying her age, it was as though a wilting plant had been well watered. Her white hair, no longer held in a knot at the nape of her neck, fell in rippling white waves to her shoulders.

*Just like the mill race,* thought Mattie, taken aback by this transformation. *It's really beautiful.*

"The mill race is so beautiful, don't you think?" Anna asked, looking at her slyly sideways, her spectacles glinting in the sunshine. Mattie blushed at this half echo of her thoughts. Anna always penetrated her defences, always put her at a disadvantage.

"Are you warm, my dear? You look rather flushed." Removing her spectacles, Anna turned her incredible eyes, searching Mattie's face. Apparently satisfied with something seen there, she whisked her hair back into a knot, put on her spectacles once more, slipped her feet into sensible shoes, and was again an elderly woman ready to shop. "Before we leave, we will just check such furniture as is here. There is very little of it I would have about me."

Her expression disparaging, she glanced at the old Boston rocker, glowing dully where the black paint had been worn away by generations of hands clasping the arms; at the sturdy pine table, smoothed, by many years of use, to a patina which only time can provide; at the plain lines of a pine hutch.

"Peasant stuff!" Anna scoffed. "Upstairs the bed looks as though it is made of old cotton spools."

Mattie explained that it was an old spool bed and these things were hard to find, and very valuable.

"Not to me!" Anna touched the dark carved chest lovingly. "This is what we are going to look for. Things such as this."

"Mr. Watson must have been collecting local antiques," Mattie explained. "This far from being rubbish, Anna."

"Do *you* like things of this sort, my dear?"

"Why, certainly!"

"Mmm," said Anna thoughtfully. "Well, let us be on our way."

She was very hard to please. Her tastes were for the ornate, the heavy, the dark. They were able to find a Victorian sideboard, large and heavy, all the drawers carved with fruit, figs, pears, and grapes. She bought a large gilt mirror, probably from some Edwardian barroom, for the carving was gilded and overblown, the sidepieces being full-bosomed caratids.

"Now, I need a table and some chairs."

Exhausted by Anna's capriciousness, Mattie suggested they wait and try another day.

"Well, we will have a quick lunch then," Anna conceded ungraciously. "I must have at least one large chair immediately. But I *must* have it today! The rest can wait until next week. I *must* have a chair. Large, opulent." Anna's voice rose. "Throne-like!"

"Throne-like" rolled thunderously round the show room, causing startled heads to raise, Mattie flushed self-consciously as the other shoppers turned to see what was happening, but as usual Anna had her way.

"Wants it for the stage, does she?" the proprietor asked Mattie. "Likes her own way, too?" His tone was low and confidential.

"Do you know of such a chair?" asked Mattie, snatching at straws.

"Try Treasure Trove over by the highway. They buy old theatre props. Perhaps the old lady might find something there. My Aunt Ethel is difficult like that," he added cosily. "You try Treasure Trove, m'dear." He nodded knowingly, looking askance at Anna, winking heavily at Mattie.

But he was absolutely right. In irritable silence, they drove to Treasure Trove, and there it was! Huge, throne-like, cushioned, gilded, upholstered in crimson plush, complete with footstool.

"At once! Deliver it at once! At once! At once!" Anna, delighted, was all warmth and generosity. "I knew I could count on you! Yes, you have done wonders!" she gushed. "And you will come again. Say you will work for me! We make a good team."

Her smile, her enthusiasm promised riches untold. Mattie shook her head, determined not to be beguiled.

"Anna, I earn my money in real estate. Beth and I get on very well and I hope to make a life here."

Anna's face went blank, her mind busy with a new scheme, as she drove them back to The Old Mill. Mattie fell silent, too, her heart sinking at the thought of spending more Saturday afternoons like this.

"I need to stop at the hardware store," said Anna. "I wish to buy some wood enamel, in rich bright reds and greens. Maybe some gold paint, stripper, brushes. I mean to be busy."

*Anything,* thought Mattie, *as long as I can go home.*

Back at The Old Mill, Anna coaxed Mattie into carrying her parcels inside, then spreading them out on the chest, she looked around at the furniture. "Now you can help me choose. Which shall I paint first? The rocker? The hutch? I think the hutch will be good in a bright red and the chair green. I shall paint the spool bed, each spool with a different colour, gaudy as a Gypsy caravan."

Shaken out of her torpor, Mattie horrified, cried out, "Oh no, you can't! You mustn't!"

"My dear child, I certainly can and will! Unless," she paused, "unless you will undertake to come every Saturday *or* Sunday to be my assistant. In which case the furniture is yours."

"I am not asking for it, Anna," said Mattie stiffly, "but this lovely old furniture is priceless."

"Well," said Anna blandly, "it's up to you!" Thoughtfully she held the crimson colour chip against the hutch. "Maybe blue and crimson, do you think? Then the knobs gold."

"Oh! Stop!" said Mattie angrily. "Saturday or Sunday each week."

"My! My! Hoity toity! You like it, I don't, everybody is happy! There's more in the barn shed."

"I know," said Mattie, defeated. She would never be free of an obligation such as this.

"So we shall have many happy days together, shan't we?" purred Anna.

Mattie gathered her things and made for the door.

"Now, don't forget, Mattie," Anna's voice had changed from teasing to forbidding, "we have an agreement. Let me see, where shall I keep this paint?"

*Every time!* Mattie seethed, driving too fast down Mill Road. *She wins every time.* Slowing down to a reasonable speed, she tapped at the steering wheel impatiently. *She knows just how to pull my strings. It's as though she could get inside my skin.*

Shuddering at the thought, she drove thankfully back home.

Bookie looked up from the packing crate of boxes "Well?" he asked eagerly.

"Oh Bookie, I have no idea what she's up to. No good, I should think. Of all the capricious, difficult, self-willed...."

At Bookie's expression she broke off, laughing. "I'm just tired, Bookie."

"She sounds *fascinating!* She must be full of talent! She could teach you all sorts of things, Mattie."

"I know," said Mattie slowly. "That's what has me afraid – ending up another Anna Waters. I'm going to call Beth, tell her all about it. Beth is so *solid*, such a comfort. Yes, I'll put a call through to Beth."

Reassured, feeling better already, Mattie went off to make some tea. Maybe she could join Beth for supper, and a breath of sanity.

After Mattie had left, Anna sat in the despised rocker, full of hope, dread, confusion, as she awaited the arrival of her new furniture. In truth, she was at war with herself, with an ancient past now full of uncertainties, with her present full of conflicting impulses and with the dreadful enigma of her future-If only her chair would come!

"I paid well to have it delivered today. It must come or...." a feeling of malice, quickly extinguished, caused her hands to clench, her eyes to darken. With relief, she saw the deliveryman staggering up the path with her chair, assisted by a grinning teenager.

"My son, Danny," Sid Heddle proudly introduced him as Anna directed them to place her chair near to the fire alongside her carved chest. Father and son were ridiculously alike, Danny being just as dark, easygoing, and comfortably built as his father, and both observing the world with knowing and inquisitive eyes.

"Like a throne, is that," said Danny admiringly. "Is it a throne, I mean, I saw one like that in a movie. Let me see, what was that movie called? It was about this old queen...."

Sid nudged him sharply, grateful for the large tip, and as they left, nagged Danny all the way to the truck.

"You learn to mind your own business, m'lad. You'll see a lot in this trade that's best left unnoticed."

"But *you* tell all sorts of stories." Danny objected sulkily. The family spent many an evening regaled by Sid's tales about what he had seen on his travels.

"That's my business, not yours! You mind me now!" Grumbling, albeit good-naturedly, they set off home.

Anna, alone at last, sank back in the chair, which looked grotesquely out of keeping with the simplicity of the room, then rousing herself, prepared a fire in the large hearth, and standing briefly in silence, her hands clasped to her breast.

Muttering huskily, "I must prepare myself," with a light step she climbed the shallow stairway to the gallery, going softly to her bedroom.

"First, the cleansing."

Bathing ceremoniously under a warm shower, her face relaxed, filled out, grew luminous with an inner light. Gently smoothing sweet oil over all of her skin, she loosened and brushed her beautiful hair. Going over to a sandalwood chest, at the foot of her bed, she took out a brocaded robe. Sea green, long, silky, loose-sleeved and flowing. The back intricately embroidered with a motif of scarlet flame, it hung in heavy folds, as she slid it reverently over her head. Around the hem, was a curving pattern of waves, in brilliant peacock blue. Interwoven throughout with gold thread, it was dazzling, magnificent.

Slowly she went back down the stairs. Going to the dark chest, she took out matches, and a long white wax taper. Lighting the taper, cupping it with her hands, she went to the hearth and carefully set light to the kindling, stepping back once the flames were rising steadily. Taking up a heavy translucent goblet in her right hand, raising her left in a wide gesture of supplication, she spoke, her voice resonant with emotion, "Ahuro Mazdao, the wise! Ormazd, primal spirit. All Father, who brought forth the world with your foreseeing eye. It is I! Anahita. Anaista, Daeva of Water. Must I still follow Ahriman? It is I! I am here as I was before, as you have guided me. I am here! I await!"

Drinking the contents of the goblet, apparently exhausted, she sank into her ornate chair near the glowing hearth, set down her empty goblet and sank into a deep sleep.

# CHAPTER 5

"Yes, come over right away. We will finish up this bit of ham. I want to hear all about it. Bring a salad."

Mattie's 'phone call had found Beth in her comfortable living room, taking her ease, the only time she felt free to be herself. Beth at home, relaxing in a housecoat and slippers, looked very different from the woman she presented to the commercial world. She looked, felt, and in fact was fifty-two years old.

*Oh, Mattie can get used to me the way I really am*, she thought, glancing in the hall mirror, making a grimace at herself. *Alec liked me this way, anyway. He would never recognise me in my war paint. Nor, come to think of it, with a double chin.* She patted it despondently for a minute or two.

Mattie arrived tense and full of frustration, her expression set in lines which had no place on her usually calm face. Beth's glance took it all in.

"Here, take a load off," she said, kicking the pair of slippers she now kept for Mattie. "I'll make up a couple of plates, and we'll eat in the living room. That's what Alec and I always did. He was a great one for the comforts of home."

Muttering, "I can see she has had a hard time with that impossible woman," under her breath, off went Beth to rustle up some supper. "No wine tonight, and she certainly doesn't need caffeine, by the look of it. We'll have some ginger beer."

Feet resting unhygenically on the coffee table in front of the fire, they ate in companionable silence.

"Now," said Beth, as they finished, "shoot."

In this friendly house and pleasant room, the whole long day seemed in retrospect hilariously funny.

"She's bought a *throne,*" spluttered Mattie. "An honest-to-God gilded *throne.*"

In great detail, she recounted the episode leading to the Treasure Trove, and the conniving salesman. Her laughter verged on the hysterical.

"I think she must be something to do with the theatre – oh dearie me!" Mattie wiped her eyes. "Oh Beth, thank you! I feel so much better."

Sobering, she described how Anna Waters had decided to paint the lovely old furniture already in the mill with garishly coloured enamel.

"I just couldn't stand it," Mattie said. "But now I have become really involved with her." She went on to describe how it happened. "I have to keep at least one day open at the weekend for selling houses, as you well know that's when clients are free to come, but the other I shall be spending with her."

Sighing, she felt herself tightening up again inside and noticed that her thumbs were tucked inside her clenched fist, as was always the case when she was worried..

"Now, Mattie! Relax! She has a genius for winding people up! Why, that first day…." Embarrassed, Beth described in part her reaction to Anna's first arrival at the office.

"Even you weren't quite yourself, Mattie. She just plain isn't good news. Still and all, you're committed now, and we'll work something out. Frankly, I think she could be a bad influence on you. You watch out, my girl!"

Mattie laughed it off, feeling uneasy at the confirmation of her own fears.

"Forewarned, forearmed, Beth," she said seriously. "I am going to find out what she's up to, what it is she has to do. You keep me sane and I'll keep you informed! Now, let's talk about more pleasant things. I do believe you have lost some weight. It suits you."

The rest of the evening passed in inconsequential chatter, and by eleven o'clock, Mattie was back in her apartment, at peace with the world.

Every day Bookie's eager questioning evoked the same answer.

"I don't know, Bookie! For Heaven's sake!"

Until Anna's arrival, the two of them had never talked so often, but now Mattie was spending much more time with him, wandering round the shop, browsing through the old books.

"Tenant's perks, Bookie," she laughed. "Tell you what, you let me read these and I will smarten you up. The clothes you are wearing have earned their rest! And the shop needs brightening up."

"What do you mean?" said Bookie, clutching protective arms round his old grey pullover.

"Oh, just dusting, a bit of paint. A pot of flowers or a plant would be nice on the desk. And cut your hair. Let's go on a self-improvement binge. You, me and Beth Oxner."

"But I've *always* looked like this," wailed Bookie.

Mattie laughed and left for work. "I've a good mind to match-make! He and Beth! They are both good people, both lonely – both *totally* unsuited to each other. They'd have that in common."

She was sniggering at the idea as she entered the office and waved off Beth's inquisitive look

Inevitably Saturday came again and another day of accommodating Anna. That day they searched for dining room chairs and a table. They encountered just as many difficulties and frustrations, as before.

"It must be something different, something unique, as are my other things," Anna stipulated. "Something lavish, ornamental, different – *regal.*"

Gradually relinquishing her role as elderly spinster, her manner was imperious, her hair, still drawn back but loosely, becomingly framing her face. The June weather being warm, she wore slacks and jacket of Delft blue linen, looking poised, self-assured. However, her spectacles were always in place, impenetrable, baffling.

As before, they drove from bric-a-brac to antiques, farther and farther afield. Then Mattie had an inspiration.

"Wait! Just stop a minute, Anna, I want to make a suggestion."

Anna pulled over impatiently.

"You have already wasted too much of my time today, Mattie, and I have found nothing."

"Well," said Mattie slowly. "While we were in that last store, and you were telling them exactly what you wanted–" she shuddered inwardly at the memory– "I looked around. Over to one side I found an old wrought iron table. The design is elaborate, leaves, flowers, and there are six chairs. I dismissed it, as too heavy, but–"

"And you said nothing?" interrupted Anna angrily. "We will go there immediately. I will have it sent, this very day. Really, Mattie, you must try not to waste my time."

Mattie bit her tongue rather than snap back.

The purchase made, Anna was all graciousness as they went back to The Old Mill. "Such a clever girl. This is working out very well! Now, you may run back to your little office, and we will meet again next week. Off you go."

On this, she swept into the Mill, oblivious of everything but her own plans. whilst Mattie, hungry and full of unresolved hostility, drove back to Calderford, snapped at poor inquisitive Bookie all agog in the bookshop, made her way upstairs, and grumpily ate yet another peanut butter and jelly sandwich.

*Just to rescue some furniture. Why am I doing it? She always brings out the very worst in me! I feel thoroughly disagreeable. Poor Bookie. He didn't deserve that! I am becoming as ill humoured as Anna! It's like a contagion.*

She laughed ruefully, remembering Bookie's comical look of dismay.

*Time for a visit to my family attic*, she thought.

Her "attic" was the only family treasure she possessed, a blue leather jewel box, gold tooled and worn. In it lay a necklet of old, dark gold, and on the necklet a pendant, in the form of a fish, intricately carved in lapis lazuli, with inset emerald eyes. Mattie stroked it gently, then fastened it briefly round her throat, but only very briefly, for it lay there like a halter, constricting her, as though holding her against her will.

*I wonder who my parents were. I wonder where they came from.*

These unanswerable questions had haunted her all her life.

*One day*, she promised herself, *Beth and I will talk about it. I wonder if she knew her parents. She was a foster child too.*

Neither she nor Beth ever talked about their early days.

Lunch over, in a better mood, she shamefacedly apologised to Bookie, promising to tell everything she found out about Anna Waters, as soon as she had anything to tell.

"Which is nothing at all, Bookie, except that she is a very difficult and temperamental person!"

That done, she went to keep an appointment with some clients, a nice, sensible young couple, whom she felt quite capable of helping. It would smooth her ruffled feathers if she managed to satisfy them.

On Monday, Beth asked her if she could spare a minute.

"You know I can, Beth! Good Heavens, who do you think I am, Anna?"

"It's really about The Old Mill transaction that we need to talk. There seems to be a bit of a spanner in the works."

This came as no surprise to Mattie; the whole business was fraught with complications.

"What now, Beth? I thought all the payments went through and all was well?"

"Oh absolutely! No question there, but now there is this." She tapped the letter on her desk. "I have a letter from Bob Haswell, Kurma Watson's agent. He apologises profusely, but says he has overstepped his mark. Mr. Watson had no intention of selling the furniture. Apparently there is more in the barn?"

"The agreement stipulated that the furniture be included, Beth, and yes, I do believe there is more in the barn loft, but Anna seems to have mislaid the key – or so she says. I believe it's another delaying tactic."

"Well, it appears it is a collection Kurma Watson has been working on for years, and Bob Haswell is investigating the possibility of getting it back."

Poor Mattie! Had all her efforts with Anna been in vain? But then had she ever wanted to possess the furniture, or just to save it? She flopped down disconsolately into her chair.

"Is Kurma Watson back in the country, then?"

"No! No! Not yet, but we can contact him through Bob Haswell."

Beth studied the mixed emotions on Mattie's face

"I know Anna won't sell it back. She is enjoying the situation too much," Mattie said slowly. "However, it is rightfully mine."

"Have you signed an agreement, Mattie?"

"A sort of one. But you are right, I must get this on a business-like footing. Then we could let Mr. Watson have his collection back, right away."

Beth shook her head slowly from side to side.

"Hold your horses, Mattie, and listen carefully, while I explain the whole situation to you. Kurma Enterprises is – or was – owned by Kurma *Deulkar*. Kurma Watson is his nephew, named after his uncle. Clear so far?"

"So?"

"As soon as Bob Haswell e-mailed Anna Waters' offer, Kurma Deulkar signed over the company to his nephew, lock, stock and disputed furniture. We should all be so lucky!"

"So that's what caused the delay? The courier service must have been very busy. When was the uncle in Nova Scotia?"

"Never! But Nova Scotian property was becoming very desirable and somehow he knew all about the mill. He sent his nephew – that's Kurma Watson, in case you are getting confused!– to negotiate a deal. He was very determined to buy this particular property. Of course it was quite cheap at the time.

"Why was that, Beth?"

"It had long been neglected, and then a rumour started that it was haunted. Goodness knows why! Alec had it on his books for years – that was before we were married. Anyway, Kurma Watson, laughing, at the very idea of ghosts, went ahead and spent a lot of money on restoration."

"Even so, I couldn't *profiteer* at Kurma Watson's expense, it wouldn't be honest, somehow."

"Well, I will e-mail Bob Haswell, tell him that we are working on recovering the furniture. How that woman has invaded our lives!"

"But it does look as though we are taking advantage of poor old Mr. Watson, doesn't it, Beth? What a muddle."

"Whatever gave you the idea that Kurma Watson is old? Just because he is well off, it doesn't necessarily follow at all! I tell you he is the *nephew* According to Bob Haswell, he's thirty or thirty-two. Something like that. Anyway, he'll be back home from India in a few weeks, and we'll find out for ourselves. He's coming to see us. By the way," she called as she made her way back to her own desk. "How are you fixed for Thursday night? It's my fifty-third birthday and I feel like company."

"Great! I have something I have decided to show you."

"What? What? Don't be so mysterious."

"Oh, it's nothing much. I'll show it to you on Thursday."

With that, Beth had to be content.

Whereas Mattie had succeeded in regaining her peace of mind, Anna had been pacing around the living room at The Old Mill, full of indecision and nervous energy. For many minutes she stood in front of the hearth, where a small fire burned in spite of the late June day. With sudden determination she picked up a small basket and strode out of the house towards the woods behind the barn.

*I wonder if I can remember where they were. They were early that year, that warm spring,* Anna murmured to herself. *But it has been so long! Some trees have grown and some trees have gone. Where are they now? So few there were, in their sheltered corner, shy and full of promise.*

Here the woodland was open, with filtered sunlight, the ground soft beneath her feet. She wandered on, scanning the ground carefully, drawn by a compelling need.

*Just to see them! Just once.*

At last, there they were, scattered in small clusters beneath the pines, Amanita Muscaria, Fly Agaric, in hues varying from yellow through orange to red, flaunting, tempting, deadly.

"I must not touch them! I made a vow!" But her voice was thick, husky, yearning. "There will be more, it is still very early for them."

Her eyes voluptuously caressed the plump, colourful caps with their white warts. Some, newly emerged, were fat, squat; but others, taller, wore a frivolous white frill round their throats where the veils had ruptured from the caps, and each squatted on a bulbous base. Several times Anna's hands reached out towards them, and then drew back. At last, as though unwilling, she reached down, looking furtively from side to side. With a gloved hand she carefully plucked five, placing them gently in her basket, before taking them back to The Old Mill.

"Now, Ahriman – now, Ormazd," she intoned, as she laid them on her carved chest.

Immediately, the small fire leapt up, licking towards her. Trembling with shock and alarm, she threw them into the flames, which immediately subsided. Anna cowered in front of the hearth.

"Ahuro Mazdao! Ormazd, all-seeing eye, hear my plea! For Ahriman is strong."

She lay there weeping. Then rousing herself, she took out her goblet, filling it with water. Returning to her chair, she drained it, placed it reverently on the carved chest, and sank, as before, into an exhausted sleep.

# CHAPTER 6

Mattie had given a great deal of thought to Beth's birthday present, keeping an eye open for possibilities as she went round the antique and secondhand shops with Anna. Eventually she chose a plain sampler. It was irresistible. "Mattie Willet age seven 1898" it said in bold red wool. She made believe it had been embroidered by her great-aunt, and that she was giving a family heirloom.

*Well, it could have been, who knows?* she mused, running her fingers dreamily round the old-fashioned frame, smiling at the crosses in each corner to keep away the Devil.

*Anyway, it will be perfect for Beth's birthday.*

She put it, carefully wrapped, next to her "attic", on the seat beside her, then sat for a while irresolute.

*I don't know whether this is a good idea,* she thought, regretting her decision to reveal her enigmatic past. *Maybe it would be better to let well alone? No, no! I think it is for the best.*

Nevertheless, she drove thoughtfully and carefully, taking her time.

"Why Mattie, it's perfect! Oh, it has your name on it! How clever of you!"

A delighted Beth tried the sampler out in different locations, then set it aside.

"I shall have a lovely time deciding where to hang it! But first things first. Satisfy my curiosity. What is it that you have to show me?"

"Not yet, Beth." Still full of misgivings, Mattie decided to postpone it a little while longer. "Let's have dinner first. It smells so good."

Never had time passed so quickly. With dinner over and cleared away, they sat glass in hand, their feet on the long suffering coffee table.

"Now," said Beth.

"No, you first, you tell me. Did you know your parents, Beth?"

"You'd better believe it! What a pair! The less said about my dad the better! Ernie Oxner, that was his name, a big bruiser of a man, free with his hands. Mother did nothing to make things easier. She seemed bent on provoking him, what with drinking and fooling around. I was in and out of care since I was very small. Then Dad hit me a little too hard, and was put inside for aggravated assault, out in Calgary. That's the last I ever saw of him. He's dead now. Well, they both are. Mother drank herself to death, and everyone blamed Dad, but I knew better. I was in care all over the place until I was seventeen. Then I tried to cope with Mother, worked in a supermarket and took night courses. At twenty, I gave up and left for good. Ethel, that was her name. Ethel and Ernie Oxner." Beth sighed, looking around her pretty living room for reassurance.

"Now you can't have anything worse than that. Tell me!"

"You haven't told me about Alec."

Beth's face softened.

"I got out of the city, and came out here. Alec took me on as an assistant, and just about saved my life! A gentle, kindly man, of great patience and understanding, he was snuffed out by a drunk driver on highway 103." Here Beth paused for a moment, remembering that night. "He was twelve years older than me. We just seemed to grow naturally together, and were very happy. I'm leaving it on that note, Mattie, I don't want to feel sad."

They sat quietly, each thinking for a moment of the life Beth had led.

"Now, tell me all about you. No holding back! You know all about my background. Now it is your turn."

Mattie took out the blue jewel case and ran her fingers thoughtfully over the surface.

"The suspense," said Beth dryly, "is killing me."

Mattie started, as though shaken from a dream.

"It's so strange, Beth. I have nothing really to tell, but I'll do my best. I never knew my parents at all, you see. But then, no one did." She laughed self-consciously. "It's like a Victorian penny dreadful. I was literally left on a church doorstep, well, in the porch really, a noisy little bundle on a cheap plastic sled. It was St.Peter's Anglican Church in Atterbury. They used to say that I must have floated down the Atter River, like Moses in his basket of reeds! No one really believed this, of course, since it was winter and the little Atter river was frozen almost solid. It was very odd, for although there had been a heavy snowfall, there were no tracks – perhaps they had been covered, since snow fell overnight. Someone had been very clever."

Beth's eyes widened and her mouth fell open as Mattie recounted her sad little tale. She pulled herself together.

"Where is Atterbury?"

"It's a small town in Eastern Ontario, south of Ottawa. At one time it was quite an important centre There is still a local fair there each summer. It's a pretty little place."

Slowly she opened the box taking out the necklace, and the note.

"This was fastened round my neck and I was wrapped up in an ordinary flannel blanket, long since loved and washed to pieces. It was a real 'Linus' blanket! Then there was this note."

She handed the necklace to Beth, who examined it with fascination, holding it this way and that.

"Why, it's beautiful, Mattie! Eastern I should say. Middle Eastern most likely, and very old. Could it be Egyptian? Put it on."

Mattie shook her head.

"I'd really rather not, Beth, not now. Let me finish my story. Maybe later."

She laid the necklace carefully in the blue box.

"The vicar, Kendrick Gibson, was at a loss what to do with me. A widower, he felt quite unable to deal with it himself. The jewellery box held a note, typed and unsigned. Here it is. As you see, the paper could be bought anywhere."

She handed the faded note to Beth, who read it aloud. The words were just as Mattie had said.

*This is Matsya, my little fish. Christen her if you must. I will be back for her.*

"No name, no date, no address," Beth commented.

The two women looked at each other in silence.

"Nothing else?" asked Beth.

"Nothing. Now the problem was that sentence, *I will be back for her.* That meant no one could adopt me, or even be willing to foster, long term. There were a lot of service people locally, being near Ottawa, and they were frequently posted to new duties. I went from one foster parent to another. Christmas and Easter I spent at the vicarage with the elderly vicar and his sister, who always visited for those holidays."

"And were you Christened?"

"Oh, yes. The vicar decided it would be best, so he Christened me Matsya Peters, after the church. 'When your mother comes back Mattie,' he explained, as I grew older, "she can add her family name after Peters, you see! I really miss old Kendrick Gibson."

"He's dead then?"

"He must have been in his late fifties the day he found me. He was such a kind, gentle man, rather vague and absent-minded. Of course the sled got lost! But he kept the necklace safely in a strong box for me, and left me

$2000, enough at the time to help me through school as long as I worked too. I owe a great deal to Kendrick Gibson."

She paused, remembering those times. Beth, leaving her for a while in peace, went out to make some chocolate, coming back with steaming, fragrant mugs. She was full of questions.

"Didn't anyone try to find out where you were born? Birth registrations? The sled? The blanket? Surely, the necklace?"

"Of course the authorities searched! It's a crime to abandon a child! They could find nothing, it was uncanny. No one had seen my arrival. No one remembered a pregnant woman. The sled and blanket? Well, they could have been bought anywhere! As for the necklace, that caused some excitement for a while, or so I was told. The box, you see, has the name of a Nova Scotia jeweller inside the lid, with a Halifax address. They signed a statement that such a thing had never passed through their hands. Someone must have found the box from somewhere. They tried the antique stores. You can imagine how intrigued everybody was, but – nothing!" She dropped her voice to a whisper. "That's where I came from, Beth! I'm really Miss Nobody from Nowhere! I came to Nova Scotia because of the slender tie to my mother, having none at all, you see, in Atterbury, after Kendrick Gibson died."

"Nonsense!" said Beth, stoutly. "Well, not anymore! You are now Mattie Peters, and I would be proud if you were my daughter!"

Neither being given to emotional displays, Mattie and Beth smiled shakily at each other, and sipped their chocolate reflectively.

"Just one more thing, Mattie. When did they find you? Do you know the date?"

"The date I was found, yes. The date I was born, no. I celebrate – if that is the word – the day of my arrival. 'DOA' It sounds like the result of a terrible accident, doesn't it? Dead on arrival." She laughed shakily. "Perhaps I am."

"And when is this DOA, Mattie?"

"One thing first, Beth. The name Matsya is an embarrassment to me. Promise me you will just call me Mattie?"

"Agreed, if that is what you want. So when is this DOA? Did anyone know how old you were?"

"They estimated not more than two weeks old, at the most. 1976 was a leap year and February 29th, 1976 was a Sunday. That's when Kendrick Gibson found me, Sunday, February 29th, 1976, so next year I celebrate my twenty-fourth, or maybe my sixth, DOA. It will be leap year in February 2000, too."

"Mattie, that is the most curious mixture of circumstances I have ever heard! I don't think much of my background, you know, but at least it is something I can deal with. I think maybe I would just like to sleep on this. One thing I *would* like you to know, Mattie, is that you have found a place to be now, a home."

Beth gave her a quick, awkward hug. "Shoo now! Go home and get some sleep, and I'll see you in the morning. Thank you for my sampler."

Mattie drove home feeling comforted, knowing that by sharing the story of her past with someone else, she had lessened her burden of loneliness. Remembering Beth's reaction to her necklace, she took herself to task.

"I should really put it in a strongbox, at the bank. Since coming here, there are a good many things I have just let slide."

Parking her car, she went thoughtfully into Once Read Books, almost bumping into Bookie, who was just coming out.

"Bookie, what ever are you doing here this late?" cried a startled Mattie. "It's half past eleven!"

"You're pretty late yourself." Bookie sounded nettled. "Here I've been creeping around all evening, not to disturb you. I thought you had gone to bed early, with everything being so quiet."

"I've been over to see Beth. You must have come back after I left. Sorry!"

"It's these books, you see, Mattie. Poor old Eustace Wilkie's they were." Lovingly, he patted a pile of various old tomes, raising a cloud of dust.

"Oh Mattie! They are full of wonders! Ancient cities, old beliefs, ancient rites, old-fashioned illustrations!"

His face alight with enthusiasm, his voice over loud, his gestures so wide they sent a little pile of books toppling to the floor, Bookie was rejuvenated, as though he had shed some musty old shell and broken out, newborn.

Mattie helped him to pick up all the books, laughing, "Bookie! Control yourself! I've never seen you so excited!"

"A special shelf! I shall have a special shelf, at the back – with a lamp – and a good chair! You must read them, Mattie! You must share them. I will–"

"Yes, yes, Bookie," Mattie said soothingly, propelling him inexorably towards the door. "It's all amazing. Now off you go! I'll see you in the morning."

Amused, shaking her head, she went up to bed, going over in her mind all that had happened.

Next day she and Beth were very busy. By common consent neither of them referred to the previous evening.

"Just one thing, Mattie, before you go off on your travels, I've been giving some consideration to that furniture. I think it would be better if *you* wrote to Mr. Watson. Explain the circumstances and tell him how you intend to handle it. If you don't wish to sell it back to him, perhaps you could act as his agent? Give it some thought, and then we will forward the letter through Bob Haswell. Now, I shall be in the office until one o'clock, and you take over then."

Each day, Beth gave her a little more responsibility, which was just what Mattie wanted.

*I was right to come to Nova Scotia,* she reflected. *I'm sure my mother must have been here once, because of the jewel box. Of course it could have been sent to her. Still, it is at least some sort of link to her, and I am happier here than I have ever been, more at home, that's for sure.*

Anna, unwillingly, was echoing the selfsame thought as she wandered once more under the trees behind The Old Mill.

"I was happier here, at that time, than I have ever been, before or since. But I am not happy now. It is too hard a battle to fight. I try! I try!"

She fell silent, still and quiet under the trees.

"Which shall I follow? The ancient ties are so strong! How many times have the stars followed their courses? From the days before Polaris, when Thuban was the pole star, when great rivers, Numeirah, Eval, Kerahi, filled the large inland water, now shrunken to become the Dead Sea. Life was young. I, even I, Anahita, Anaista, was young. Then I was the mistress of all the known waters."

The heartbroken remorse of the night before receded with each word, to be replaced by a wilful desire to exert such power once more, to have the authority to give or deny, in generosity or malice. Her eyes taking on an upward slant, like those of a cat, she produced the same small reed basket from a capacious pocket in her dark green smock. As though not wholly of her own volition, she made her way languidly to the small scattering of Amanita Muscaria. Deliberately, she pulled on her gloves and took out her small golden scissors. Snip! Snip! Snip!

"Three will be enough! It takes very little! Oh, the dreams that will be mine! And maybe – perhaps Mattie will dream too."

She looked around, her expression furtive, guilty, then put the bright caps in her little reed basket. This time she avoided going into the house, making instead for the barn. There on the workbench she had placed a blue dish, large and lustrous, gleaming dully in a shaft of light. With careful precision, she cut the caps into fine slices, smiling slyly. The hot late June sun, shining through the barn window, fell across the dish, casting small, dark, ominous shadows where the sliced mushrooms lay in a circle on the pale blue surface.

"There! Lie there for the sun to dry you!"

She covered them tenderly with a thin piece of white gauze.

"Tomorrow perhaps, but if not tomorrow, they will keep. Oh yes, they will keep."

Full of suppressed elation, Anna went back to The Old Mill. Masking her feelings, she ignored the small fire glowing as always on the hearth and sat, complacent and secretive, in her great chair, the powers of good and evil dangerously unbalanced in her heart.

# CHAPTER 7

Early on Saturday morning, Mattie called into the office to see Beth before heading off to meet Anna at The Old Mill. The day, already hot, promised to be a scorcher, and Beth, slumping behind her desk, fanning her face, straightened up self consciously, when Mattie spoke to her.

"Oh, I'm so glad I caught you, Beth. I have been thinking some more about Mr. Watson's antiques. I want to have moved them safely out of Anna Waters' reach, before I write to assure him as to their safety."

"Smart move, Mattie, and don't forget to have it all properly agreed and signed."

"I was wondering, you see, Beth," Mattie went on diffidently, "if I could store them in your barn? There isn't too much. Maybe I could fit the rocker in my apartment, but–"

"Good idea. Think no more about it. Get on to Sid Heddle right away. He likes Saturday work, because his son is there to help. He doesn't charge too much either. Here," she ferreted in her purse, producing a key to the barn. "Don't lose it!"

"Oh, thank you, Beth. What a relief. I'll pay of course."

"Not for the storage, Mattie, but you can pay Sid Heddle. Get it back from Mr. Watson. Phone Sid Heddle right away. He'll be there. You can always rely on good old Sid. We put a lot of custom his way!"

Waving away Mattie's thanks, she switched the phone through to her.

"Just get on with it," she urged. "Anna Waters strikes me as a shifty customer. You never know what she's up to."

Anna was, in fact, pacing restlessly about the Mill yard, waiting impatiently for Mattie.

"You're late!" she cried accusingly as Mattie drew into the drive.

Mattie, refusing to let herself be bullied, called a cheery, "Good morning, another lovely day!" Producing an inventory of the furniture, along with an agreement that it should be payment for Mattie's services, she asked to have it co-signed. Anna sulkily complied.

"Sid Heddle will be coming by later to take it all away, Anna. That way you need not worry about it anymore. Now, what have you planned for me to do today?"

For a moment Anna was disconcerted, for she had planned nothing. Her intentions were a different matter, those having been clear to her from the beginning. She needed Mattie's youth and strength, she needed her heart and mind, she needed to subsume Mattie's whole being into the old beliefs. She looked at her with all the doting longing of a hunter for its prey. Her own powers sinking, Mattie was to be her hostage to Ahriman, the purchase price of her freedom. The difficulty for Anna was the curbing of her impatience, the need to school herself to friendliness and subtlety, when her whole impulse was to drama and coercion. Suddenly aware of Mattie's look of bewilderment and enquiry, she smiled away her ungraciousness.

"There! What do these old sticks of furniture matter? You're here now, and we have disposed of all those little matters. We must make the most of the time before Mr. Heddle and his gauche offspring arrive."

Such was Anna's attempt at affability.

"What I now require of you is another inventory," adding spitefully, "you seem to be expert at writing those!"

As she made her way into The Old Mill, Anna explained that she needed to check that everything had arrived safely.

"You write what you find and I will check it against my list later"

"Have they come far?" Mattie asked. "Where were they before?"

"Oh, here and there! Here and there!" Anna waved her hands vaguely.

"Were you with a theatre company, Anna?" *There,* thought Mattie. *That's for you, Bookie!*

"My! My! Aren't we full of questions today?" Mattie flushed.

"This will take you some while, Mattie, more than today. As we check things off, I will tell you a story. We will begin with this chest."

Anna lovingly traced a finger round the carvings on the old chest near the hearth.

*It's strange,* thought Mattie, *but the furniture, which seemed too bizarre for this old place, now looks perfectly at home! More than suitable – in fact absolutely right. How odd.*

Anna produced a handsome old volume, bound in leather, tooled with curious devices in gold. When Mattie commented on the beautiful binding, Anna, giving her a plain foolscap binder, snapped impatiently, "Yes! Yes! I only enjoy the rare and intricate, as you will learn to do. Now, let us begin."

Mattie was fascinated, enthralled by the colours, textures and exotic designs of the things that lay before her. The first to come to hand was a heavy goblet with handles on either side, opalescent where it caught the light.

"Oh!" she gasped. "It's so beautiful. I fear I may break it."

"No one can break it. It will never break!"

"But isn't it glass?" Mattie asked wonderingly.

"More questions, Mattie? Just note it down as a 'lustral goblet'. See, I will fill it with water and we will drink together! A purification ceremony."

This she did, thinking. *Water only, for now. Maybe it will be enough? If not, then we will drink haoma together.* The now shrivelling strips of Amanita Muscaria, curling wickedly on the blue plate, flashed across her mind's eye.

Mattie shyly sipped from the goblet before handing it back to Anna.

"No! No! You must drink deeply!"

Mattie obeyed, her feelings of animosity towards Anna already lessening as she drank ceremoniously from the beautiful goblet.

*It's sort of like communion*, she thought, stifling a giggle. *But Anna is so serious about it.*

Anna placed the goblet reverently on the wrought iron table, holding it briefly as though in blessing.

"You see how magic these old things can be, Mattie? Relax and let them speak to you. That is what they are for."

She turned her brilliant eyes on Mattie, dazzling her.

"You are a wonderful actress, Anna! You make me feel as though all this is real."

"Ah, what is reality?" Anna replied.

It was slow work, as heavy silver gilt dishes – *They must be imitation,* Mattie thought – were followed by old-fashioned knives and spoons, with heavy silver gilt handles.

"There are no forks," commented Mattie. "Are they lost?"

"No, my child, there were no forks. There are ladles, jugs and ewers."

As the morning progressed, a closeness grew between the two of them. Partly it was a love of beautiful workmanship, partly a sense of sharing the moment. It was like a dream. Then Sid Heddle arrived. Anna heard his voice at the porch doorway.

"Where's it at then, Miss?" he called. "The furniture that's to go."

Anna hastily shut the chest before Sid could see the contents, throwing a rug over the items spread on the mat.

"See to it, Mattie," she snapped.

Mattie, shaking herself, for it was like wakening from a delicious sleep, went hastily to the porch, intent on intercepting Sid Heddle. Already she felt immersed in the atmosphere Anna had created, already protective, secretive, as if she and Anna were in some conspiracy together.

"Oh Sid!" she said as though surprised. "Good Heavens, is it that time already?" Turning to Anna, she said regretfully. "I must go with him, Anna, to show him where to put the furniture, as I have the only keys."

She looked dispassionately at the lovely old rocker, seeing it through Anna's eyes as no more than quaint. Anna observed her with sardonic and watchful eyes.

*It has started to work!* she exulted. *Soon she shall find the seal.*

Well content with her day's work, she ignored the confusion and bustle about her.

"You know there are one or two things in the barn, Mattie." Suddenly, remembering the mushrooms, she became full of energy. "Wait! I need to see to those myself."

Crossing to the barn, she hastily covered the blue plate with its precious contents, then carefully steered Sid and his inquisitive son, Danny, towards the back, where stood one or two chairs and side tables, all in need of repair.

*Rubbish,* she thought dismissively as the Heddles carried them out. *No better than kindling.*

She turned her back as Mattie and the Heddles drove away. The further they left Anna and The Old Mill behind, the more Mattie's appreciation of the lovely old pine returned, her spirits rising at the realisation that they were safe. It was as though she had been watching a B movie, full of melodrama and excess, and had now left the darkness of the theatre.

*Anna has always known how to jerk my strings*, she mused thoughtfully as she led Sid towards Calderford and Beth's home. *I must be on my guard. Anyway, the furniture will be safe here, and soon my obligations will be at an end, or so I hope. Tonight I will write to Mr. Watson, and see if he can come up with anything.*

After paying Sid, and slipping the keys through Beth's mail slot, Mattie drove thoughtfully home, trying to sift through all the impressions and emotions of this strange day. Too confused to feel like making supper, she went down The Snicket to Tim Horton's, for soup, sandwich, and coffee, enjoying being amongst other people, all intent on their own family life; no goblets, platters, or silver gilt extravagances, just good, hot food, simply served. Here was the warmth and friendliness she so badly needed. Afterwards, grateful to find that Bookie was busy at the back of the shop, she escaped upstairs to compose a letter to Mr. Kurma Watson.

*Dear Mr. Watson,*

*I understand from Mr. Haswell that there has been an unfortunate misunderstanding about the lovely old pine pieces you have left behind at The Old Mill, i.e. you had not intended to include them in the purchase price.*

*This could have caused some difficulty, since Mrs. Waters is a rather unusual woman, and quite fails to find any quality or beauty in such furniture. Her intentions were, in fact, to enamel them in garish reds, blues, greens, even to paint the knobs metallic gold. Finding this very hard to accept, I took the liberty of intervening. Not being in a position to purchase it, I managed to arrange that I should render certain services to her, which is what she already wished me to do. By these means, I have retrieved the furniture and it is safely stored in Mrs. Oxner's barn. I have not, so far, taken any for myself.*

*Perhaps you would be kind enough to give the matter some thought as to whether you wish to regain possession, and, if so, how this might be managed.*

*Sincerely*

*Mattie Peters (agent)*

*There, that covers it. What a load off my mind! I hope he decides to take it off my hands and the sooner the better! Maybe I can buy my way out of this mess. I do find my association with her very unsettling. I'll get Beth to include this in her correspondence to Bob Haswell. I expect he will e-mail Mr. Watson. What a day.*

Stretching, she thankfully went off for a hot shower and a well-earned rest.

# CHAPTER 8

On the following Monday morning, Beth searched her young assistant's face, interested to know how the time spent with Anna had gone, but finding Mattie's expression non-committal.

"Well," she asked at last, unable to contain her curiosity. "How did it go? I suppose the furniture is all safe? I found the keys. Thank you."

"Oh, sorry, Beth," said Mattie apologetically. "I should have let you know, but it was such a strange day! I have written to Mr. Watson, by the way. Can you put this with the mail to Bob Haswell?"

"Thanks." Beth put the letter aside. "Now, what does she have you doing? She must have all the furniture she needs by now, surely"

"She has me doing inventory." Mattie found herself unwilling to go into greater detail.

"And…." persisted an increasingly inquisitive Beth, "*is* she in the theatre?"

"She didn't say. I did try to find out, if only for Bookie's sake! However, she has a great many beautiful and exotic pieces. They are either stage props or else worth a fortune as antiques. I have never seen anything like them! They certainly appear authentic. It's very puzzling. A lot remains to be done. I shall have to go at least one more time, next Saturday, to complete the inventory. I must admit it's fascinating."

"Oh, do be on your guard, Mattie! She's using you, you know. It's as bad as being indentured. Well, never mind that for now, we still have a living to make, and it's going to be a very hot day. We really do need rain, don't we? You hold the fort at the office, I have an appointment. We have someone interested in that old place on the La Have islands. If I am not back, have lunch sent in. We are doing quite well, these days, we should make the most of it while it lasts."

Beth gathered up her things and took off in a rush.

Mattie found settling back into an everyday routine soothing. Whenever she had spent time with Anna, she felt in an emotional tug-of-war, out of balance, and routine work set things straight.

Anna, on the other hand, was in a mood of discontent and impatience. She prowled listlessly along the bank of Kingfisher Creek, which the heat of July had reduced to an inconsequential little stream, quite unable to stir the big mill wheel. Prolonged lack of rain always caused her to have lowered spirits and loss of vitality. Her shoulders drooped, and she ran her fingers languidly over the dusty foliage of an alder.

"The trees are just as dispirited as I am." Suddenly she turned, looking about her despondently.

"I must leave," she said restlessly. "I must seek other waters. I will return recharged, to meet with Mattie on Saturday. Yes, I must leave here at once."

Immediately, she went back to the barn and The Old Mill, locking them both before walking resolutely to the bank of the millpond, where the water was deep.

Thus it was that when Mattie, against her better judgement, drove over to The Old Mill one evening, she found no trace of Anna, although her car was still there. Gingerly trying the doors of both house and barn, she found them both locked.

*That's curious,* she thought, then shook her head, as though freeing herself from doubts. *It's nothing to do with me. What made me come?*

Looking around once more, she drove home, where Bookie greeted her delightedly.

"Look!" he said. "I've bought us each a window fan! Get rid of some of this stuffy air. Don't go! Don't go yet! You must look at some of these old books! You must."

He urged her to the back of the shop, which he had set up as a little reading room, with an old pine table and four chairs. It looked cosy and welcoming.

"Well, maybe just for a minute, Bookie, but I am too hot to be intelligent about them."

"Oh dear, oh dear, you poor thing! But I won't keep you long. Look! Look!"

His face shining with the happiness of a true enthusiast, he grabbed her hand and drew her with him. More to humour him than out of interest, Mattie allowed herself to be persuaded into a chair by the old pine table, where Bookie sat beside her.

"Look at these," he said. "Old ceremonial vessels."

Reverently, he opened a worn leather volume of colour plates. Mattie obediently gave him her attention, as he turned the pages.

"Wait!" she cried. "Turn back to the other page."

There, large as life, was a black and white drawing of a platter with the same design as those Anna had shown her. Intricate, wonderful, with a central sun surrounded by deeply chased figures, it depicted lions, goats, men with formal curly beards, carrying bows, arrows, spears, and all interwoven with vines and foliage.

"Why! What?" said Bookie excitedly.

"I believe I have seen this design before somewhere, Bookie." Some reticence held her back from telling him where. "Maybe I'm mistaken." Slowly she read the inscription.

*A design believed to have been taken from an ancient Middle Eastern platter, probably Old Persian. Now lost.*

Looking through the book, she found nothing further of similar interest.

"Thank you, Bookie. You have some real treasures here. May I look through them all sometime?"

"Of course, of course, you know you may." Bookie glowed with happiness. "I love to show my treasures. They are meant to be shared with friends."

"May I bring Beth with me? I know she would find it interesting."

"Beth would be welcome any time." His manner was gracious. "I have always had a high regard for Beth Oxner."

Next day he went to the barbershop for a haircut, surprising both the barber and himself by finding more hair had been scraped back into his bootlace than either of them had expected. It sprang about his head quite vigorously. He turned this way and that, admiring the barber's handiwork in the mirror. After paying, he left, whistling happily, taking his old ponytail with him, his step springing and full of confidence. For years his diffidence had kept him from pursuing a friendship with Beth Oxner, and now here was his chance. It was well worth all the teasing he received from Mattie that evening concerning his youthful appearance and curly hair.

By Wednesday, Mattie was her usual serene self. Now, in retrospect, the things she had seen at The Old Mill seemed tawdry, flashy. At a loss to understand her earlier feelings, she turned to a humdrum explanation.

"I was probably just hungry. Next Saturday I will be sure to have a good breakfast. She truly is an exhausting person to be with for any length of time. I often feel quite light-headed after spending any amount of time there."

On Wednesday, she began telling Beth about the volumes at Once Read Books.

"I thought you might be interested to see one plate in particular. There is an illustration of a platter very like one of Anna's. Why not come over to my apartment on Thursday evening? That is if you wouldn't mind my cooking!

I know Bookie would be happy to show the book to you. He's so proud of his finds – but I haven't told him where I saw the platter."

"I really would like that, Mattie. I have always thought it would be interesting to know Horatio Bean better. Whatever would make his parents give him a name like that? It sounds so old fashioned! It does have a fine heroic ring to it, though. Do you remember 'How Horatius kept The Bridge'? I just loved that poem. 'Then out spake brave Horatius, the Keeper of the Gate.'" She broke off. "Don't look at me like that! Didn't you learn that at school?"

"No, Beth, but I'm most impressed!"

"'To every man upon this earth, Death cometh soon or late!'"

She was still spouting away when Mattie left.

On Thursday, a flushed Bookie joined Beth and Mattie for dinner. It was simple enough, just chile, homemade biscuits and fruit.

"No coffee, thank you," said Beth. "I will never go to sleep tonight if I have coffee now."

Bookie was delighted.

"That's so true! I just get so excited if I have coffee at night."

They smiled understandingly at each other. After dinner, they trooped down to the bookshop. The space at the back looked homely and inviting, with the glowing old pine and ancient books.

"We'll have a candle. It's more in keeping," said Bookie.

"But we won't be able to see the colour plates," protested Beth.

He immediately took the candle away, switching on a reading lamp instead. The three of them sat happily together, browsing through the same volume Mattie had examined previously.

"Why, it's gorgeous!" exclaimed Beth, looking at the drawing of the platter. "Lost, is it? Perhaps Anna found it! I wouldn't put anything past her!"

"It was lost hundreds of years ago, maybe thousands! She can't have anything to do with it!" Mattie laughed. "It is a very good copy that she has, though. That's where I saw it, Bookie. Sorry, I should have told you that."

"She's capable of anything," Beth said darkly. "Now, I must get off home. We must do this again. Thank you, Mattie, and you too, Horatio."

Giving him a hug, she laughed wickedly at his embarrassment as she went out to her car.

On Friday, there was a thunderstorm. Heavy rain fell for most of the day, and the Calder River looked full and turbulent.

"I wonder whether Kingfisher Creek has overflowed its banks? Beth, do you think that's likely?"

"Oh, I shouldn't think so! It has been very dry and the mill pool needed filling up, I'm sure. Anyway, you'll find out tomorrow. I wonder what else you will find? The Koh-I-Noor diamond perhaps!" Beth laughed. "It's really good of you to do this, Mattie, for the firm's reputation. You aren't getting much out of it for yourself. It's all really Bob Haswell's responsibility. We should hear something from Kurma Watson by next week though."

By Saturday morning it was sunny and warm, the whole world looking freshly washed, the sun sparkling like a million stars on the wet leaves. Nevertheless, Mattie took her rubber boots with her, just in case, and Kingfisher Creek was indeed just as full as the Calder River. As she drove into The Old Mill yard, she was surprised not to see a wisp of smoke curling up from the chimney, for Anna always kept a small fire burning, in spite of the heat. Shading her eyes, she looked once more. No smoke was to be seen. She tried the door and found it still locked.

*That's odd*, she thought. *No message or anything.* Turning to leave, she saw Anna right in front of her.

"I can't believe what I am seeing," Mattie whispered aghast, for Anna gave every appearance of emerging from the swollen creek, fully clothed in her blue linen suit. Closing her eyes briefly, Mattie looked again. There was Anna, standing beside, looking fresh and immaculate.

"I thought – I thought…." whispered Mattie.

"Whatever is the matter with you, woman? Has the heat affected you?" Anna asked, taking out her key and moving towards The Old Mill. "Better come in and sit down! Next thing you know, you will be imagining things." She looked slyly at Mattie and laughed.

Shaken, Mattie followed her followed her silently into the cool of the house, rubbing her eyes.

"What you need is a long cool drink of water. Nature's best restorative."

After lighting the usual small fire, Anna took out the goblet, filled it with water and handed it ceremoniously to Mattie.

"Drink," she said. "We will pledge each other."

As though hypnotised, earlier resolutions to withstand Anna's blandishments forgotten, Mattie drank deeply. Anna followed suit.

"Ahuro Mazdao," she murmured, holding the goblet towards the hearth before placing it once more on the wrought iron table.

"What does that mean, Anna? 'Ahuro Mazdao'?"

"Oh, Mattie. Ahuro – sublime, awful, divine spirit. Long before Zarathustra called him Ahuro Mazdao, there were many gods and goddesses."

Her voice trailing away, she looked towards the fire, her wide eyes reflecting the flickering flames.

"All-powerful, divine," her voice became low, vibrant, compelling. "Long ago, there was the one divine spirit. Long before the time of Phoenicians, Babylonians or Greeks, when the ancient Accadians and Sumerians studied their flocks of stars, there by the mighty Euphrates, when Thuban was the pole star. Before Ki-din-nu of Babylon even, whom the Greeks called Cidenas, observed and measured the spin of the constellations."

"Wait! said Mattie, sitting on the floor by the hearth. "I need time to absorb all this."

Anna, barely acknowledging the interruption, sank into her great chair, the throbbing voice continuing the tale, her eyes remaining fixed and still, in the glimmering light.

"The Sun they called 'the Old Sheep', the planets 'Old Sheep's Stars'. Great luminous Arcturus they knew as 'the Shepherd of the Old Sheep's Stars'. Those early people watched the wheeling skies, eyes wide with wonder, measuring, recording. Even long before those early days there was One Divine Spirit, when the Dead Sea was a great water, and the Black Sea new. He it was who ordained the precession of the constellations, the mighty astral clock, that spinning cone of light around Earth's spindle. I know him as Ahuro, Ormazd."

She fell silent. Mattie, mesmerised, looked questioningly at her face. Anna spoke again.

"At that time, there were the nature deities, half mortal, when all was new, they who were known as the Daeva."

Her face darkened and her voice slowed, thickened.

"Zarathustra's vision changed it all. Now Daevas must serve Ahriman."

Rising, she strode to the hearth.

"Ahriman, the antagonist! Ahriman, who in temporal time limits the power of Ahuro Mazdao, tempting men to evil." She paused. "But after death! Ah, then Ahuro Mazdao shall judge, and none but he!"

"And the Daeva?" Mattie asked softly, unwilling to break the spell.

"They are called the children of Ahriman." Anna's voice became tragic, "Alas that it is so! Except Mitra, whom some call Mithras, God of fire. His light is joined to the light of Ahuro Mazdao. He is one with the All-Powerful"

A sob caught in Anna's throat. She opened her hands in supplication.

"But why? Why only Mithras? Is water not pure? Does it not cleanse and refresh?"

Mattie waited breathlessly to hear more, but suddenly Anna, becoming aware of Mattie's presence, brushed a hand across her face and lowered her gaze, breathing more calmly.

"What wonderful stories, Anna!"

"Stories?" cried Anna, her voice echoing round the ceiling beams. "Stories?"

Mattie stood up in alarm.

"Why yes, of course, such stories," Anna said, more calmly.

"You tell them so well," Mattie said quietly. "But you should not exhaust yourself."

Anna fell silent, gazing into the fire, while Mattie waited. Presently Anna looked up. Her smile was gentler, warmer.

"You are right. I feel a great weariness. We will leave the inventory for another time."

Mattie gathered up her things, schooling her mind to blankness, aware of Anna's uncanny ability to read her thoughts.

"I will see you next Saturday, then," she said.

Anna, in her great chair, simply nodded, turning her head away.

The air outside, freshened by the rain, cleared Mattie's head, and once more she felt relieved to be leaving the tense atmosphere of The Old Mill behind her.

*Perhaps Anna is a little unstable,* she thought. *I always find her very emotional. She must have been enormously charismatic in the theatre. Whew! I couldn't handle it for very long. What a presence though, and what wonderful legends.*

Returning to the office, she spent the rest of the day in the comfortably prosaic world of real estate, happy, for once, that Beth was out.

After Mattie left, Anna sat brooding in her great chair. Then slowly she rose and as though in a dream, turning her back on the fire. Resolutely, she left the room and strode towards the barn. Unlocking the door, she went over to the blue dish where, like dark question marks, the pieces of Amanita Muscaria lay. She trailed her fingers round the blue rim, just as troubled and disoriented as she had ever been.

*To use them, or not? To drink haoma, or to wait? To stay with Ahriman, or hope for Ahuro Mazdao?*

The gentle expression which had been softening her face faded away. Slowly her eyes narrowed, her mouth tightening into an imperious curve. This transformation, at least, Mattie had been spared.

# CHAPTER 9

"Bookie, what do you know about 'precession'?"

"You don't mean 'procession', do you, Mattie?"

"Oh, come on, Bookie! I'm not that ignorant!"

Bookie waited indulgently. Mattie was very much in his good books these days, since bringing Beth Oxner into his life.

"Ah now, 'precession'. 'Pre' you see, meaning 'before'."

Mattie rolled her eyes. "Give me some credit, Bookie! I understand the word as such, but what I want to know is, what is the 'precession of the stars'?"

"Why Mattie? You have hidden depths. Are you interested in Astronomy?"

"No, not really, Bookie. I heard the phrase and just wondered what it might mean."

"This may take some time, Mattie, tell you what, why don't you come to supper on Thursday? I'll have cold salmon and salad. I'm a very good cook, you know! Yes, that would be best. Come then. Bring Beth."

Amused, Mattie agreed and hurried off to the office feeling like Cupid, to extend the invitation to Beth.

"This could become a habit, Mattie. You know how these things start!" Beth tried to sound severe but was smiling, in spite of herself. "Yes, well. Why not? Stars now, is it? Anyway, there is a letter of sorts from your Kurma Watson. It came by e-mail. Via Bob Haswell. Kurma will be here by the end of August, if not before. Bob is very apologetic and thanks you for your trouble. Here, I ran off a print for you. I should reply, if I were you. Let him know how things stand."

Mattie read the letter eagerly, hoping for some relief from her Saturdays with Anna.

*Dear Miss Peters.*

*Thank you for your letter about my old pieces of pine. I appreciate the concern and consideration you have shown. The confusion arose when my uncle was adamant that the right moment had arrived to transfer Kurma Enterprises to me. Caught by surprise (I might say amazement), I failed to make matters clear.*

*It is difficult, at this distance, to make any sort of restitution, but I hope to meet with you in person in the near future, at least by the end of August, at which time we should be able to settle matters more comfortably. I could, meanwhile, have money transferred to Miss Waters as recompense, and to relieve you of these extra duties.*

*Sincerely.*

*Kurma Watson.*

"He sounds very reasonable," Mattie observed, handing the copy back to Beth. "Some people might have been angry, and blamed us for the mix-up."

Beth nodded.

"I don't suppose Bob got off so lightly! Still, there you are. Mr. Watson couldn't have been clear in his instructions either. Why the sudden interest in things astronomical, by the way?"

"It's Anna, you see, Beth."

"Naturally! Why do I even ask? Who else? Just be careful, my child, that she doesn't become an obsession."

"Nothing like that, but she does tell the most fascinating stories. I want to find out what basis they have, if any."

"Well, let's leave it aside. We have a business to run. There seem to be a good many people interested in our waterfront properties. There always are in the summer. It doesn't seem right, does it? They have so much more money than us Blue-Noses."

This, said so casually, gave Mattie, a 'come from away', without family, a feeling of belonging, of having found a home. She smiled warmly at Beth, in complete agreement.

"That's true, particularly if they are only used as summer places. To be fair though, many local people are only too willing to sell."

They furrowed their brows over this conundrum for a little while, then shrugged and went about their business. First, Mattie wrote a reply to Kurma Watson.

*Dear Mr. Watson.*

*Thank you for your letter.*

*First I should explain the reason I chose this particular way of safeguarding your furniture. Miss Waters' first name is Anahita, tho' sometimes she calls herself Anaista, sometimes both! This is not the only unusual thing about her. My belief is that she may have been on the stage, or in some way connected to the theatre. Her preference in the things she has around her is for the exotic. This means that she dismissed your beautiful old pine pieces as worthless. She gives the impression of having plenty of money, and would not be interested in returning your furniture on that basis. She was, however, very interested in having my help with shopping, inventory taking, chores of that nature. This I will continue to do, until we are able to resolve the situation in person. I would advise against sending her money directly. She is very unpredictable.*

*Sincerely.*

*Mattie Peters.*

*There*, thought Mattie. *I suppose I'm stuck with Anna for another week or two – or three.*

She was unwilling to admit, even to herself,, how attracted she was to this strange woman, or the ambivalence of her feelings towards her, half fascination, half aversion.

*I can't understand for one minute,* she mused, *why she should be so determined that I should help her. She obviously already has a complete inventory of all her things. She could easily check it herself.*

Sighing, she finished her letter to Bob Haswell. *It would be simpler to deal directly with Kurma Watson, but I suppose he wants to keep his whereabouts to himself, although....* here she smiled, *Bob hasn't proved to be very useful by any means!*

Gladly she put the whole business out of her mind, occupying herself instead with the mundane office work.

On Thursday evening Bookie had outdone himself. The little 'reading room' looked cool and inviting. He had installed a small refrigerator in one corner to keep the food cold, and Mattie looked admiringly at both the blue bowl of old-fashioned yellow roses on the table and the spiffy real linen napkins in an echoing blue.

"Why, Bookie, you are spoiling us!" she said. "You should move in and live here!" She looked at him curiously. "Why don't you live in the flat, Bookie? I've often wondered."

"I found a nice little apartment out at Hestler's Settlement, Mattie."

"Why though?"

"Because I might never go to bed, that's why! I would sit and read, and mess with books all night, and day too! Oh good! Here's Beth."

He pulled out a chair with a flourish, inviting Beth to sit down. It was all much more civilised than Mattie's little supper, and when they had finished,

Bookie cleared everything away into a large basket, rejecting all offers of help.

"I will take this home with me. Forget all about it! Now," he wiped the table and waited expectantly, "you wanted me to tell you about the precession of the stars, Mattie, is that it?

"Yes, professor," said Mattie, smiling. "I thought you would be bound to know all about it, Bookie! If not, surely it's somewhere in all these books."

Bookie tapped his head knowingly. "No need of books, it's all up here. Just a minute, I need to get something from the shop."

He came back carrying a short whip.

"Good Heavens!" gasped Beth. "Whatever is that for?"

"Nothing to be alarmed about! See what I have here." In his other hand Bookie held an old-fashioned spinning top.

"Have you ever played whip and top?" he asked. Pushing back the chairs to make some floor space, he wound the whip round the spindle of the top, steadied it with one hand, then pulled the cord sharply. The top spun merrily.

"Oh! I haven't seen one of those for years, Bookie," cried Beth happily.

"Notice how it spins," Bookie instructed them.

"It doesn't stand straight up anymore," said Mattie. "It's slowing down."

"The upper part makes a bigger circle than the toe," added Beth. "Aren't you going to whip it up?"

"No, because I have some thing else to show you. Now watch this! Don't you love these old toys?"

"Why, it's a gyroscope!" said Beth, at the same time as Mattie asked, "Whatever is it?"

Bookie handed it to her, so that she could examine it. A metal disc on a central spindle was caged in two intersecting metal rings.

"They look like lines of latitude and longitude," joked Mattie.

"Smart girl! Here, see this little hole in the spindle? Now, if I adjust the end cap just right, thread the string through the hole and wind it up, I can spin it."

Beth clapped her hands.

"Oh! I love these things! See how it leans, Mattie, and keeps on spinning. Hear it hum?"

Bookie looked smug.

"That's it," he said. "The central mass causes the spindle to spin in a cone from the base."

He put the gyroscope away. "Now pay attention, children. The mass of the Earth causes the same cone effect. The result is that the star year is over twenty minutes longer than the solar year."

He looked at their dazed faces. "Don't you see? It's like a huge clock. The constellations rise a little later each year."

Bookie, far too interested in his subject to be self-conscious, looked at Beth and Mattie to see if they were still interested.

"Go on," said Beth.

"It's after the vernal equinox, you see, March 21st. That's the starting point. Now Hipparchus noticed this around 130 BC. when he compared his observations of longitude with those done in Babylon by Ki-din-nu some two centuries earlier. The equinoctial points moved clockwise, you see." He paused, watching Mattie. "Am I boring you?" For she had gone quite pale, and drew in her breath sharply. "Perhaps that's enough for now. I do get carried away with the equinoxes, and I will only confuse you."

"No, Bookie, it's not you. It's Miss Waters."

Beth groaned. "Oh! Not *that* again, Mattie, please! Forget her!"

"But Beth! She knows all this stuff. It is what she was saying. I remember the name 'Ki-din-nu'. She was very convincing! It was as though she had *been* there."

"That is odd," agreed Beth. "She doesn't look the type of person who would have read much, does she?"

Bookie looked from face to face, and fiddled with his gyroscope

"Let's leave it at that for now, shall we?" he said at last.

"Yeah, come on Mattie! Stop worrying! Accept it! The woman is weird," said Beth "I'm off home. Thank you, Bookie, this was great fun. I'll bring supper next week."

Bookie flushed with surprise and pleasure as they gathered their things together. Beth was coming again.

"Till next time then, Horatio!" said Beth mischievously. "Go to bed, Mattie. Forget the woman, do."

But Mattie, finding it impossible, tossed restlessly for a long while before falling asleep, her dreams full of stars, clocks and spinning tops.

On Saturday morning, she stolidly worked her way through cereal, egg, coffee and fruit, determined to fortify herself against another day of discomfiture. On arrival at The Old Mill, she checked the chimney for the small plume of smoke.

"Ah! The Pope has been elected, I see." Pleased to be able to laugh at her small joke, she went warily towards the door, which Anna flung open, calling.

"Come in, my dear, come in!" Her manner was warm and welcoming.

Mattie, realising that she had been holding her breath, relaxed. Anna seemed to be in a good mood today.

"To work! To work! We have been wasting time. First our toast."

Once more she held out the goblet to Mattie. As she did so, the quiet little fire flared angrily, causing Anna to step back, snatching the goblet from Mattie, her face full of alarm.

"Now it will be spoiled! There will be ash in it."

"I don't see any, Anna. I'm sure it's...."

But Anna had swung away from her and gone to the kitchen. Mattie heard the tap running before Anna returned with the freshly filled goblet, looking discontented but no longer alarmed.

"A toast, Mattie!" she said dully. "Ahuro Mazdao Ormazd!" Her manner was perfunctory. "Come, we will go upstairs to check my jewellery and robes."

In the closet were several long flowing robes. The fabrics were beautiful silks, richly dyed and patterned. As they hung side by side they seemed to ripple and flow like running water under varied skies. Mattie longed to run her hands through them, to feel them against her skin. Her eyes shining with delight, she turned to Anna.

"Why, they are gorgeous," she cried. "Under the stage lights they must have glowed like jewels."

"You always talk about acting," Anna said impatiently. "Count them, check them There are still others; in this cupboard, there are a four more."

On opening the door, Mattie gasped, for the four robes hanging there were magnificent.

"There is one for each season, as you will be able to tell. All are many-coloured, but as you see, Spring is mostly greens and blues, Summer has more rose and yellow, Fall has rich reds and gold, Winter, white, silver and grey. But all have blue in all its shades and hues, like water running through the landscape."

She held each one up in turn for the entranced Mattie to admire. Nowhere to be seen were the nondescript clothes Anna had worn when they first met. She watched Mattie's dazed expression with pleasure.

"And you shall wear them all, Mattie. They will be yours! Not now, but all in good time."

She saw the consternation on Mattie's face, and ran her hand softly down her cheek.

"Not yet! Not yet! There is nothing to fear."

"We should check your jewellery," Mattie said stiffly, "before I go."

She turned away from Anna towards the heavy ebony jewellery chest standing on the windowsill. Following her, Anna took out a slender key with an ornately fashioned head. Her eyes slid to Mattie's face.

"Open it," she said.

Mattie opened the heavy lid and almost laughed out loud, the effect was so theatrical, so gaudy. She stood back, hands clasped, suppressing a giggle, feeling like one of the thieves in *Ali Baba*. The more apt idea of *Pandora* never crossed her mind.

"It's like an illustration from *Arabian Nights*," she said apologetically as she saw Anna's offended expression. "They look so opulent, they seem unreal, and there are so many."

It took them two hours of checking and rechecking, and still the tally was wrong.

"There are these," said Mattie, holding up a small cedar box. It was beautifully made, the lid fitting so closely that it gave a small sigh on opening, as if unwilling to reveal the contents. "Not one of these pendants is listed. They look different, to my inexpert eyes. The gold doesn't look so old, or soft, and is not so dark, though the settings are lovely. Amethyst, I recognise, and amber. What is this green stone? It is such a beautiful colour."

"Peridot. So they are extra. Perhaps I didn't value them. I must have picked them up somewhere or other, and never worn them."

"Then there is this." Mattie held up a beautiful black opal pendant, her eyes glowing with pleasure at this quieter, less flashy jewellery.

"So, take them! I don't want them." Anna pushed them into Mattie's hand. Mattie retreated, dropping the pendants to the floor, her reaction one of dismay, almost of fear. Wishing to have no further obligations to this woman, she put her hands childishly behind her back.

"No! No!" she cried. Slowly becoming calmer, she retrieved the jewels and held them out. Anna ignored them. They stared at each other for a moment, looking very alike, eyes wide, mouths set, hair unruly, then Mattie put the jewellery carefully on the table.

"It is very generous of you, Anna, but the furniture is all I wish to have. Now there is just this box of signet rings, incised with names."

The signets, in obsidian, were unusually large and impressive, the rings wrought gold.

"See, we will try them," said Anna. From the box she drew out a stick of red sealing wax, and matches. Dropping sealing wax on to a card, she tried each ring in turn. One after another imprinted "Anahita" in a circle, until the last, which, as with the pendants, looked newer. It made an imprint of a fish, surrounded by a name. The colour fled from Mattie's face, for the name was "Matsya".

"Why are you so concerned, Mattie?" Anna tones were silky. "That's only Matsya, my little fish. My own little fish." She laid her hand against Mattie's face, her expression a mixture of love and malice.

Unreasoning, Mattie fled downstairs, Anna's laughter echoing in her ears as she ran. Snatching up her purse and car keys, she drove, far too fast, back to Calderford, impelled by her racing heart.

When Mattie had left, Anna sank on to the bed, her rejected gifts beside her, her laughter turning to tears, she hugged her arms around herself, rocking back and forth.

"Matsya! My little fish! Alexander, what have I done? What shall I do now?"

# CHAPTER 10

Mattie drove unsteadily down Mill Road, pulling to the side near Kingfisher Creek. Getting out of the car, she walked to the bridge and leaned on the parapet, watching the water purling between the rocks to the Calder River, letting the serenity calm her nerves.

*How does she know? Why did she laugh? Who is Anna Waters? Can she possibly be...?*

Unwilling to give her suspicions a voice, Mattie went shakily back to her car. Driving home to Calderford, leaving fantasy behind her, she headed as usual for the comfortable reality of Tim Horton's, revelling in the chatter and laughter around her. The warm feeling of shared food and friendships combined with the smell of the coffee welcomed her and as she sipped, her feeling of trepidation lessened.

*I imagine things*, she told herself firmly. *It is obviously a very old name, maybe from Europe! Why did I run?* The coffee was helping. *Of course! No wonder she laughed! What a fool I must have looked.* Mattie, giggling self-consciously, turned her attention to her sandwich.

"What are you laughing at? Come on! Share it with me! I could do with a laugh."

Sid Heddle sat down heavily in the seat across from Mattie, Startled, she shook her head.

"Oh. nothing special, Sid. How's she going?"

"I'm doing all right, thank you very much! It's these barbecues, you see, everyone wants a brick one now. They still have their fancy gas ones, to do the work of course, but the brick ones 'look so nice and natural.'" Sid affected what he thought was a citified way of speech. "They'll be lucky the Fire Marshall isn't after 'em." He shrugged.

"Sid, that's dreadful! Don't you build in safeguards of any sort?"

"Oh! It's not as bad as I make it sound, m'dear," said Sid sheepishly. "It's a properly designed thing, you see, but there, so are cars. It's those using them," he finished darkly.

"Nice side line though, for you and Danny."

"Danny's in school – or at least he better be. Had to do summer school, to make up, didn't he? I could do with his help too. Still, he'll be home Saturday, and he can help me with that Miss Waters."

"Is she moving?" asked Mattie, her voice full of hope. Anything was possible with Anna.

"No, she wants one of those barbecues, 'So many things we can do outside, Mr. Heddle.'" Sid's falsetto was grotesque. "'So many, many things that we can't do inside!' I'll bet she was a goer in her time." This last was in his own voice. "She reminds me of someone, but I can't call it to mind."

"Well, Sid, I must leave you to reminisce. I'm off to the office. See you."

Her earlier fears dismissed as fantasy, Mattie settled down to make phone calls, arranging viewings for the following day. People are always available on Sunday. At first, she did not notice Beth, who was looking critically round the office.

"Something wrong, Beth?" Mattie felt twinges of her old feelings of incompetence.

"No, nothing like that, Mattie, but just look at this place! It's a mess!"

"I like this old office, Beth. It's so much more welcoming than the new shiny ones."

"Oh, I agree, but there's old and then there's down at heel. We spend quite a lot of our lives here, Mattie. Why should we spend it in squalor?"

Mattie laughed.

"It's not that bad, Beth! It would cost a fortune to look like – your house, for example."

"Oh, pooh!" Beth waggled her fingers, letting her diamonds sparkle in the sunlight. "I have a small fortune here and what good are they, pray tell me? I bought them to console myself for Alec, as though anything could. No, they served their purpose, I suppose, but I'm not really the diamond type." Beth examined her hands critically. "They look so cold and hard, don't they? And that's how I felt, for far too long."

Mattie laughed at her.

*It's true,* she thought. *Beth is changing. Her hair is softer, and she smiles more. She has even lost a little weight. She looks – motherly.*

"I could get enough from these to make the changes, Mattie, without ruining the business. It would," she struck a pose, "be a new influx of capital!"

Once more they laughed together.

"Well, it would be fun. I could learn a lot from you about old places, Beth, but I am afraid I haven't any capital to help."

"Look, Mattie. You aren't involved, really. I own the property. I'm really just protecting my investment. *You* can put in some sweat equity, if you like.

I'll see someone or other and start making plans. Now, what are you pulling out of the hat to ask Bookie this Thursday? I really look forward to that, don't you? He's much more knowledgeable than I suspected."

"I'll come up with something, Beth," said Mattie slowly. "He may know something about my name. I wont tell him it's *my* name, of course."

"Why ever not, Mattie? You talk as though it would harm you, somehow! You know the way some people think a photograph will rob them of their souls? No, Rumpelstiltskin! That's it! You are like Rumpelstiltskin!"

She laughed gleefully, Mattie unwillingly joining in.

"I know it's absurd. I've always been that way. It's such an outlandish sort of name, and my background is outlandish enough."

"There are names here from all over the place, Mattie! I think Matsya is a lovely name."

"I suppose I am being quite irrational about it," Mattie said, "but I have always felt that way. Anyway, Bookie would be sure to guess. I'll tell him."

The following Tuesday, there was another letter from Kurma Watson. This time it came directly to Mattie.

*Dear Mattie.*

*(Please excuse the informality) Thank you for your letter. I now understand the situation more fully and will happily follow your advice. I shall, meanwhile, remain indebted to you.*

*Miss Waters does seem to have her own ideas about things, but then, which of us hasn't? Her name Anahita (or Anaista) is very old indeed. Thousands of years ago, Anahita or Anaista was the name of the Daeva, a nature Goddess of Water! Whoever named her must have known this, I should think. I have dubbed her 'The Water Witch'. This is very unkind of me, isn't it? Just because she doesn't appreciate my antiques....*

*Keep in touch with me. Bob has my number.*

*Sincerely.*

*Kurma (Watson)*

Mattie smiled as she read it.

*'Water Witch'! What a wonderful name for Anna. It just about sums up my feelings for her exactly. She's so – so – disquieting*"

She had found the letter comforting in some way, allowing her to view Anna's eccentricities differently, and it was in a light-hearted mood that she proposed her name as Thursday's topic of conversation. Bookie was delighted at the challenge, his eyes gloating over the old volumes.

"You are so interesting, Mattie, always coming up with a challenge. Matsya is a lovely name. I know it from somewhere! Oh, bother, here's a customer."

"Isn't that what the shop is for, Bookie?" Mattie teased.

"Well, partly, I suppose. Good evening, Madam, may I help you?" He turned busily to the customer, adding hopefully, "Or do you prefer to browse?"

Mattie escaped upstairs, still wondering if she had made a mistake. Almost reluctantly, she took out the jewel case with the necklace, holding it tightly. Closing her eyes, she willed the box to give up its secrets, then sighed ruefully.

*I'm growing weirder by the minute!* Opening the lid, she studied the necklace in minute detail.

*The fish is exactly the same as Anna's! What was it she said – "Matsya, my own little fish"?*

A shiver ran down her spine. Quickly snapping the lid shut, she dropped the box hastily into the drawer, as if it were too hot to handle.

"Water Witch," she whispered. "Water Witch."

On Thursday evening, Bookie greeted them with suppressed excitement at the discoveries he had made.

"May I say how particularly lovely you both look this evening?" he said, pulling out the chairs.

"Oh, do!" Beth was laughing. "As often as you like."

She and Mattie looked at each other, and found that it was true. To Mattie, Beth looked warm, happy, loving. To Beth, Mattie looked young, fresh, untouched. They looked away self-consciously, busying themselves with supper, their eyes following Bookie to a large volume bound in dark red.

"Now," said Bookie, "I have something to tell you. First about the books. This volume, which I bought from Eustace Wilkie's sale, has another name on a bookplate inside, and I am concerned that I should return it. The name inside is Kendrick Gibson."

Beth looked sharply at Mattie, who sat transfixed, shaken by the coincidence.

"No need, Bookie. I knew Kendrick Gibson very well and he died some time ago." Tears came into her eyes. "He was very good to me, and helped me a great deal."

"Well then," said Bookie, "now he is about to help you again. I have found your name, Mattie. Let me read it to you. 'Matsya, literally meaning fish, the first Avatar of Vishnu.'"

"Hold it right there, Horatio!" cried Beth. "Explain, explain."

"An Avatar is a visible form of a God, Beth. It says here, 'Hindus believe in one all-embracing, neutral spirit, Brahma. His works are carried out by three personalities, two of them are masculine, Brahma the creator and Vishnu the preserver. One, Siva, is feminine. She conceives, reproduces and destroys."

"Whew! Busy lady," said Beth irreverently while Mattie sat quietly listening.

"So these personalities pop up in different forms, or Avatars, you see, Beth. Now the first Avatar of Vishnu was Matsya, the fish, and the second was Kurma, the tortoise."

"What?" gasped Mattie. She turned to Beth. "I wonder how Kurma Watson got his name?" Her head was full of wild suppositions. She felt drawn against her will into an intricate pattern of coincidence – or was it more than that?

Looking from one face to the other, Bookie continued, "Vishnu has already had nine Avatars, At the end of the ninth age, the tenth Avatar of Vishnu will arrive as a winged white horse, Kalki, to destroy the Earth."

"So *anyone* might know the name 'Matsya' means 'fish'?" asked Mattie diffidently.

"Of course! It's right here!" Bookie assured her

Mattie let out a long breath of relief. Beth looked at her quizzically.

"See, Rumpelstiltskin?" she chaffed.

"Now you've lost me," said Bookie. "Rumpelstiltskin?"

"Oh, it's a long story, Horatio!" Beth leant over to Bookie, and kissed him roundly on the cheek. "Thank you," she said. "You always give us something to think about. You're a treasure."

Bookie's hand touched his cheek in wonderment.

"There's just so much we don't know, isn't there, Bookie?"

"That's why I love these old books, Beth."

He looked round the shelves with pride, his self-conscious mannerisms falling away. "There is so much to know. Would you like the book, Mattie? I feel you should have it."

Between Bookie and Kurma, Mattie went off to bed, immensely re-assured. The Water Witch receding to manageable proportions, she slipped off to sleep as soon as her head hit the pillow.

Next day she sent off an e-mail via Bob Haswell to Kurma Watson.

*Dear Kurma,*

*I am presuming to use your first name, because I have just found out that Kurma is The Tortoise, second Avatar of Vishnu. The reason*

*I find this so amazing is that my name, Matsya, is the first Avatar of Vishnu, The Fish! I wonder how we came by such names?*

*Anna seemed quite dismayed when she first knew that you were called 'Kurma'. I have never used 'Matsya' in my dealings with her and, for some reason, never will.*

*Sincerely.*

*Matsya Peters.*

*There,* she thought laughing ruefully. *The way things are going I suppose it was inevitable that our paths would cross.*

# CHAPTER 11

After Mattie had gone, Anna sank discontentedly into her great chair, holding the rejected gifts in her hands, a tangle of gold, amber, amethyst, peridot and opal.

*And so I am left with the opal. The unhappiness will be mine.*

Rising, she went over to the fireplace. Crouching before the small fire, she stirred the embers, as though searching them for a message, murmuring to herself, "How to free myself of Ahriman, if not this way? How to shed my mortal self? How to become one with you, O Ahuro, Ormazd? I know only one way. One way only. I must find another, someone young, acceptable to Ahriman, to take my place."

Standing with a sudden resolve, she cried.

"A sacrifice! As in ancient times! Then it was blood that was shed to placate Ahriman, now I only demand her will. Only then would I be free to be one with your spirit, Ormazd. Mattie" – she sneered at this corruption of the name – "Mattie shall be my sacrifice, Mattie shall purchase my freedom."

As she spoke, the fire belched out smoke, as though wet leaves had fallen on to it, immediately quenching the flames. Then, in spite of the heat of this mid-August day, the room itself became dark and cold. Anna, shivering, escaped to the barn, away from the ominous warning, consoling herself with thoughts of the uses to which she might put the amanita. Once more she was caught in the snare which tied her to Earth. Only by choosing warmth and light, only by leaving the dark paths of the past, would she ever be free.

*Mattie must be reassured. From now on, I will plan more carefully,* she promised herself. *I must make haste slowly. Gain her confidence. I showed her the stone too soon! 'Matsya' – I thought such a name would help me break the circle. But must I surrender her? What must I do? And that woman – Beth,* she thought venomously, *if only she were the one.*

In a fit of petulance she threw the box containing the pendants into Kingfisher Creek, crying, "Take them! It is I, Anahita!" She watched as the little box bobbed on the water, then she walked restlessly along the bank of the creek, muttering angrily to herself.

When at last she re-entered the house, the small fire was burning fitfully.

Sitting in her Great Chair, the shadows flickering across her face, she stared at the hearth.

*Solve me this riddle, Ahuro Mazdao. Make it plain. But what redemption is ever to be found, except by our own strivings?*

By the time Mattie and her friends met for supper on Thursday, Anna had schooled herself to patience. She was indeed quite gracious to Sid Heddle, who had failed to show up on Sunday, arriving instead on Tuesday morning. She offered no interference and pleasantly indicated where the barbecue should go, midway between the barn and Kingfisher Creek. Her intentions in having this fire out of doors were unclear, even to herself, but the possibility of increasing the influence of Ormadz lay before her.

*I need not light the fire, after all. First, I must consider it carefully.*

Even at the thought, her fingers drummed impatiently on the newly laid brick, her volatile emotions overwhelming her.

*I need rest, to gather my strength, calm myself. I shall put distance between us for a while, foster security in her. I will return to my well-spring.*

So saying, she went upstairs, locked up the ebony chest, changed into her blue linen suit and left the house. Going towards the head pond, among the trees, she disappeared from view.

Mattie, on the other hand, had spent her time peacefully working in the office. She felt both tranquil and confident, and why not? Work was going well and she no longer felt her name to be taboo. Why, anybody who could read would know about Matsya! Besides, Kurma having named Anna the Water Witch diminished her, lessening her hypnotic attraction.

"Another sale, Mattie? I think I'll retire, and leave you to it!" said Beth, not for one moment meaning it. "A sleeping partner. Doesn't that sound peaceful? Would you like to be a partner, Mattie?"

"You know I would, Beth! As soon as I can divvy up my share, but not before. Have you decided what to do about the alterations yet?"

"I have a contractor coming next week, a cousin of Sid Heddle's, Garnet Romburg. He'll look things over, and we'll decide whether we need an architect. I intend to have some of these old dividing walls removed. They spoil the proportions of the building, don't they?"

"Aren't they supporting the upstairs rooms, though?"

"Not really. Knock on them – see? – they are quite hollow. If I renovate, I could make an apartment upstairs, easily. Alec used to live over the office years ago, but it's very shabby now. I should be ashamed of myself. There are all sorts of old things up there. I still feel I am prying when I go through them! Silly, isn't it?"

"Be careful you don't remove a supporting beam, Beth! Kendrick Gibson did that! He managed to have it supported in time, but what a disaster that would have been."

"Mmm," agreed Beth. "Maybe an architect would be better, if it is not too expensive."

Mattie, leaving her happily doodling on an office pad, went off to show another property.

*One day*, she promised herself, *I will have a home of my own, an old house with personality, a place that has been lived in and loved.*

Dreamily, she pictured to herself different visions of just what such a house would look like, but always ended up with The Old Mill.

*I'm obsessed*, she thought. *I used to love the place before Anna came. I wonder whether she has spoiled it for me. But if I were to live there, it would look so different. I would fill it with old pine pieces. But then again it would be a very dangerous place for active children. I would need a fenced play area.*

Breaking off, laughing out loud at her daydreams, she speeded up to meet her client. Over the months she had spent in Nova Scotia Mattie had grown to love the old houses, recognising the different styles, the Lunenburg bump, the simple, beautiful proportions of the old barns, the Cape Cod houses, the Victorian homes resplendent with their gingerbread.

*It makes such a difference. These homes have had time to become part of the landscape. Look how beautifully they are finished, too. Such fine carpentry and lovely old wood, and the colours!*

Her enthusiasm was infectious as she showed people around, particularly when she found a home with the old pine floors intact. If a house had been brutally modernised, with Luan mahogany panels for example, she used her imagination to describe how it would look restored. She sought out Sid Heddle and his cousin Garnet Romburg, enquiring about restoration costs. In her own way, Mattie was intent on conserving the old homes, imagining what it would be like to live in each one.

*I will never find my family, I know that now*, she thought, *but I do feel I have found a home at last.*

Throughout the day, as she worked, one part of Mattie's mind remained in this dreamlike state, and as she drove back to the office, her thoughts bore fruit.

*All these years*, she mused, *I've been yearning for the family I lost. But I can have a family! I can have a family of my own! Why not? A home of my own, a family of my own! I must stop brooding about the past, and consider the future.*

Arriving at the office, finding Beth there, alone, she called out to her, impulsively.

"Beth, I'm so happy! I love my work, I love this place! I even–" here she hesitated, flushing– "I even quite like you."

"Humph," said Beth, equally inarticulate. "Then we are both happy."

Neither one of them belonging to the touchy-feely school of thought, they were quite content with this modest interchange of feeling.

"Here's something else for you. Another e-mail from Mr. Watson. Signs himself 'Kurma' now, does he? My! My!"

Beth looked slyly at Mattie's face, sniggering as she handed over a printout.

"Well, he *is* a client," retorted Mattie, defensively, "and I do have all his furniture, you know."

"Of course you do. Why ever else would he write?"

Beth, all innocence, picked up her purse. "Coming?"

It wasn't until she was safely in her own apartment that Mattie was able to read the letter.

*My dear Matsya.*

*This really is an amazing coincidence! Now I know my future is safe – sorry, I meant my furniture! What are you now? My alter ego? My doppelganger?*

*I am fascinated to know why your parents called you Matsya. Now about my name. Kurma Deulkar is a good friend of both my mother and my father. They met at McGilll, spending a great deal of time together as a threesome. However, when Mum and Dad suddenly got married (I have always suspected I was the reason for the haste) Kurma left quite abruptly for India and has not been back since. Anyway, I have always known him as Uncle Kurma, and was named after him. In return, he named his son Victor after Dad. So, in Canada there is a Kurma Watson, and in India, a Victor Deulkar! Mostly, of course, everyone calls him Vickram, so it fits in nicely. I wasn't so lucky, my friends call me Kermit or Froggy.*

*I think it would be as well if you had my e-mail number, and I had yours, then we could communicate directly. My number is at the foot of the letter. Please write soon!*

*Avidly Avatar,*

*Kurma (Froggy) Watson.*

At first smiling over the letter, Mattie later felt dismayed. How would she be able to explain her background satisfactorily by e-mail?

*Bother!* she thought. *Just as I have become more or less reconciled to things. Still, it is a very friendly letter. I shall certainly reply, one way or another.*

She re-read it several times before going to sleep that night.

"Mattie!" Next morning, she heard Bookie hammering on the handrail of the apartment stairway, their agreed signal. "Are you decent? Here's Sid Heddle to see you."

Mattie hurried downstairs, looking flustered

"Oh, I know I'm late, Bookie! I slept so well last night, I overslept! Good morning, Sid. What can I do for you?"

"I got a letter for you here." He was pulling an envelope from his pocket. "See? Anyone would think there aren't any telephones! Here." He thrust the envelope towards Mattie. "It's from that Miss Waters of yours."

"Good Heavens! What now?" Surprised, Mattie took the envelope.

"I should rightly have brought it last night, but I was just beat. I wanted to finish the barbecue, you see, before she left.

"Left? Has she gone?" Mattie clutched the envelope.

"Oh, she'll be back, but wouldn't say when. Anyway, there it is, and I'm off. Look, she sealed it up! Did she think I would open it?" Sid laughed at the very idea, offensive though it was.

Mattie hesitated before she opened it, studying the seal, relieved to see that it said "Anahita". Not "Matsya".

*My dear Miss Peters,* (Mattie pulled a face at the formality)

*I will not be here this weekend. After your extraordinary and unprovoked behaviour last Saturday, I feel you may have been doing too much. Really, my dear, you must have more control over your emotions. It was quite upsetting.*

*I feel you still have an obligation to me, and will notify you of my return.*

*Anna Waters.*

Mattie pulled a wry face at the flamboyant signature. *I should control my emotions!* Try as she might to dismiss the letter as vintage Water Witch, she found her spirits considerably deflated. Putting Bookie out of his agony, she told him that Anna would be away for a while, and went off to work. Offered the letter, Beth laughed when she read it.

"Come on, Mattie! Don't let the woman get you down! What ever did you do to her? Never mind," she added, seeing Mattie's expression. "It certainly can't have been more than *I* would have done, whatever it was. So you will have a holiday on Saturday!"

"No, Beth. I shall come in to the office, of course."

"No such thing. I'll tell what we'll do. Let's all play hooky! We'll get Horatio to close early on Saturday and go down to the beach! We haven't been once this year. Let's try Cherry Hill, it isn't so crowded as Risser's or Crescent. I'm told it's a good year, very little seaweed, and so no flies. We could toast hot-dogs there. I'll bring the buns."

"Horatio can bring the coffee. We'll need it! The water there is so cold. You tell him – well, ask him – we can all work Thursday night instead."

"You like Bookie a lot, don't you, Beth?"

"He's full of surprises, isn't he, Mattie? Yes, I do quite like him. Do you know he went back to school after his wanderings? He took English Lit at Mount Allison, as a mature student."

"Why, Beth, you've been going behind my back!"

Beth waved her away.

"Just talking with him over coffee. Let's get on with our day, shall we?"

To Mattie, Anna's absence felt like the calm before the storm.

*I do hope Kurma comes back soon, I want to be free of her. I'll write tonight, and try to find out when he is coming. I needn't go into details about my name, why should I? I'll write it out tonight, and send it first thing tomorrow. I vow I wont let Anna Waters sour my life. I think hot chocolate would set the mood, warm and undemanding.*

Soon she settled down to answer Kurma's letter.

*Dear Kurma.*

*Froggy indeed! Thank you for your letter. I wonder whether your father knew he was calling you 'Tortoise'? Of course, Kermit wouldn't have been around at the time, would he? So frogs didn't enter into it. My real concern in writing to you is to ask if you know when you are likely to return? The atmosphere between the Water Witch and myself is becoming very tense. Thank goodness she has gone away to points unknown, for an equally unknown period of time. I will be happy to finish with her.*

*I too have often wondered why I was called Matsya. Maybe I look like a fish! (Do you look like a tortoise?) However, in my case it is a long story, better told in person than written. Which brings me to my main concern in writing. Have you decided yet?*

*When you come, we will be in the throes of renovations. We have a good all-round contractor lined up, but we are trying to decide whether we should hire an architect, or if it is a needless expense.*

*I feel we should, in case we remove some necessary supporting wall. All this is no worry of yours! But it would feel good to have a disinterested opinion. You did such a wonderful job at The Old Mill.*

*The W.W. decided to leave well (no pun intended) alone with the dam. She seems curiously well (that word again!) informed about water! It must be her name.*

*Thank you once more for your friendly letter.*

*Sincerely,*

*Mattie.*

# CHAPTER 12

"It will seem strange not meeting on a Thursday evening, Mattie," Bookie complained. "Why don't we meet for a snack, at say 8.30? That wouldn't take too much time. I have, as the song says, 'grown accustomed to your face'. That doesn't really fit, does it?"

"Never mind, Bookie. It's a good try. I'll run it by Beth. It's so difficult in the summer. It's really our busiest time. I sound as though I know what I'm talking about, don't I? It's hard to realise that I haven't been here one whole year yet!"

"It feels like a lifetime," said Bookie gallantly. "Oh Heavens, that's wrong too, isn't it? See if Beth agrees to Thursday evening."

"You two are as thick as thieves. Why don't *you* ask her?" Mattie was all innocence. "It would probably carry more weight."

In the end they all agreed to meet for an hour or so, and Thursday evening found them sitting, once more, around the old pine table in Bookie's 'reading room'. With no particular agenda, they started talking about Beth's renovation plans.

"I wont be easy," she said. "I own the whole block and it would mean including the little shop next door. I don't know how Emily Hiltz will feel about that."

"I think she would be a very lucky woman. Would you be putting up the rent?"

"I hadn't considered it. I might need to. But then, I could rent out the apartment upstairs, if it is fixed up. What an expense!"

"Better than waiting until the roof leaks, or something worse. It may even be a fire hazard," said Bookie.

"Oh Bookie, don't say that. It's my worst nightmare."

Mattie looked from one to the other

"Well, *I* think you will need an architect. It would be worth it in the end," she suggested.

Even though the evening was still warm, Mattie had brought along a jug of hot chocolate milk, three mugs, and cookies. It was all very comforting and cosy.

"I had an architect to look this over, years ago," said Bookie. "No need to look so surprised! I'm not just a pretty face, you know. Did quite a bit to it in fact, before opening the apartment upstairs. I had to satisfy the Fire Marshall, you see. You had better get on with it, Beth."

"Oh my! Aren't we masterful?" Beth fluttered her eyelashes in mock humility. Bookie ignored her.

"If you have a problem, it would be possible to organise this place a bit better, and *then*," he paused, looking around, "you could temporarily use this room as a makeshift office, if yours becomes uninhabitable."

"I don't know what to say," said Beth. "It's a very generous offer, but I hope it won't come to that. Thank you very much. I will give the whole matter some serious thought. Yes," she concluded, shuffling her feet back into her shoes and reaching for her purse. "The more I think about it, the more necessary it becomes. One of these days I really might have the Fire Marshall after me. I hadn't thought of that."

Mattie collected the mugs and the jug.

"I'm really glad you spoke up, Bookie," she said, when Beth had left. "I was very nervous about letting Garnet Romburg loose on it, good though he is at his own work. You really are a friend."

"I've always liked Beth," he said, smiling reflectively. "Goodnight, Mattie. Thanks for the chocolate."

On Friday morning both Beth and Mattie were very busy, and it became obvious that closing down on Saturday afternoon would just be too costly.

"It would seem a pity to spend all that time driving there and back. What a shame! I was really looking forward to it," Mattie said sadly.

They sat silent for a moment, then Beth brightened up.

"I know what we could do! Go to the quarry!"

"Oh Beth, I don't know about that. Isn't the water very deep?"

"Well yes, in the quarry itself, but there is a nice little pool just above it, fed by a small stream from Kingfisher Creek. All the kids used to swim there, but of course they went into the quarry too, kids being what they are, and one boy drowned. That's why it is all fenced off now, but I know old Seth Adler and he lets me have a key. I haven't been there for years, Mattie. Let's go there! We can go to the beaches when the tourists have left. We had a little stone fireplace there too, I remember."

"Sounds good to me, Beth. I'll tell Bookie tonight."

"Oh, no need for that." Beth's manner was elaborately casual. "I'll slip over on my way out."

"Good idea," Mattie agreed, suppressing a knowing smile.

Their evening picnic was a great success. Bookie, thoughts of the Fire

Marshall always with him, had brought a hibachi, insisted on supervising the cooking.

"Men are so much better at this sort of thing, don't you agree, Mattie?" Beth, spreading herself luxuriously on her beach towel, winked at Mattie. Nevertheless, she watched everything Bookie did, her manner possessive.

"I don't like the name Bookie," she pronounced, at last, "and Horatio sounds too formal."

"Just try shortening it," Bookie said. "Think of it. 'Hore' – that's out! 'Ratio'? Too mathematical. 'Rat'? No thanks. One friend tried 'Nelson', but of course that was shortened to 'Nellie'! If you can come up with anything better, I shall be very grateful."

"'Cuddles'?" suggested Mattie. "'Curly'? You like cooking, how about 'Cookie'?"

"Mattie, I thought you were my friend!" protested Bookie.

"You could offer a prize," Mattie went on. "Hold a competition! What an advertising gimmick. 'Name Horatio'. Ballots here!"

While Beth and Mattie giggled like naughty children, Bookie went to the little stream, intent on filling some cups with cold water to throw over both of them. As he knelt by the bank, his eye was caught by something floating in the water.

"Hey! Look what I've found! See? At least somebody loves me!"

As he waded into the stream to fish out his treasure, he was joined by Mattie and Beth. Then Mattie shivered and her face paled.

"I know what it is, Bookie. Open it up. No! Wait a minute! Let me tell you what may be inside. Four pendants, each on a gold necklace, one amethyst, one amber, one peridot, and one opal. A black opal."

Bookie eased up the close-fitting lid, then turned to Mattie, open-mouthed. Beth put an arm round Mattie's shoulder protectively.

"I'll bet it's something to do with Anna Waters," she said. "Come over to the hibachi, it's still warm. Bring her sweatshirt, Horatio. Now, what's this all about?"

Mattie's teeth were chattering.

"I can't get away from her! She knows where I am! Kurma is right when he calls her the Water Witch. She gave those to me!"

Bookie held out the box.

"No! No! Take them away!" Mattie thrust her hands up her sleeves for warmth. Recovering a little, she told them about the day she had left The Old Mill, and how she had been followed by Anna's laughter.

"It's as though she wishes to bind me to her forever," Mattie whispered. "I don't know what she wants from me, but it is something I feel unwilling to give."

Bookie and Beth looked at each other over Mattie's head, their eyes full of concern.

"What shall I do with these?" Bookie asked, helplessly. "Shall I throw them back?"

"No," said Mattie, stonily. "What's the use? I shall take them with me. Later I will decide."

Then she and Beth described her necklace to Bookie, without telling him about Mattie's past.

"I'll show it to you, Bookie, then you will know why I was so interested about my name."

"Why *are* you called Matsya?"

"Do you know, Bookie, I haven't any idea. But all that is for another day."

Beth and Bookie, collecting up their things, shepherded Mattie home to bed, tucking her in as would concerned parents.

"Hot chocolate!" decided Bookie. "That'll be best."

"That's your cure-all, isn't it, Bookie? Now are you two going to tell me a good-night story?"

"She's feeling better. They always get sassy when they perk up. Now, once upon a time...."

So the evening ended in laughter after all, and Mattie slept dreamlessly. Next day, the little cedar box joined the blue jewel case in Mattie's drawer.

*Time enough to see about these. After all, I don't want them.*

She gave a wry smile.

*She probably just threw them away. I'm getting too fanciful,* she thought, little guessing that this was the truth. *What with one thing and another, I am right back where I started, wanting to know who my parents are – or were.*

And it was in this frame of mind that she went over to join Beth in the office. Beth, too, had been thinking things over, puzzling out how to persuade Mattie to visit Atterbury again, to see if that would settle her mind a little. They were both lost in their own worlds when the 'phone rang.

"Oxner's Real Estate," Beth answered automatically.

"Is Mattie Peters there? This is Kurma Watson, I wonder if I might have a word with her?"

"Are you back home, Mr. Watson?"

"No, not yet. I am calling from India, so–"

"I'll get her." Beth covered the mouthpiece. "Kurma Watson," she said, "from India."

"Good Heavens! Whatever time of day is it there, I wonder." Puzzled,

Mattie picked up her extension.

"Mr. Watson?" she asked.

"Froggy to you, Mattie, yes. This is urgent. Don't go hiring an architect yet until I am home. You see, I am an architect myself, and here is a way I can recompense you and Mrs. Oxner for your kindness. Let me speak to her. Please send me more mail, Mattie, though."

Dumbfounded, Mattie handed the 'phone to Beth, too confused to switch through. Beth listened in amazed silence.

"When may we expect you back, Mr. Watson?"

"Soon after Labour Day. May I have another word with Mattie please?"

"Mr. Watson?"

"Kurma, please."

"Kurma then. Whatever time is it there? It's 9 am here."

"About seven o'clock in the evening. We should do this more often! I'll see you in early September. Now, remember to write "

Mattie hung up the 'phone, dazed.

"Will you wait?" she asked Beth. "To get an architect, I mean?"

"Why, certainly! He did a good job with The Old Mill, didn't he? Now that brings me to something else, I think you need a break."

"I haven't been here a year yet, Beth. No way."

"I don't mean a long holiday. I think you should make one more trip back to Atterbury, see if you can quieten your mind. Get right away from Miss Waters. Look, Mattie, she petrifies *me*, and I hardly see her."

"I haven't too much put by yet, Beth. I'm saving to buy into the firm one day."

"Time enough for that. Take a few days. Settle yourself. Look what you are saving me! It's by your efforts with the furniture that I lucked into free architectural advice!"

"I'll think about it. Right now, I have an appointment with a client. Maybe you are right, Beth. I could take the train or the bus."

Beth shook her head.

"Not economically sound, Mattie! You would waste about five days travelling! We'll talk about it later."

"It's pretty difficult, anyway," Mattie said. "It's really harder to get to Ottawa than Toronto. In any case, I would have to drive down to Atterbury. Perhaps it would be better not to go just now. Later I could drive there."

"Do that anyway. Borrow my car."

"I wouldn't like to do that, Beth. When I came up here, I came through Maine by the 'airline to Canada' Do you know that road? I used my own car and it was fine."

"Highway 9! Oh, I know that road all right! There was only one place to eat on the whole length. They called it the 'airline to Canada' because of all the ups and downs. It's much better now, but I don't like all the lumber trucks, and the huge containers of wood flakes. I've come across more than one ditched. Once we had to detour about twelve miles through a logging trail."

"I must hurry. I have to keep that appointment."

"Don't forget, we are going to settle this tonight," Beth called after her.

As Mattie drove along, she was remembering her time in Atterbury, and how had she left.

*I only went back once or twice after leaving high school, then only to see Kendrick Gibson. I suppose, if I went, I would come back here and start afresh, may be I could come to terms with my arrival at St. Peter's and with my childhood. Yes, I will go. It's very kind of Beth, and I will make it up to her many times over. I have been very lucky with friends, good friends, first Kendrick Gibson, and now Beth. Even Bookie is a comfort. What do I care about Anna?*

That evening, she and Beth talked it over.

"Take six days, two to go, two to come back and two to stay," said Beth. "Take the ferry to St.John, to save driving."

"It would save driving, but the ferry is so expensive now. If I start early enough, I could go round through Moncton and Sussex. I would be in St.Stephen in time for supper, stay the night and cross to Calais, Maine, first thing in the morning."

"Have lunch at Miller's Red Lion in Bangor! My treat. Remember how difficult it is to find lunch on Highway 9. No, better make it on the way back. It will be too early for lunch on the way out. It's only about a hundred miles from Bangor to St.Stephen."

"I'll stay in the U.S. I know the route, you see. Maine, New Hampshire, Vermont, New York State, over the border. There are scads of hotels in Cornwall. Thank goodness I have just had the car inspected."

"Leave tomorrow morning, Mattie, you will be back by next Sunday. With luck Anna will still be away somewhere, sulking." She laughed. "I would have liked to have seen her face when you refused those pendants! She's used to having her own way, that woman."

Beth had never really recovered from her initial reaction to Anna.

"Meanwhile, Mattie, I'll have fun fiddling around with plans for our renovations. I must talk to Emily Hiltz, see what she wants to do. Her lease is soon up for renewal anyway. Heavens, is that the time? I must get on. Have fun, and come back feeling better."

Giving Mattie an awkward and unaccustomed hug, she hurried away.

That night, Mattie told Bookie she would be away, got a few things together, made some sandwiches and filled a flask with orange juice. Why pay for lunch? Going over the route in her head, planning what she would do, she drifted off to sleep.

# CHAPTER 13

Early on Tuesday morning, Mattie set off, anxious to be on her way before all the tourist traffic started.

*Please*, she begged an uncaring Fate. *No Wally Byam caravans or convoys of trucks.*

She liked driving, enjoying the feeling of independence and control. The morning was clear and bright as she headed along the 102 to Truro, and the traffic was light, since the commuters were still eating breakfast and the school buses were still in the garages for the holidays.

*So far so good. I shall take the new bypass and avoid Wentworth. It's a shame really, it's so pretty along there, but I need to make time and distance. Goodness knows this is costing more than I can afford, and much of it in American dollars. I'll get to Sussex and have my sandwiches there. I may take a break at Amherst, or just beyond, for coffee. Meanwhile, I had better concentrate on what I'm doing.*

To keep her company and to stop her mind from wandering, she turned on her radio to *Information Morning.*

*Whatever would we do without the CBC? It will be a bit of a trick keeping tuned in as I travel, but by then I'll be into my stride, and perhaps won't need it.*

By concentrating on the immediate she hoped to forget her worries for a while, letting the driving, the traffic, the route, the radio, occupy her full attention.

As there were more cars on the road she decide against stopping in Amherst, and by the time she reached Moncton the traffic had thickened, even on the by-pass. She was thankful to pull over for a rest in Sussex, eat her sandwiches, stretch her legs, go for a coffee, and relax for a while, still keeping her mind on practical matters.

*I should be in St.Stephen in good time, but I'll call ahead, this being the holiday season. Thank goodness for credit cards and cell-phones.*

By the time she reached St.Stephen, it was a relief to get from behind the wheel, so she made straight for a motel.

"Heading for the States, Madam?" the receptionist asked.

"Yes, first thing tomorrow, but I need to buy travel insurance. When does the Blue Cross office open?"

The receptionist pushed across a leaflet.

"Not until nine o'clock, so you won't need to hurry in the morning."

Mattie had wanted an early start, but in the end was glad of the extra sleep, even though it would mean there was a long line of traffic at the US Customs waiting to cross into Calais, Maine. This proving to be the case, she resigned herself to the delay.

*It's a matter of hurry up and wait today*, she thought. *But I should be in St.Johnsbury by tonight. I'm just going to relax and enjoy the trip.*

As she made this resolve she was watching the St.Croix River, running between Canada and the USA All at once she was overwhelmed by the old familiar feeling of dread. Her palms sweating to the wheel, she drew a sharp breath.

*Anna is everywhere. Now all the water I see reminds me of her.* Trying for a smile, she added, *If only her name were 'Hope'.*

"Something wrong?" asked the American Customs official, ever sharp-eyed for signs of nervousness.

"Yes, Officer, there is, I'm very concerned about my parents," Mattie said this in all sincerity, meaning every word. "That's why I am travelling to Atterbury, in Ontario. I shall be there about a week."

The official handed back her passport with no further query.

"Have a good trip. I hope you get good news."

Mattie drove away, berating herself.

*Start adding a phobia to your obsession, you'll soon be paranoid, my girl. Pull yourself together.*

But Route 9, undulant and winding as a snake, had its own consolations and Mattie's tangled feelings started to unravel, unwinding like the road behind her. After pausing for a coffee in Bangor she was in a much better frame of mind, and from then on it was plain sailing, the traffic flowing steadily, allowed her to reach St.Johnsbury in good time. Before falling asleep she had momentary qualms about all the water crossings ahead of her, a frisson of her old fears. The thought of crossing Lake Champlain at Rouse's Point and the St.Lawrence River filled her with dismay, then she shrugged it off.

*Cut it out, Mattie my girl!* she admonished herself. *Anyone would think you had hydrophobia. You aren't frothing at the mouth yet.*

And if her laughter verged on hysterical, it was nonetheless laughter, and against herself.

She set off early the following morning, her nervousness lessening with each mile to be replaced by a fragile hope. By day's end the last long stretch of the journey through Upper New York State found her driving with scarcely controlled impatience. Perhaps it was for this reason that the sight of the mighty St.Lawrence River, flowing inscrutably between the two countries, filled her with such a rush of confidence. For a brief moment it was as though the river surged through her veins, bringing new life.

"Yes," she whispered, "I know this is where I began. But it all started long, long before that. Oh. long before. I feel it. I know it."

With a start she came back to her surroundings, the flash of thought – or was it only a sensation? – forgotten as swiftly as it came.

*Time for a good night's sleep*, Mattie thought, shaking her head to clear it. She set off next morning heading for Atterbury.

*I'd forgotten how straight the roads are!* she marvelled. *It's like geometric geography!*

She pictured the early surveyors, at the time of the white settlement, squaring off the maps, grid-like, for the concession roads.

*It's an efficient way of doing it, I suppose, but they are boring to drive down – especially if you miss the concession number! It's much more interesting in Nova Scotia.*

She took the turn – right-angled, of course – along the road to Atterbury, slowing as she neared the small town, long before the speed limit required it, even following a farm tractor for several miles.

*Here's the sign. 'Atterbury – population 4,200'. Why, that has never changed all the years I've known it. I wonder who has taken Kendrick Gibson's place? It's going to feel very strange.*

She passed the old cheese factory, bought out by Kraft, now housing a farm co-operative. Brightly coloured farm machines, new and shiny as massive toys, lured the hard-pressed farmers to buy.

*Some wives will go teaching, or waitressing, to help pay for those,* thought Mattie. *And here is the church.*

St.Peter's church looked much older than it could possibly be. Built by the Scottish stonemasons, who had built so many of the fine old stone houses in the nineteenth century, it looked stable, robust, safe. Parking the car, Mattie walked over to the churchyard. In late August, the grass had a dusty, used look. Someone with a practical mind had evidently been working hard in the garden, late summer roses and canna lilies stood side by side with ripe tomatoes and squash. Opening the lych-gate, she wandered round to the back of the church yard where the Atter River, low in its banks, dawdled along with summer languor, she tried to picture it as it must have been, that long-ago February day, frozen hard, the alders along its banks almost buried in snow. Gazing out over the water, lost in thought, she was startled by a voice behind her.

"Can I help you? I'm sorry. I didn't mean to alarm you! I'm Foster Harrington, the vicar here. Are you looking for something?"

"I have been admiring your garden," Mattie answered evasively, wondering, now that she was here, what she should say.

"Oh, that's all Beryl's doing. My wife, you know."

"You are so different from Kendrick Gibson," Mattie blurted out.

"You knew the former vicar then?"

"He was a very good friend to me, and oversaw my girlhood. I spent every Christmas and Easter with Mr. Gibson and his sister."

Remembering this vague and elderly man, her eyes filled with tears. How could this tall, red-haired young upstart possibly fill his shoes?

"Why, you must be Mattie! Mattie Peters! Kendrick told me all about you. Do come in and meet Beryl."

The vicarage, no longer the austere home of an elderly man, looked bright and welcoming. Children's voices could be heard from behind the house, and as they stepped into the cool of the hallway Mattie felt a sense of peace, of safety, as though her old friend and adviser would appear at any minute. Instead Beryl Harrington came out of the kitchen, her fair hair carelessly falling across her face, bearing a tray with cups and saucers. She looked tired, busy, happy. Foster kissed her flushed cheek.

"Come and meet Mattie Peters, Beryl. Remember me telling you about Mattie? She used to live here when Kendrick Gibson was vicar."

"Oh, how nice! Someone for tea! I'll go and get another cup," she said.

Mattie explained that she had been fostered in the parish, but had not lived at the vicarage, "although I spent every Christmas and Easter here."

They chatted pleasantly over the teacups, until Foster Harrington cleared his throat.

"I'm sure you came for more than a cup of tea, Mattie? May I call you Mattie? Thank you," as Mattie nodded. "That's much too long a trip to come for a cup of tea! Would you like to tell us?"

Beryl jumped up. "Oh! I must see to the family, Foster! Why don't you take Mattie into the study. That's the best place for peace and quiet – believe me, I know! We have two boys, you see, six years and three years old. They don't hold with peace and quiet, Mattie! Just listen to them!"

Laughing, she collected the tea things and left them to make their way to the study.

"For one thing, Foster, I have brought a book with me. It must have belonged to Kendrick Gibson. See, his name is inside it."

"I wondered why you were carrying that mighty tome around. I'm sure he would wish you to keep it. But you didn't come all this way to bring that book, I'm sure."

Haltingly, but with growing confidence, Mattie explained her whole situation, from her arrival in the church porch to her re-arrival at the same door.

"It is an amazing tale, Mattie. You are really troubled by this woman?"

"Yes, yes, I am."

"Now. I suggest you stay here with us tonight. You've had a long and exhausting two days. Would you like to talk about this again tomorrow?"

"Oh yes please, yes, I would. I need help understanding my feelings. I feel – lost."

Over supper she met Ben – "I'm five and I can bathe myself!" – and three-year-old – "No! No! Let me do it!" – Dickie. It was like finding new relations. Already, as she went to bed that night, her heart felt easier.

*Never judge by appearances,* she thought, as she had about Beth all those months ago. *Foster Harrington looks so young, but is very good at what he does. Besides, not being involved in my day-to-day life, his advice will be totally unbiased.*

The hours of driving having taken their toll, Mattie considered drowsily what she would say on Thursday morning, her last thought before drifting off to sleep being, *How kind they are, Foster and Beryl Harrington! Perhaps Kendrick still keeps watch.*

Breakfast was a noisy affair, with two rambunctious little boys, tactless, hungry, full of questions. Mattie, revelling in it, resolved again to have a family of her own. Foster shooed them away.

"Now, come on Mattie! I have left the morning free. Clergy's middle of the week, you see. Maybe Beryl will join us later. We work as a team."

"Now, where were we?" he asked, once they were settled in the study. "You have told me that your name has always concerned you, and your parentage too. I know much of this already, from Kendrick, you see. You say you were very upset to find the signet ring, and had rejected the pendants offered to you?"

"Yes."

"Why?"

"I have no wish to increase my sense of obligation to Anna. I feel strongly that she is laying claim to me, as though in some way it is her right to do so."

"Yes, very difficult. Now, tell me Mattie, what is your fascination with Anna, your fear of her? Be honest."

"Every time she recites 'It is I, Anahita, Anaista, Daeva of Water, O

Ahuro Mazdao', I become more convinced that it is all true. I think of her as having powers beyond the ordinary."

"Well, let's consider this," said this surprising young cleric. "Let's assume that it is true."

Mattie's eyes widened in alarm. "*True*?" she echoed.

"You see, Mattie, everyone, every civilisation has always acknowledged one thing – still do."

"And that is?"

"That there is an energy, a source, beyond our understanding. The more we discover, the more there is to know. For simple folk, this is much too difficult to live with, and we try to simplify it by personifying. We try to find a name, where there is none. 'The Great Spirit', 'Manitou', 'God', 'Buddha', or 'Brahma'. There are as many words as there are cultures. The destructive force, in the same way, may be 'Siva', 'Satan', 'Ahriman'. 'Satan', you know, comes from the Hebrew word for 'adversary'. We sense the inevitable tension, you see! Yin and Yang."

Mattie sat quietly, pondering what had been said.

"Where does someone such as Anahita fit into all this?"

"People are fearful, and certainly through the ages have striven to placate, propitiate, striving to control, or even negotiate with the uncontrollable, to know the unknowable. Hence the anthropomorphic Gods and Goddesses, half human and half divine, therefore half predictable, half understood."

"So Anahita, Water Goddess, is one of these."

Mattie's palms felt sweaty, her face paled.

"Do you really believe, Mattie, that this is the case with Anna?"

There was a silence before she spoke, and then only reluctantly.

"I don't know what I believe. That or she is mad. Out of touch with reality, at least."

Foster Harrington did not question what Mattie had said. He spoke thoughtfully, and with conviction.

"The ancients considered that such a divinity lost power if people ceased to believe in them. If you think about, you will see that this is so. There will always be distance between those who have given such things some thought, and those who have not."

Mattie still sat withdrawn and silent. Foster Harrington leaned forward, taking her cold hands in his.

"But that is not your real fear, is it, Mattie? There's more."

They looked at each other, each trying to read the other's mind.

"No," she whispered, at last.

"And your real fear is?"

"That she is my mother. That I will become like her."

At last it was out in the open, the reason for her fear and fascination.

Beryl, who had come quietly into the room, held out her arms to comfort as Mattie wept uncontrollably, as though tears could wash her foreboding away.

"Let's leave it there, for now," said Foster. "Later, Beryl will talk things through with you. My field is theology. Beryl is a psychologist. We often work together."

Mattie, overwrought, welcomed the break. She still had the afternoon to fumble towards some understanding of her feelings, before facing the long trip home.

While Mattie was helping to clear away the lunch, Beryl hailed Foster.

"Hey, Fosse! Your turn to be a parent. Here you are, Daddy-o, over to you. Mattie and I are going to chew the fat. Come on, Mattie! You're a Godsend! I can leave the washing up. 'Bye Fosse! Have fun!"

This time it was the two women who settled in to the study.

"All right. Talk," said Beryl, leaning back in her chair.

"Foster was a great help, Beryl. He made me recognise something I had been denying, that Anna may be my mother."

"Nothing like looking something in the face," Beryl said. "Now let's think about this. Just supposing...." She held up her hand to halt Mattie's protests. "Just supposing she is. So what?"

"Beryl, you should meet her. She is very strange indeed. She is emotional, capricious, demanding, and does some very weird things. I don't want her as a mother."

"Had you known her all your life, what then?"

"I'm not sure," said Mattie, slowly. "Would I have grown used to her? Would I have emulated her? Fought with her? Left home? I don't know."

"Would you still be Mattie, do you think? I mean as you are now."

"That's a poser, Beryl."

"Well, consider it for a while. I'll be here."

Picking up some knitting. "Mittens," she said, "for the boys."

Some time elapsed before Mattie spoke again, pausing now and then to reflect.

"All my life I have been adjusting to other people," she said, at last. "All those foster homes. Of course for many years there was Kendrick in the background."

"Did you change as your homes changed, Mattie? Did you bring to each your own values and ideas?"

"Oh always! I grew up very young, in that way, Beryl. Somehow I could be myself. It was very interesting really, studying other people's ways. I learned a great deal."

"So then, think about it. You are you, whether Anna is your mother or not. Do you feel you must change if you are her daughter?"

"That has been my greatest dread. I feel threatened by her personality, her power."

"We haven't time to be fancy about this, Mattie – your time here is not long enough. Let's take a shortcut. Suppose you say to yourself, 'I am *not* Anna. She cannot change me. I realise she does not have that power. She is a woman, as I am. This I believe.'"

Then Mattie, head on one side, as though viewing the idea from a different angle, nodded.

"Yes, that I do believe – *now* I believe it. Thank you, Beryl, for helping me put it in perspective. It may take time, but I can do this."

"Oh, don't get up to go, Mattie! Let Fosse baby-sit. Tell me about Nova Scotia."

By the time Mattie was ready to leave on Friday morning, she felt she had known the Harringtons all her life. They said good-bye amid mutual assurances of seeing each other soon.

"It's your turn," Mattie called as she went to her car. "Bring the children to Nova Scotia. It's Canada's Ocean Playground, don't forget!"

# CHAPTER 14

Before leaving Atterbury, Mattie stopped at Sadie Hallam's Select Gift Items, smiling at the old-fashioned name of the store. As soon as she went through the door, Sadie Hallam recognised her.

"Well, land sakes, it's Mattie Peters! Now haven't you grown into a pretty young thing!"

"Oh Sadie, it's great to see you again. You haven't changed at all."

Indeed Sadie had changed very little in all the years Mattie had known her. She was one of those people who look middle-aged at fifteen, and still look middle-aged at sixty, a plump, comfortable woman with a timeless Sadie look all her own. Mattie wandered round choosing gifts for Beth and Bookie. The store was well named. The items were indeed very well selected. For Beth she bought an old pewter tankard, costing more than she could afford, and for Bookie a twist of wrought iron holding a tall blue candle. A sudden impulse caused her to pick up a small cranberry glass jug for Anna, for reasons too complicated to understand.

"Shall I gift wrap them, Mattie?"

"Better not, Sadie. I am driving back to Nova Scotia via the States, and Customs may want to see them."

"My, Nova Scotia! I wondered where you had taken yourself off to! I haven't seen you for, what, five years? At least."

They chatted for a minute or two, then Sadie suddenly slapped the side of her head.

"What am I thinking of? There was someone in here only two or three months ago, April was it? After Easter anyway. An elderly woman, dark glasses, was looking for someone. I thought she meant you, at first, but she said the name was 'Maxi', 'Matsi', something like that – didn't know the second name. Up to no good I shouldn't wonder. Funny, isn't it? And now you come in here, large as life! Could it have been someone you know, Mattie? Maybe she did mean you, after all."

"If I have met such a woman, I can honestly say I don't know what she can possibly want with me."

This she spoke with the conviction of truth, for of course it had been

Anna, and of course Mattie had not the least idea what was expected of her.

Leaving the store, she paused, waiting to see whether her spirits plummeted once more at the thought of encountering Anna here. Perhaps for a second she wavered, before a surge of relief made her hold up her head, thinking, *I really can handle this.*

Even the little cranberry glass jug was, in its way, an equaliser, a leveller of terms. As she drove south to Cornwall, on the long journey home, she was smiling, soon she was humming and then singing.

"Going home, going home," she sang, "I am going home!"

Strains of Dvorak's 'New World' symphony seemed very appropriate. In a sense she *was* entering a new world, a world of far greater confidence.

Beth Oxner, missing her in more ways than one, had found herself spending a lot of time with Bookie.

"Mattie does more than I realised, Bookie. She's so quiet and unobtrusive about it, I didn't realise. What ever impulse brought her here, it's been good for us both. Business has really picked up with her help."

"You are missing her companionship, Beth, admit it, never mind the business."

"Oh, I know *that.*" Beth sounded angry. Since Alec's death she had taken solace in being "one woman against the world", her manner becoming gradually more contentious and self-centred. Now, aggravatingly enough, her little business was thriving on co-operation and friendliness. In her better moments she freely admitted to herself that this was only natural, but just now, feeling combative, she looked at Bookie with disfavour.

"Bookie! What a ridiculous name! 'Bookie Bean'." She mouthed the words derisively. "It might as well be 'Haricot Bean'. Horatio sounds like haricot anyway." Her face cleared. "That's it! That's what I'll call you. 'Harry'. We will be the only ones to know it's short for Haricot. Now, Harry, are you good for a coffee at Tim Horton's?"

"Too late, Beth. I'm used to 'Bookie' Bean, so is everyone else. You wouldn't want me to call you Lizzie, would you?"

"That's very different, I was christened Beth."

They went over to the coffee shop, bickering amiably.

Later, checking both her own and Mattie's e-mail, she was amused to see Kurma Watson's repeated messages.

*Where are you, Mattie?*

*Why haven't you mailed me, Mattie?*

At last, on Thursday, he 'phoned and Beth explained that Mattie had been called away.

"We all miss her very much, here," she said brightly. "I expect she will mail you when she gets back."

"I shall be in Nova Scotia a week after Labour Day," said Kurma. "Have you postponed your renovations? Yes? Oh good! See you then, Mrs. Oxner."

Putting down the 'phone, Beth sighed.

"That's another thing. I must speak to Emily Hiltz. It's only fair to her. I'll ask her to lunch at the River Restaurant, splurge for once. Silly though she is, she's nice little woman, Emily Hiltz. I hope we can work something out."

The River Restaurant was an 'up-market' dining room on Lower River Road, next to River Park. Emily Hiltz jumping at the chance, Beth booked a table for two, for Saturday.

That was the day that Anna came angrily into Calderford looking for Mattie, whom she regarded as neglecting her manifest duty. Beth had left a sign saying the office was closed, omitting her cell phone number, in order to concentrate on her business with Emily Hiltz. Anna swept over to the bookstore, so far completely unaware that Mattie's apartment was overhead. Bookie, having no intention of enlightening her, greeted her pleasantly with offers of help.

"I am looking for Miss Peters," stated Anna imperiously. "Where is she?"

"I can't help you there," Bookie replied blandly. "I believe she is away for a few days."

Amused, he watched as Anna stalked out without a word of thanks. Thwarted, she returned to The Old Mill in a blind fury, her resolution to take things calmly already forgotten. Sitting in the Great Chair, she stared wrathfully into the glowing heart of the fire.

*Were I able to strip away my mortal half, such things would leave me untouched. Perhaps, O Ahuro Mazdao, it is you."* – defiantly she rejected the ceremonial 'thou' – *"It is you who frustrate me, who keep me as I am. Ahriman tempts, coaxes, lures, prevails. But you ignore me, reject my pleas for acceptance.*

She valued herself far too highly to understand that this was not a competition for her favour. She must make her own decision. Sadly, as the day wore on, realising how much she missed Mattie, how much she needed her, she stared resentfully at the fire, muttering to herself.

"I still have not bent her to my will, and now she is not even here."

Going upstairs, she moved round her room impatiently, touching the things that Mattie had touched, at last taking out the signet ring with the fish, she idly melted some sealing wax, impressing it again and again.

"Matsya, Matsya, Matsya."

Blissfully oblivious, Beth was enjoying her lunch at the River Restaurant. She chose cold poached chicken breast with orange and cranberry relish, accompanied by a salad, watching with amazement as the tiny little Emily Hiltz worked her way through a large mixed grill, apple pie and ice cream. Over coffee she broached the subject of the renovations.

"You see, Emily, it might be very difficult for a while, and I might need to close up for a week or two. How do you feel about that?"

"Oh, don't worry about me!" said Emily breezily. "I have been meaning to talk to you about my lease for a month or two now. Remember my sister, Polly? She's Polly Marsh now, of course. She runs that gift and craft shop over in the mini-mall. It's called 'The Basketfull' Do you know it? Dried flower arrangements, dolls, and things like that?"

"Of course, yes, I do. I didn't know your sister ran it."

"Oh, yes, and doing very well. But she has more room than she needs, and we've decided to go in to together. Isn't that a good idea? Ever since Uncle Arnold left us all that money a year ago, we've talked about it. We have a nice little bit of capital to put into, it, and…."As Emily chatted on, Beth nodded and smiled, thinking ruefully how gullible she had been.

*Now she tells me! On the right side of a good lunch! Well, never mind, it* was *a good lunch, and maybe it's all for the best. Wretched woman! Always owing me the rent and all the while nursing 'a nice little bit of capital'.*

"So there it is, Beth," Emily concluded. " I wont be renewing my lease! I overlooked the three months' notice but I know you'll understand. I just never got around to telling you about it before. Wasn't that good of Uncle Arnold?"

"Much too good," Beth said, fuming at the way the leasing agreement had been broken. "Well, Emily, I would have preferred the three months' notice, but in the circumstances, as we are such good friends, I will accept just one extra month's rent, plus the two you owe" She smiled sweetly, knowing that Emily would miss the irony. "I know you'll understand."

They parted on reasonably good terms, Beth doing new mental arithmetic about costs and losses. Why ever had she started all this?

*Bookie and his Fire Marshall,* she thought, before shamefacedly admitting to herself that it had all been her own idea in the first place. *I wonder why I'm always picking on him these days? Poor old Bookie.*

Mattie arrived back, worn out but contented, late on Saturday afternoon. She found Bookie and Beth waiting impatiently for her, with a cold supper. There were the usual exchanges. "How was your trip?" "How have things been here?" "Oh, what a lovely tankard!" "Candlestick!" "Oh, you shouldn't have," and so on, until an exhausted Mattie threw up her hands.

"If I don't go to bed soon, I shall never get up in the morning. Sorry, folks, we can talk again tomorrow."

"Anna was looking for you. Will you go over to see her?"

"Next Saturday is soon enough, Beth. I want to come into the office. Now, I love you both, but I'm off to bed."

Mattie was still unsure how much she would say about her time with the Harringtons, but knew that she owed the confidence to Beth.

*Just think*, she mused drowsily before dropping off to sleep. *I didn't go running over to The Old Mill to apologise to Anna. I* can *handle this.*

On Sunday morning she called Beth.

"Sorry to rush off to bed last night, Beth, but I was so tired! Can I possibly drop over to see you this afternoon? Will you be in around three p.m.?"

"Why, Mattie, aren't you rushing over to The Old Mill?" Beth teased her. "Miss Waters will be *most* annoyed."

"Not my day, Beth. I go on Saturdays."

"My! My! All this independence. Yes, come over by all means. I want to know what you found out."

"Not much, as a matter of fact, but yes, I can tell you what happened."

"I have something to tell you, too. You know how sorry I have been feeling for Emily Hiltz? I even lowered her rent!"

"I didn't know you had done that."

"Well, I had! More fool me. And all the time she was sitting on – what did she call it? – 'a nice little bit of capital', left to her and her sister by their Uncle Arnold! *She* gave *me* notice."

Mattie burst out laughing, Beth reluctantly joining in.

"Oh, it is good to be home again, Beth! See you at three or so."

Beth put the 'phone down thoughtfully.

*She said 'home' so convincingly. I wonder why? Why, out of all the world – out of all Nova Scotia, does she feel so at home in Calderford? That's something else I'd like to find out.*

Mattie spent a leisurely morning, tidying up, washing a few clothes, going over her day planner, thinking of the past week. She penned a hasty letter of thanks to the Harringtons, thinking of their kindness and saying how happy their family had made her feel.

*I'll send the boys some T-shirts. There's one I've seen around saying 'Someone in Nova Scotia loves you very much'. That would be good.*

At last she went to her chest of drawers to get her pendants.

*I know, I'll take them back to her next Saturday, and – and I'll take the cranberry glass jug. It's childish really, a game of one-upmanship!*

It was in a light-hearted mood that she set out for Beth's house, pleased at the opportunity to talk with her on her own.

*Of course she'll pass it all on to Bookie, but that's different. It's easier to tell her these things alone. Good old Beth.* She looked round appreciatively at the old houses, at the trees, at the blue sky, at the river.

*Home*, she thought, looking for the loon that lived along this stretch of water.

*The tide must be up, the Calder is high,* feeling knowledgeable, experienced, a real Maritimer. *Think of all those poor people in central Canada who have never seen this – and here's Beth's house, quite one of the prettiest.*

She tootled her horn merrily and drove round to the barn.

"Come in! Come in! We'll go through to the terrace and have some iced tea." Beth was all smiles and eager curiosity. "And then tell me everything! Or at least, as much as you want me to know."

"It's more a matter of what I remember, Beth, but here goes."

Haltingly at first, but with growing confidence, Mattie recounted her adventure, explaining as best she could her fears and doubts about Anna. One thing she could not bring herself to speak about was her dread that Anna might be her mother. She spoke of her fascination, of her conviction that Anna had powers that were out of the ordinary.

"My intelligence rejects it, Beth, but my gut feeling doesn't."

Beth nodded in complete understanding.

"Why I should have a similar feeling, I don't know, Mattie. I have hardly met the woman. When she came into the office, I understood for the first time the saying, 'my blood ran cold'. It was quite extraordinary, as though a wave of antipathy amounting to malevolence flowed from her. What have I possibly ever have done to offend her? I do agree that, one way or another, she has a very powerful personality. If she really is, or has been, on the stage, I can imagine her taking the part of some unrelenting figure in a Greek tragedy."

Beth shuddered in retrospect.

"Well, I think I may, just may, have found a way to counteract all that, Beth, thanks to Foster Harrington."

"And how may that be, pray tell?"

"Just refuse to believe she has such power. I refute any claims she has to them. Everything giving her such an ascendancy is in her mind, and in mine. It takes us both – she to control, me to accede. Well, I won't! I must show an equal power myself."

"Mattie! It sounds like a western movie! Showdown at The Old Mill!"

"It need never come to that, I hope it doesn't, but I will not accept a subservient role any longer. Why should I?"

Beth looked at the young woman sitting beside her. It seemed incredible that this was the same meek Mattie who had first come to see her, in answer to her advertisement. This Mattie had large and sparkling eyes; her hair, falling loose, shone with dark red lights in the sunshine. She held her head and shoulders with an air of self-assurance bordering on authority, and when she spoke, her voice was round, firm, full of confidence and control.

"Mmm," said Beth dryly. "Well, rather you than me! You'd still better be prepared to hold my hand if she comes into the office, because frankly, I'm scared to death of the woman!"

"Oh Beth," Mattie protested, laughing. "You aren't scared of anything! Now tell me why you wanted to call Bookie, 'Harry'. I like it, by the way, but I won't get used to it!"

"Bookie told you? Well, he won't change it, you know."

"Why should he?"

Beth filled her in on this, and anything else that had happened during the week.

"Oh, and then there is Kurma Watson! He's going to be here the week after Labour Day. He keeps calling you up! What's going on?"

"Oh nothing, Beth. He's become very friendly, but I have just too much on my plate to worry about e-mail friendships! They very seldom survive a face-to-face meeting, anyway. I will answer him, maybe tomorrow, but there isn't much to tell him that's new."

They sat contentedly, side by side, enjoying the warm sun and the quiet, idly watching the chickadees chasing each other around the feeders, until Beth broke the silence.

"There is one thing that has really been puzzling me, Mattie. I never gave it much thought until recently, Why here? Whatever brought you to settle here in Calderford? It's just as mysterious as Anna settling here. I mean, I love it, it's my home, but you?"

"I told you about looking for my family, didn't I, Beth?"

Beth nodded.

"It's all part of the picture. As I grew up, going to the old Atterbury school, I was driven to get on with it, to be off. The older students are taken off by bus to big high schools now, but in my time the school was quite small, and very good. Small classes, the personal touch, the whole nine yards. This sounds unbearably cocky, but I turned out to be very bright and whizzed along. There were still thirteen grades in Ontario at that time, meaning that an undergraduate course was only three years. The top ten percent of students were given scholarships, so I was well away."

"You never told me all this!"

"Beth, have you ever been turned down for a job as 'overqualified'? Don't laugh. It isn't funny when it happens."

"Why did you choose business studies?"

"Figure it out for yourself – I had no money, no family. What could be more practical? As soon as I was old enough, I had worked part-time to pay for a business course in the summer. That's where those diplomas came from – typing, bookkeeping, computers. The result was, I had a head start in university, and was able to add extra courses – urban planning, heritage buildings, that sort of thing. Of course, I worked too, as a waitress. It's amazing what you can make in tips! Don't look so appalled! Young, ambitious, bright. I enjoyed it. See what you have achieved yourself! Remember how you urged me to exert myself, keep my elbows out?"

Beth laughed at herself sheepishly as Mattie pumped her arms back and forth.

"I didn't know you were a *genius*, Mattie. Truth to tell, I thought you were pretty stupid, and slow on the uptake, too."

"I was at the end of my rope, Beth, and almost out of money. You saved my skin."

"Oh, pooh!" Beth said uneasily. "So why here? There's more money in Ontario!"

"When I first arrived in Nova Scotia, on the ferry from St.John, I took the trip all along the coast, including, of course, the 'Lighthouse Route', gradually making my way to Halifax. I spent all my time searching, pointlessly. But this is where the jewel box came from and I went on looking, hoping. I was drawn back to the South Shore, though I have no idea why. When I saw your advertisement, that settled it. This would be my home. It was as if I recognised it, as if I had been here before. I can't explain it, Beth."

"I can't stand it! Not another woman of mystery. Isn't Anna enough? Anyway, I'm glad you came, and I hope you stay. Now let's go and polish off the rest of that cold chicken in the fridge. There's a bit of potato salad and some cranberry dressing."

For the rest of the evening, they chatted about local news, speculated on the weather, the apple crop in the valley, the rising cost of living. They might have known each other for years.

# CHAPTER 15

On Monday morning, as Mattie read her e-mail, an amused Beth watched her covertly, aware that there were several from Kurma Watson.

"Importunate, isn't he?" she said at last. "Is that the word? He called you on the 'phone too, you know. He'll be here the week after Labour Day."

"I'd forgotten all about Labour Day, Beth. Shouldn't it be today?"

"Oh, wake up, Mattie! It's August 30$^{th}$ today! I thought you said you were bright?" Beth teased. "Labour Day is late this year, September 6$^{th}$, so he won't be coming until at least the 13$^{th}$ or 14$^{th}$. You will have to be patient."

"For Heaven's sake, Beth. What is that supposed to mean? I have too much on my mind to think about Kurma Watson! It would be good though to get the alterations done before winter comes though, wouldn't it?"

"And that's all?"

"What else could it be? Look at all the work piling up! I meant to ask you, will having the shop next door standing empty spoil your plans?"

"I need the rental money, but in some ways it will be a relief, not having to negotiate around Emily Hiltz. That little craft shop wasn't going anywhere, whereas Emily's sister will see to it that they succeed. I'm not sure what to think, shall I make the office larger or not?"

"Frankly, I don't think there is the volume of business, do you? Not locally, with those big offices in Lower Calder, just down the road. Maybe another apartment would help."

Beth nodded thoughtfully.

"You know what *I* would like to do, Beth? Start a business to do with restoration. I would like to open a warehouse somewhere, and stock it with those things so often lost in demolition – clawfooted bathtubs, Victorian 'gingerbread', old pine mouldings, windows, doors…." Mattie's face grew dreamy

"There wouldn't be room for that here, Mattie, but it sounds like a wonderful idea! Bookie's building would be much better for it. He has all that space behind, where there used to be a market garden and orchard. They are long gone and most of it is now a car park for the Save Easy. Bookie fenced off a good big piece though. You must have seen it!" she broke off.

"Get with it, Mattie. You're still half asleep!"

"I don't think I know – oh, you're talking about *Bookie.* Wouldn't that work out nicely for everyone, I mean, just think, he could have his bookshop next to you. Think how cosy you would be!" she rolled her eyes lasciviously.

"Cut it out. Anyway, I expect the Save Easy would be gobbling Bookie's place up as a car park if he would agree to sell."

"I heard they were building a new store between River Road and School Road. If they do, then we could use the old store! That would be wonderful space!"

"Meanwhile, come down to earth, Mattie! I would like you to return these calls. We've fallen a bit behind, you know."

Conscience-stricken, Mattie set to work, all thoughts of Kurma and salvage and restoration put firmly away. She gave no thought at all to Anna, who could not bring herself to go in search of Mattie again until Wednesday. All the way into Calderford, she remonstrated with herself.

*I must not be too eager, I must not push. I must play her carefully, as the little fish she is. But time is running out. All must be arranged before the winter, before the ice, while water is still running freely.* She shivered. *One winter was enough. One month of winter, all those years ago.*

Mattie was not in the office.

"Where have you sent her?' Anna demanded angrily.

Beth mustered her courage to look Anna blandly in the face, striving to penetrate the screen of dark glasses.

"She has arranged a very tight schedule for herself, Miss Waters, wishing to make up for lost time."

Anna's annoyance washed over Beth in cold waves of hostility.

"And why, may I ask, was she away at all? She should have been at The Old Mill on Saturday. She is obligated."

"Really, Miss Waters." Beth's voice was husky, so clearing her throat, she started again. "Really, Miss Waters, you must take that up with Miss Peters. She is a very independent and capable young woman." Furtively she wiped sweaty palms on her slacks. "I suppose she will come out to you on Saturday. Isn't that the usual day?"

"You suppose! You suppose! Doesn't that girl work here?"

"That is so," Beth said quietly. "Now, if that is all, I am very busy, as you can see, and I must wish you good day."

Anna swept to the door. No longer assuming the guise of an old lady, she made an impressive figure.

"You!" she cried. "You! At every turn you thwart me! You took what was rightfully mine!"

Beth watched her, open-mouthed, as the door slammed.

*She's mad! Raving, staring – I need some coffee! Holy Moly, no wonder Mattie comes home so confused. We must put a stop to this, for once and for all.*

Anna drove back to The Old Mill, a danger to herself and everyone on the road, muttering under her breath as she drove.

"I must rid myself of her! She is so stupid, it should be easy, but my powers are weakening, I can feel it. Before long it must all be done. Mattie! Mattie is the key. Why does she resist? Why is Ahriman failing me now, when I am turning more to him?"

Sweeping into the driveway, slamming on the breaks, she ran to the barn. There on the blue plate lay the shrivelled pieces of Amanita Muscaria. Seizing one, she crammed it into her mouth, then walked triumphantly back to the house. Standing before the fireplace, she drank deeply from her goblet.

"Hear me, Ahuro Mazdao, hear me, Ormazd! I see beyond you! You are not all there is."

Flushed and defiant, she gazed at the glowing embers. Suddenly, the fire flared, filling the room with acrid smoke, driving Anna outside. Wildly she ran through the woods, tearing off her clothes, then plunged into the mill pond, laughing, crying, shouting, as the dark water closed inscrutably over her.

By the time Mattie came back to the office, Beth, having regained her equanimity, was able to describe Anna's visit dispassionately.

"It's a wonder she didn't hear my knees knocking, she carried on so." Beth shuddered. "Mattie, she really is a troubled woman. You must tell her that you have compensated her enough. Be done with her."

"I will soon, Beth. Kurma Watson will be back in a week or two, and then we can straighten things out. Did you know that Vishnu is the Preserver? Isn't that fitting for Kurma, since he has such an interest in old buildings and furniture, and such like? He isn't a Hindu, so I don't know how that works out. Still, what a relief it will be to have all this settled for good."

"Anna is so hostile, Mattie. To me, at least. Is she with you?"

"Not exactly, but it's as if she lays claim to me in some way. At times she is quite likeable!"

"*Likeable!*"

"Yes, and interesting. But she is so volatile. I find her impossibly difficult. I think I am getting a handle on her now, though, and I find it very important that I deal with her myself. Are we getting together with Bookie, this Thursday?"

"Why not? I enjoy it, don't you?"

"Yes – and it's my turn to cook supper, so I'll apologise in advance. I'm not much of a cook."

"You'll learn, Mattie. All you need is the ability to read recipes, and freedom from paralysis! I wonder if you would like – no, let me re-phrase that – be willing to help me clear out the rooms upstairs? I've been up there so many times just to look, and come down again, defeated. Alec wanted to go through it all himself, but never got round to it. Poor Alec."

"What's the difficulty, Beth?"

"Well, it's Alec's place, not mine. I never lived there myself, and he just turned the key on it. 'Let the past stay in the past,' he used to say, laughing. I feel I am intruding. Silly, isn't it?"

"Well, I don't mind giving a hand. It's an awful job to do alone. Let's start this Thursday evening, I know Bookie wouldn't miss it for the world. He loves rooting in old things."

By Thursday, Oxner's Real Estate was busy clearing up a nice little crop of summer sales. Beth, delighted, warned Mattie that it wouldn't last, now that there was a Canada-wide real estate firm in Lower Calder.

"There will be a bit of a lull next week, because of Labour Day. People like to do their moving before school starts if they happen to have children, unless they are transfers from some other part of Canada. After that it will be older customers, retirees, empty-nesters, migrants from central Canada, often from out of Province, so I hope you haven't blown all your savings on that trip to Ontario. The big real-estate companies do so much of the inter-provincial business, you know. We can't compete."

"Do we have any rentals coming up, Beth?"

"Not much in that line at all, one or two lease-to-purchase. I don't want to join up with any of those big firms, but it is getting harder to be a small office."

At that moment the 'phone rang.

"Kurma Watson," Beth mouthed, switching through to Mattie.

"Where ever have you been, Mattie?"

"I was in Ontario, Mr. Kurma. Family business." In a way, it was.

"You should have waited for me, we could have gone together! At least, I will be calling in there before I come to Calderford. I must see my father first, in Toronto, but I should be there by September 14$^{th}$. Let's see, that's a Tuesday; I could possibly be in Calderford the following weekend. Will you be around?"

"Oh, we will both be here."

"Both?"

"Beth Oxner and myself. This is her property, you know, and her business. She is very happy with your offer to help."

"Aren't you happy about it, Mattie?"

"I'm happy for her, yes."

"That's all? Well, I will look forward to seeing you."

Mattie hung up the 'phone, confused. What had he expected her to say? He must have meant the furniture, of course.

"Kurma says he will possibly be here by September 14$^{th}$. I will be interested to meet him and see his plans, won't you, Beth?"

Mattie's interest was not strictly to do with the renovation of Beth's property, as she was well aware. There were so many things teasing her mind. Why had Kurma come to Nova Scotia? Was he really looking for a special fish? Who had been meant to join him at The Old Mill? Why had Anna reacted so strongly at the mention of his name? But then, who knew what Anna would do next? She reacted strongly to everything! Shaking her head to clear it of all these idle speculations, she pulled her appointment pad towards her and picked up the 'phone. There were real people waiting for her, with real needs.

On Thursday evening the three of them ate a hurried supper, then, armed with a dustpan and brooms, garbage bags and empty cartons from the liquor store, went over to Alec's old apartment above the real-estate office. Bookie rubbed his hands in anticipation as they went up the stairs.

"I do enjoy a good clear-out, Beth! It'll be like looking through an old attic." Just then they reached the landing. "Jumping Jehosophat!" cried Bookie as Beth opened the door. "What a treasure trove!"

Scattered on the floor were some old Christmas cards spilling from a cardboard box full of letters, calendars and other jetsam washed up by the tides of time. Oddments of old furniture stood about, abandoned and disconsolate.

"This is what we'll do," decided Bookie. "We will put all the old letters, cards and calendars together in one box, and all the old photographs in another. We can – sorry, Beth, I mean *you* – can go through them at your leisure. Let's get to grips with the other stuff first." His eyes glazed in happy anticipation.

Beth trailed her fingers along a small tabletop, leaving a trail in the dust.

"They all look like rejects from a Salvation Army store, on the way to the dump, don't they?"

"Not so fast, Beth. Look, this is really good wood. It looks like maple-bird's eye maple at that! We'll separate out the good stuff, and put it on one side."

Bookie was in his element, checking, sorting, discarding. They bustled around with the garbage bags in hand, calling out to each other.

"Look at this old bed-head! Is it brass?"

"This lamp is past fixing, isn't it?"

"Do you want this picture frame, Beth?"

"Look! This is a lovely little mirror!"

Beth relaxed. The task she had so dreaded was turning out to be a party! Bookie constituted himself Chief Adjudicator, seeing value where Beth saw rubbish. Mattie, with her love of old things, was a big help, too. One trunk was full of old clothes, smelling of cedarwood.

"Look! This old trunk is brass-bound, and cedar-lined! It's lovely!" Mattie exclaimed.

"You want it? You can have it."

Mattie, taking out some of the old pants and shirts, tried them on. Soon they were all dressing up in Alec's old clothes, capering giddily among the muddle on the floor.

"He must have liked clothes, Beth. He has a lot of them, hasn't he? Even hats!"

"Not when I knew him! He liked his old favourites, and wore them all the time."

Exhausted, they sat there looking at each other, rather like a troop of down-at-heel clowns, hot, limp and dirty, awaiting their next performance.

Bookie produced three bottles of orange juice, some straws from one of the boxes, and some 'Tim Bits' There was an appreciative silence as they munched away. After a while, Mattie looked around, puzzled.

"Why, Beth? Why did he leave here? Why leave all this behind?"

"He was adamant about it. I once asked him, had he not been happy here? 'Once', he replied. 'Once, briefly, I was happy when I lived here.'"

"Woman trouble," said Bookie knowingly.

"We were so hard up," went on Beth, ignoring him, "that I wanted to keep some of these things. 'We're better off without them,' Alec said. Then, after selling some, he just locked the door. To me it became like Bluebeard's den, until at last I just ignored it." She smiled wanly. "But you are quite right, Bookie, this is a firetrap! Anyway, Alec always said, 'The past is over and done with, Beth, We have each other now'. Poor Alec! He always meant to clear this out, you know. He thought he had plenty of time – he should have had plenty of time."

"Well, we've made a good start, Beth. Next time we'll bring the vacuum cleaner. Do you want a hand down with these boxes of letters etc.?"

Bookie was full of cheerful efficiency.

"Thank you, Bookie. They would be better at home, I suppose. Thank you both very much – you don't know what a relief it is to root out the bogeyman! You are good friends."

Laughing, they gathered up the boxes and brooms, locked up and left the building. Bookie drove back with Beth, to help with the boxes, but Mattie went back to her apartment.

*Who would have thought that Beth had all that on her mind all these years? It's amazing how complicated life can be. Look at my problems with Anna. I shall go on Saturday and return the jewellery – and take the cranberry glass jug. That should clear the air a bit.*

She was quite unaware that Anna was having plenty of problems of her own.

For a whole day Anna had been silent, sitting in her Great Chair, wan and withdrawn. Her hair dishevelled, eyes dilated like those of a cat in a windstorm, her manner tense and anxious, staring, mesmerised, into the heart of the fire.

"I am weakening, Ormazd! Weakening. Hear my pleas, for Ahriman is strong."

But when had these pleas ever been answered, except by her own wilful heart? What voice did she hope to hear, other than her own?

"This I know. The water freed me only with reluctance. Me, Anahita, Anaista, Daeva of Water. My own element turned enemy. How will it be possible to trust myself to it now?"

Shuddering, she felt again the cold relentless grip of the running creek, feeling the fear that others had felt so often, others whom she might have saved with a thought. For the first time, she felt pangs of remorse. Immediately the fire glowed with a diffusion of soothing warmth, reaching out around her with a comforting embrace, easing away her tension. For one brief instant of luminous clarity, she saw what she must do. For she was not waning as the moon wanes, in another's shadow; rather she was diminished by her own withdrawal into the dark. For just that instant she saw clearly, understanding what was required of her, one instant only, before the illusory shadow returned.

Rising, she left the warmth of the fire, the shelter of the house. Grimly she wandered among the trees before standing silently by the creek. Time slipped by as she stared at the brown waters, wondering where the little box of jewels might be now. The day darkening, she turned back to The Old Mill House once more, her shoulders drooping, her expression resigned.

Her struggle with herself was not yet over.

# CHAPTER 16

Bookie and Beth settled for a quiet evening, taking pleasure in getting to know each other. In Beth's comfortable living room, it was easy for anyone to leave the safety of a sheltering stalking horse. She had the advantage of being at home, but Bookie's habitual nervous mannerisms fell away, leaving him revealed as a thoughtful, even wise, man.

"Bookie, you are a good friend, a good man. I haven't felt so comfortable with any other man of my acquaintance since Alec died." She held up a warning hand. "Now don't go running away with any romantic notions, whatever you do. Mattie's bad enough."

"I feel exactly the same, Beth. I never married, as you know, but I lived with a girl called Hilary Blackstock for six years. I was wretched when she went off with another man, thinking we would be together for keeps, but off she went down the road with this hulking young lad, good looking, charming, feckless. 'Aubrey', he was called. No other name that any one knew, just 'Aubrey'. I abandoned the wandering life soon after that, spent some time with my folks, then came out here. I went to Mount St.Vincent, as a mature student, working away as a stock-boy in a warehouse, part time. I was stunned when Mum and Dad left me all that money! I was able to find a home for all my books, turning a hobby into a business."

"Lucky you. It was Alec who left me the real-estate business, bless him. My parents were not that sort at all, I'm afraid. Did you ever hear from–?"

"Hilary."

"Of course, Hilary, ever again?"

"Years later. Apparently she really hit the skids, died from an overdose of heroin, in Vancouver, poor girl. So much for her dreams of freedom. I don't know what became of Aubrey."

Neither of them spoke for some time, then Bookie shrugged.

"It all seems so long ago. Another person, another life. Well, it's been an enjoyable evening, Beth, and I must be off."

"Wait, before you go. Would you be willing to come over and help with the sorting? I'm really dreading it."

"Nothing, Beth, would make me happier, for many reasons. Goodnight now, and thank you again."

*Yes,* thought Beth, watching his van pull out of the driveway. *A good man and a good friend.*

Friday passed too quickly for Mattie, knowing that Saturday would bring another visit to Anna.

*Don't start that again,* she admonished herself. *Remember Foster Harrington's advice, and Beryl's too. I have the cranberry glass jug! I'll have an early night and a good sustaining breakfast tomorrow. No more attacks of the vapours.*

After the 'good sustaining breakfast', she put herself to the first test. Taking out the little wooden box, prying open the lid, still swollen by its soaking in the water, she looked at each pendant, guiltily remembering they should have been put into the strongbox at the bank.

"They certainly are beautiful. It is almost as if she had been choosing them for me – almost as if she knew my taste! But how could that possibly be? They aren't as old as most of her things, and much simpler in design, but she must have bought them long before she knew me."

Hastily putting them back in the box, closing the lid firmly, she popped it into a basket along with the cranberry glass jug, grabbed her purse and headed for the door.

"Off to beard the dragon lady again?" called Bookie as she came down the stairs.

"Nothing to it, Bookie. Just call me Saint Georgina!"

Feeling happier because of these small jokes, she steeled herself for the coming encounter. How could she possibly know that Anna was in the exact same frame of mind?

Since her struggles in the waters of Kingfisher Creek, Anna had been very subdued, her emotions being nearer to stable than they had ever been. She spent more time quietly staring into the fire, silently and fruitlessly looking for guidance. The flash of insight she had experienced, though long faded, had left her irresolute, yearning for she knew not what.

*I gave so much of myself away. But was it really too much, or was it perhaps not enough? What I gave, I gave willingly, what I took, I took greedily, but now?*

Throwing up her hands in a gesture of despair, she went to the window, looking for Mattie's car.

*Now?* she questioned again. *What is to happen now?*

Overtaken by a sudden surge of anger, she cried angrily.

"But there is that woman! How could it happen?" Dropping her voice, "How could it have happened?" she finished sadly.

Seeing Mattie's old Toyota turning in from Old Mill Road, filled with a mixture of dread and gratification, but concealing both, she opened the door.

"So you have decided to come at last?"

Mattie smiled, as though totally unconcerned.

"Why, of course, Anna. I have been away, you know. But what does it matter? I am here now. What is it that you would like me to do?"

"We will resume the work where it was interrupted by your extraordinary behaviour," said Anna coldly.

Mattie just laughed.

"Wasn't I silly? But we can talk about that later. I have something for you. See what I have found."

Out of the basket came the little wooden box, the swollen lid still tight. At last she managed to pry it open. "See, Anna, they had floated down the creek and into the gravel pit pond. I have dried them off and they look as beautiful as ever. How is it possible they fell in the creek? Haven't you missed them? Weren't you worried?"

"Missed them? I threw them away! Tossed them into the creek. Why would I want such baubles?"

"You must have liked them at one time, surely?"

Mattie placed the box firmly into Anna's unwilling hands, saying, "I have something else for you."

Out came the little cranberry glass jug. Unwrapped, as Mattie held it up, a shaft of sunlight diffused by the patterned cranberry red glass, cast a rosy glow over Anna's face. Far from being pleased, she was furious. Holding out the box of pendants, she saw Mattie's hand held up in a gesture of refusal.

"You refuse my gifts!" she cried angrily. "You turn them away, and expect me – *me* – to accept *yours*?"

They stood facing each other, eye to eye, will to will, like reflections of each other, one hand offering, the other rejecting, standing in stiff dignity, like figures in a mediaeval painting, rigid, symbolic. Then occurred the most unexpected thing of all, Anna started to laugh, a real genuine laugh of amusement. Mattie, surprised, started to smile and then joined in.

"It is silly. isn't it? Two grown women!"

For one wonderful moment, that is what Anna felt herself to be, before her laughter subsided to a rueful smile.

"Perhaps we could exchange gifts, Mattie? I'll take the pretty little jug and you take the pendants."

"It's far too much, Anna."

"One then, choose one."

Mattie considered carefully. Would this obligate her further? No, not really. This was of her own volition, it was almost like a ceremonial breaking of bread.

"They are all so lovely, Anna, but I will gladly accept the amber pendant. See the insect trapped inside?"

Holding it up to the sunlight spilling through the window, she examined the little life held forever in that golden glow.

Then she tucked it beneath her shirt. "Amber should be kept warm. Perhaps this little creature will wake up!"

But unable to resist, she took out the pendant once more, full of wonder at the little prisoner.

"No," said Anna sadly. "It is locked in there forever," thinking as she spoke, "as am I! As am I!"

Mattie shook her head. "No, that is too sad. I shall think of it as a beautiful secret, which may never be told."

Bending her head to examine the pendant once more, she didn't see the strange expression crossing Anna's face at that moment, or the reaching hand offered in pleading, and then withdrawn. Her tone was business-like when she spoke.

"Well! Well! Time we got back to work. First let me put my pretty little jug where it will catch the light, and brighten the room."

Placing it on the wide sill, by the sunny window, she stood for a while moving her hand back and forth, letting the rosy glow play over it.

*Warmth*, she thought, *light. It's as though she has brought me a blessing.*

Upstairs in the bedroom, they took up where they had left off, Anna resuming her usual manner, amused, patronising, superior.

"Now perhaps you can tell me what happened two weeks ago, to make you run off like a silly child."

By her open smile, Mattie showed that she was not about to accept the usual submissive role.

"That was so ridiculous, wasn't it, Anna?"

"What were we doing, my child, at the time?"

"We were checking a box full of signet rings, testing them on sealing wax."

"So? You find that a strange thing to do?"

"Not generally, no. Most of them imprinted 'Anahita' on the wax, but the last one was different. The impression was of a fish, you see, and the name 'Matsya'."

"I fail to see," lied Anna, "why that should be so upsetting."

"Matsya is my name, and I have never seen or heard it used by anyone else. It felt – odd. It felt – uncanny."

"And that's all?"

"No. There was a design on it Anna, a design of a fish."

"That's as it should be, Matsya is a fish. It is a very ancient symbol."

"I know that now. I realise that it was my ignorance. Anyone might have known that! But I have a necklace, you see, with a pendant, a fish, lapis lazuli with an emerald eye, it is just like the symbol on the ring."

"Oh!" Anna said. "A pendant. But as you see now, there may be many. Why should yours be so special?"

"It's a long story, Anna, an uncomfortable one for me to tell"

"Try. I will listen quietly."

As she spoke, her gaze became impenetrable, as though a filter had been drawn over her eyes like the colour filter of a camera, screening out sensibility and emotion. Haltingly, Mattie recounted the story of her being found in the porch of St.Peter's church, of Kendrick Gibson's kindness, of the efforts to trace her parents, first by the authorities, then by herself.

"But why here, Mattie?"

The voice was toneless.

Mattie explained about the jewel box.

"Ah, yes, the jewel box," Anna sighed.

Mattie looked at her curiously.

"And you have always wondered why you had been left."

It wasn't a query, but a statement of fact.

"The word is 'abandoned'." Mattie's tone was as laconic as Anna's. "Yes, I have wondered, of course. It's certain that someone didn't want me. Unplanned, unprovided for, I must have been someone's burden."

Anna reached over impulsively, touching Mattie's hand.

"I don't brood over it, Anna. Life has, by and large, been very good to me. It's true I would like to be able to find out who my parents were, but it's their loss, not mine!"

Anna was quiet, as they looked at each other, the inventory lying neglected on the chest.

"And you say the river was frozen solid? That there was snow?"

Mattie nodded. "A heavy overnight fall, they said."

"Then let me tell you how it was done. Your foolish mother planned very cleverly. Close your eyes, we will picture it together."

Obediently, Mattie closed her eyes, leaning back against the bed. It was like having a bedtime story. Anna's voice was warm, full of feeling, lulling Mattie into a receptive mood.

"A cold winter, a cold heart. Your foolish, unthinking mother, ill equipped, unwilling to care for you but needing you for her own purposes, searched out a suitable place to leave you long before you were born. The father unaware, the mother heedless, the plan was conceived almost as soon as the child. Away she went, leaving the father alone and in ignorance. Yes, off she went to amuse herself until the time came. The time that you would be born."

Soothed by the story, Mattie listened drowsily.

"Then – then it was that the mother paid the only price she was prepared to pay. Where had she been? Where had she waited out her time? Far away, far from the father. Perhaps she had travelled the warm shores of the Mediterranean, perhaps some island in the Caribbean, knowing she must return to the cold heart of Canada, to Atterbury, her chosen place."

"So cold!" murmured Mattie, sleepily. "She must have been so cold – and alone."

"It was her choice," said the low voice, suddenly sharpening. "Back she came. She stayed in a little cabin somewhere, perhaps near the seaway, near the mighty St.Lawrence River, do you think? Yes, a small cabin of wood, in the Eastern corner of Ontario. Cold, alone, but prepared, she bore the child, the little girl – you. Alone she cleaned and dressed you, folded you into her hooded cloak, alone quelled the yearnings of her heart."

There was a catch in the voice as it continued, low, compelling.

"For one week, for seven whole days, mother and child as one, warm in that cold place, clinging together, huddled by a small wood stove, using sparingly the store of kindling and logs."

There was a long pause.

"Go on," whispered Mattie.

"Then her plans fell into place. Huddled in that enveloping cloak, heart beating to heart, the baby was carried by careful stages, here a bus, there a car, they spent two weeks, making their way slowly to the town of Atterbury, and their parting. Who notices a child being pulled in a sled in winter? Then to lie hidden, upstream, waiting for the promised snow."

"Oh, how sad for them, even the mother!" sighed Mattie, so enthralled was she, she had forgotten that she was the child.

"Alone, the mother watches the snow start to fall. Mother and child alike huddled in the warm cloak. Then, oh then, in the sheltering dark, screened by snow, she made her way, softly sliding down the icy river, her baby wrapped in a blanket and fed, tucked into a cheap sled. At last, reaching the sheltering church, she cautiously made her way to the porch. There in that cold dark place, she left the baby alone and untended!"

"Oh Anna, what a terrible thing," whispered Mattie.

"Yes, without a backward glance, she left the baby!" The voice was agonised. "Left it warmly wrapped, and recently fed, but alone! Alone! And on that lonely child's breast, a blue jewel box, a necklace, a pendant, a note. '*This is Matsya, my little fish. Christen her if you must. I will be back for her.*' See the mother looking down at her child, knowing one day she would have need of her. Then, the same steps retraced, brushed over with snow; back up the river, and away! First a promise repeated to herself, 'I will be back. She is mine.' A promise made to her child, her Matsya, her little fish!"

There was silence.

"Oh Anna, you make it seem so real! I can imagine the mother covering herself and the child – me – with voluminous clothes. I can picture her making her way to the church porch and creeping back again."

"Then," finished Anna, "the gentle, mantling snow, like a blessing, covering the footsteps, covering the world with innocence. Who better to find you than the man who did?"

"The father – my father. That would have been better."

"Yes," said Anna, softly. "Your father would have been better."

Lunch forgotten, they sat together, deep in thought.

"Thank you, Anna. To hear it in your voice, I can believe that is how it happened. I feel – comforted and at rest. I can't think why! It doesn't change the facts. You are a wonderful actress."

Anna's eyes blazed, her voice rose.

"Always you say I am acting!" Then her voice dropped. "But it is true, I have played many parts."

Suddenly business-like, she pulled the inventory back towards her.

"There is very little left to do, and I want to be away before the winter. I will not spend that cold season here." She shivered, "Oh, the bone chilling cold, the winds of winter!"

Falling in with her change of mood, Mattie sat up.

"We could have our first frost any time now, Anna. Will you be closing The Old Mill up?"

"I haven't thought so far ahead, I have some big decisions to make." Her reply was both irritable and evasive, and her voice once more imperious, as she swept to the bedroom door.

"You must go now, Mattie, off with you. I shall see you next Saturday. You can see yourself out."

Brusque to the point of rudeness, she turned her back, busying herself with the box of signet rings, which she still held in her hands. Picking out the one engraved with the fish, she stood, holding it to her breast, before dropping it to join the others in the box, ignoring Mattie, who waited at the door.

Mattie, disconcerted by the sudden mood change, watched her briefly in bewilderment, before going downstairs to the porch, turning, irresolute, she called, "Good-bye," over her shoulder. But there was no answer.

Back at her apartment, there was no need for her to avoid Bookie, since he had gone over to continue cleaning up Alec's old apartment and later would go back with Beth to help in the sorting of the old letters and photographs. Mattie appreciated having the time alone. The day had been full of surprises, of changes, highs and low. She heard the echo of Anna's story in her head, visualising again the sequence of events presented by her.

"Yes," she said, with absolute conviction, "that is how it happened. My father never knew."

She re-lived the feel of the mother's footsteps along the ice, the scramble from the frozen river, the silence and loneliness of the church porch after the mother had left. It was as though her whole body vibrated with those old sensations. She heard again her frightened wails echoing from the cavernous stone walls, her throat aching in sympathy with that of the child.

"Yes," she whispered, "yes. That is how it happened."

Feeling for her new pendant, she took it out, warm from her body, and held it up to the light.

"There you are, little fly. I wonder what deep secret you are holding."

But when at last she fell asleep that night, her amber necklace was still drawing warmth from her body, and lay above her heart.

# CHAPTER 17

Labour Day! No appointments.

Mattie stretched luxuriously. There were no appointments, nothing to hurry for. Turning over, she made every effort to go back to sleep, forcing herself to be still, to close her eyes. At last, kicking back the cover, she jumped out of bed.

"Oh! What's the use? I never liked staying in bed, and eating in bed only makes wrinkles and crumbs. I wonder why some people enjoy it so much."

Long habit found her up, dressed and busy by seven thirty.

*Time I cleaned up a bit anyway. I've neglected everything far too long.*

Facing the window, she pulled out her amber pendant, swinging it idly in the sunlight, studying the little insect.

*I wonder how old you are,* she thought. *I wonder what you would be able to tell me. What secrets do you have?*

Her daydream was interrupted by the 'phone ringing.

*It must be Beth. No one else uses my home number. She must need me to meet a client. Botheration!* As cheerfully as possible she said, "Hullo?"

Mattie never gave her name over the 'phone. Many years of living alone had taught her this basic piece of wisdom.

"Mattie?" The voice was known, but unfamiliar. "Mattie Peters? It's Kurma."

"Mr. Watson–"

"Kurma."

"Kurma. How did you come by my number?"

"It's not rocket science, Mattie! I'm back in Toronto now – in Etobicoke. Do you know that part of the city?"

"I've never been there, no."

"I'm with my folks. Dad wants to know about his old friend, of course. I haven't been on holiday exactly, you know. I wanted to study the architecture for a month or two, and meet Vickram."

He paused. At a loss, Mattie just waited. "Are you still there, Mattie?"

"Of course, yes. Do you have something specific for me to do, Kurma?"

"Now I do call that unfriendly! I just wanted to chat. Vickram, you see, was supposed to have come over to join me at The Old Mill and stay for a while. However, Fate intervened in the guise of marriage. It's odd, you know, his dad wrote to me once saying I should try to catch Matsya in the creek. He said it was some sort of fish. I thought he was joking."

"I suppose in a way it is!" Mattie was laughing. "So that is why people say you were after a special fish! Did you know it as an Avatar of Vishnu then?"

"No – not until you told me! Who knows? Maybe I will catch that fish yet!"

"Well, the creek is still there, Kurma," Mattie replied, deliberately misunderstanding his insinuating tone, "but then so is Anna Waters."

"Unfortunately! I can't think why we ever sold The Old Mill in the first place! How is the Water Witch, anyway? Casting any spells lately?"

"Sometimes she is almost human! Quite likeable, in fact, it is very difficult to understand her. It's like – it's like trying to read by strobe light, full of dazzle and darkness."

"Doesn't seem worth the effort. Now to the nitty gritty. I'm coming down to Nova Scotia one week on Monday. That's – let me see – September 15th. I'll rent a car at the airport, and drive down to the South Shore. Will you be around?"

"It will be easy for you to find the office. Calderford is only a small town. Kurma. I'll see you then."

Saying, "Don't hang up yet," Kurma rattled away for another twenty minutes.

"A smooth operator," thought Mattie, hanging up the 'phone at last. "No, that's not fair. Anyway, it will be good to clear up the furniture business. Things are beginning to settle out nicely."

Accustomed to a busy schedule, feeling at a loss at having time on her hands, and wondering how to spend the rest of the day, she heard the shop door bang open.

"Mattie!!" yelled Bookie. "Come on! Show a leg! We're all going down to the beach for a picnic!"

Beth's voice joined in. "Come on, Mattie! The picnic's all ready. Grab your swimsuit! It takes until September for the North Atlantic to warm up, you know."

"Oh, how lovely! How kind of you, Beth. What a great idea. What can I bring?"

"Oh, just bring yourself, your swimsuit, your towel," Beth said impatiently. "We've been trying to call you, but you were gabbing away on your 'phone."

"I'll be right down."

Good as her word, taking out a bottle of ginger beer, she joined them in the shop.

"Off we go then. My car this time. There's more room in the van, and it's used to sand on the floor."

Bookie drove a Dodge Caravan, not new but meticulously kept, using it to transport books back and forth. He called it 'Boanerges'.

"Boanerges! What kind of a name is that?" Beth asked.

"Very Biblical. They were James and John – Zebedee's Sons of Thunder! You should have heard this old thing before I fixed it up – noise enough for two, believe me,"

Starting with laughter, the afternoon promised well. Parking at Risser's beach, they went through the underpass and the park to the beach. Splashing at the water's edge, they looked for sand dollars, making great plans to use them in all sorts of high-flown artistic projects. At last, their T-shirts' hems tied into soggy pockets of shells, they flopped down on the beach for lunch, wondering what to do with them all as they tucked into their sandwiches. The incoming tide would soon be covering the wide expanse of sand, bringing more shells to be collected another day. They knew very well that the sand dollars would end up in a box, or basket, to be played with now and then. The pleasure lay in the collecting

"Oh well, they will be useful round the lavender bushes. Lavender needs lime," said Beth, philosophically.

Mattie traced the pattern in the flat disc of the shell, with her finger. "It is just like a daisy," she said reflectively, "or some other flower. I shall keep one at least as an ornament."

"Or you could make a pendant," suggested Bookie. "By the way, Mattie, you are already sporting a nice little pendant. Mattie's getting presents! Mattie's getting presents!" he chanted teasingly.

Mattie's hand flew up to hold the little creature encased in amber, feeling suddenly protective.

"Not a gift, a trade," she said, "for the cranberry glass jug."

"Anna," said Beth. It was a statement, not a question.

"Anna," Mattie confirmed. "This trade puts us on an equal footing, you see, each giving, each receiving. It's just amber," she added defensively.

Beth looked at her sadly, saying in a voice still quiet, still controlled, "Do be on your guard, my dear. Remember the old saying about 'a sprat to catch a mackerel', or 'a Greek bearing gifts'."

Mattie nodded, but without agreeing, tucking the pendant back under her wet T-shirt. "I hear you, Beth. You know I have been calling her the 'Water

Witch', but–"

Before she could finish her sentence, a cold gust of air swept over the beach and a tongue of angry seawater licked towards them. Hastily they grabbed their shoes, towels and the remains of their picnic.

"How extraordinary! I've never seen the like of that!" cried Beth. "Look, the sea isn't rushing in anywhere else!"

"It must be small pocket of high pressure." Bookie was always anxious to find a rational explanation. "Anyway, time to tidy up and head home. It's been a lovely day."

"We must do it again," agreed Beth.

Sandy, wind-blown and happy, they climbed into Boanerges, heading for home.

"I'll drop you off first, Mattie, then Beth.... I've been giving her a hand with all that sorting, you see."

Mattie sniggered. "I'll bet you have," she said.

"None of your snide comments, young woman! Show some respect for your elders."

"Sorry, I'm in such a giddy mood today. Thank you, Bookie. I shall be glad to be home. It's been pretty hectic the last couple of weeks. Tomorrow is a holiday too, isn't it?"

As she got out of the van she suddenly remembered Kurma's call.

"Oh, by the way, Kurma Watson called, Beth. He plans to come next Monday, September 15$^{th}$. He said he would see me then"

"I'll bet he did!" teased Beth. "–I'm only quoting you! See you on Tuesday morning!"

They drove off, grinning at Mattie's discomfiture.

*They can be really aggravating! Like a couple of teenagers, teasing me as though I'm dating! I never heard such drivel.*

Nevertheless, she was smiling as she took off her damp T-shirt, throwing it into the kitchen sink, along with her shorts and swimsuit. Lazily stirring them around to rid them of salt and sand, her mind drifted over the last two days, chuckling over Kurma's attempt to chat her up.

"Just because of our names! How silly! He uses the Water Witch as another bond. This is someone to watch out for."

Mattie had 'watched out' for several others over the years, ever since her seventeenth birthday. Determined to be independent, having worked hard for the security that lack of a family had denied her, there was no place in her plans for romantic entanglements. At last, drifting off to sleep, she drowsily re-enacted the exchange of gifts with Anna, and the recounting of her abandonment.

*She made it all come so alive for me! She gave such a sense of all the emotions involved, even the sadness as she recounted the pathetic little message in the jewel box.*

The message? The box? All at once Mattie was wide awake, recalling Anna's voice.

"'This is Matsya, my little fish. Christen her if you must. I will be back for her.'"

*The exact words! Anna knew the exact words! But I'm sure I didn't quote them to her! Nor describe the jewel box, yet she said, "a blue jewel box."*

Abruptly. Mattie threw back the covers, and got out of bed. Taking out the jewel box, she held it in her hand, unwilling to open it, to see that little note. Then, unfastening her amber pendant, she held it up, studying the insect trapped within. Roused as she had been from the edges of sleep, her fancy endowed the little creature with powers beyond her guessing. Opening up the jewel box, she dropped the pendant hurriedly alongside the other, as though it burned her fingers. They lay side by side, glinting knowingly up at her, the insect, the emerald eye of the fish.

"Two of them," she whispered, in momentary terror. "Has Anna now given me two? Does that mean that Anna is, in truth, my *mother*?"

Her lips suddenly dry, she licked them nervously.

*Not an equal trade, after all. I was wrong.*

Closing the box firmly, and putting it far to the back of the drawer, she crept back to bed, only to find that sleep had deserted her. Far into the night, she argued and reasoned with herself, finally falling into an exhausted slumber. By morning, when she awoke, the clear light of day made the whole episode seem like a bad dream.

"Too much sun," she said, looking at her flushed skin. "Too much sun and sea water! What a night! No wonder my memory was playing such tricks! But at least it wasn't all my fevered imagination, because I have taken off the pendant – when did I do that? Probably to clean off the salt. Yes, that must be it."

Shaking her head at her foolishness, she nevertheless made no attempt to put the pendant back on again as she made ready for work.

Bookie and Beth had spent the evening more productively

"First," said Beth, "we will tackle the letters, then the photographs. I can't make up my mind whether to keep them or not. They really have nothing to do with me."

"Read them first, and then decide," suggested Bookie. "It will be like having Alec back with you for a while."

"Oh, these are all from the time before we were together, Bookie. I feel

I'm invading his privacy. But you are right. We shall soon be able to tell whether they are best thrown away. We'll make two piles, keepers and non-keepers. I'll shred the non-keepers at the office, or maybe burn them."

Beth soon forgot these letters were to Alec, as all the early ones, fastened in a lavender ribbon, were from his mother, to "Dear little Alec."

"He must have been in his twenties when she wrote these," cried Beth, "still Mother's little boy! I wonder what changed him."

They were full of advice about such things as food and underwear, often ending pathetically with "hope you will come home soon." Through the letters, they followed Alec's mother's hopes and fears for him, her joy when he visited.

"Alec's mother was widowed, you see, Bookie," explained Beth.

The later letters were full of gratitude for various sums of money, then they turned to the kindness of the nurses at the Victoria General Hospital, in Halifax. The last envelope was blank, and in it a brief note in Alec's hand.

"Mother died Dec. 2, 1974. I shall miss her."

Beth dabbed her eyes.

"Poor Alec! How sad for him. These are keepers. I shall treasure them."

Re-tying the lavender ribbon, she set them aside.

Most of the letters, loose in the box, were at once more frustrating, and more interesting. Several, anxious pleas to know "why you don't call?" or "where are you these days?" were signed with such names as "Cuddles", "Lovey", "Liz", "Mandy".

"He was quite a lad, your Alec. Listen to this from someone called 'Terry'."

> *You always were a dark horse, Alec! Whenever you find a new girl, you disappear from view for months at a time! Who are you with now? Peg and I are quite different – we shall always be together. Drop us a line sometime.*
>
> *As ever, Terry.*
>
> *PS. Peg sends her love, and tells you to GROW UP.*

"Look, Bookie, I know I wasn't the first woman in Alec's life. He was tall, dark, and a looker in his own way. Remember, I was the last, and that is good enough for me!"

She handed over the letter to him.

"Put it among the non-keepers. I shan't enjoy that sort of thing. Those are strictly his affair, and I use the word advisedly."

As they each read silently, the little pile of 'Non-Keepers' grew steadily.

Beth shrugged.

"You're right, Bookie – a bit of a lad as you say. No wonder he had such a wardrobe! I wonder why he kept all this junk? I like to think it was sheer idleness, rather than sentiment."

"Do you want to keep business letters, Beth?"

"For now, anyway. They might tell me how he got started. I already have all the old tax forms and so on, of course."

At the bottom of the box was a small bundle of large envelopes, tied together with a dark blue ribbon, interwoven with gold thread.

"Hmm, beautiful, expensive paper. Handmade, I shouldn't wonder," Bookie said appreciatively, rubbing it between his fingers.

"And that looks like real gold thread, too," added Bath. "And smell that aroma, sandal or cedar wood, I should say. It all looks very up-market. Whatever was Alec up to?"

Abruptly she dropped the bundle of letters on the coffee table, rubbing her hands together as though they were cold.

"You read them aloud," she said. "I don't like the feel of the paper, nor do I care for the smell. First, let's have a stiffener."

"Oh, make it a hot chocolate, Beth. It's been a long time since supper."

"Oh, you and your hot chocolate, Bookie!"

However, it was with some alacrity that Beth went to make the chocolate, glad to leave the last bundle of letters behind, and to feel the grateful warmth of the mugs.

"All right, shoot!" she said as they sat, mug in hand

"Look at the handwriting, Beth! All capital letters! What a scrawl, and purple ink, at that."

"What else, on such exotic paper. Still, they must have been important to Alec, at the time, seeing how smartly they have been tied."

Clearing his throat, Bookie began.

*MY OWN BELOVED,*

*AT LAST WE HAVE MET AS FATE INTENDED. MY ARMS AWAIT YOU!*

*WOULD ONLY THAT WE WERE TOGETHER NOW. FIND US OUR OWN HAVEN, DEAREST ALEX, WHERE WE CAN BE CLOSE.*

*NAIA.*

"I can't believe that Alec treasured this garbage," muttered Beth. "It must be a joke. Go on, Bookie."

*DEAREST HEART,*

*ONLY LET IT BE BY WATER, BY YOUR SIDE, AND I AM CONTENT. BUT MAKE HASTE. SEE HOW TIME PASSES, AND THEN PASSIONS MAY COOL. OH, MY BELOVED, YOU MUST FIND A WAY.*

*NAIA.*

*HEART OFMINE,*

*THE EXPENSE SHOULD BE OF NO CONSEQUENCE, ALEX, IF YOU LOVE ME, SEEK! SEEK! SOMEWHERE THERE IS A PLACE FOR US, AMONG THE HOUSES YOU LIST! BORROW ONE TO SANCTIFY OUR LOVE!*

*NAIA.*

"I can't stand much more of this, Bookie! Are they for real?"

"There are only two more left, Beth."

"Go on then."

*MY OWN TRUE LOVE,*

*AT LAST YOU HAVE FOUND IT, THE PLACE WHERE OUR BODIES WILL JOIN, AS OUR SPIRITS HAVE ALREADY JOINED. NO ONE WILL COME NEAR US, NO ONE WILL DARE! FOR THE OLD MILL WILL BE HAUNTED BY OUR PASSION.*

*NAIA.*

"Really, the drivel she writes! The quality of the writing certainly doesn't equal the quality of the paper," groused Bookie, "but there is only one left."

*SO ALEX,*

*YOU HAVE SERVED YOUR PURPOSE. I HAVE WHAT I NEED. YOUR TIME OF BLISS IS OVER, AND I HAVE LEFT. YOU SURELY DID NOT EXPECT ME TO SHARE YOUR SQUALID LITTLE LIFE FOR MORE THAN A FEW MONTHS?*

*ONE THING I PROMISE, THERE WILL NEVER BE ANOTHER LOVE FOR YOU. HOW COULD THERE BE, AFTER YOU HAVE KNOWN MY PASSION? NEVER WILL ANOTHER TAKE MY PLACE, THIS I VOW. POOR, FOOLISH, SOLITARY, ALEX! YOU DO NOT EVEN KNOW ME, FOR MY NAME IS NOT NAIA ONDE! WHO EVER HEARD OF SUCH A NAME?*

*FOR YOU, I SIGN MYSELF,*

*?*

As he finished reading, they sat in stunned silence.

"Is it some sort of play?" asked a bewildered Bookie. "Was she mad?

Poor Alec was certainly bedazzled if he swallowed that piffle."

"The Old Mill," whispered Beth. "Alec must have started the rumour that it was haunted, himself. It was on his books, you see, all those years ago. I can't believe it of him."

"Think of it, Beth, how that woman used him, devious, cunning, cruel, beguiling. He must have been dazzled by her extravagances."

"The whole experience must have changed him into the gentle and kindly man I came to know and love," said Beth sadly.

"Not changed, Beth, developed his innate goodness. Remember how he helped his mother? Don't grieve so. There, there."

Awkwardly he patted her shoulders, as she wiped her tears away.

"But Alec did have another love, he had me." Beth sounded defiant. "How that woman would hate me for it, for we were very happy."

It was on this more positive note that the evening ended, and Bookie drove back home in Boanerges, full of conjecture.

It had been a long day for everyone.

# CHAPTER 18

On Tuesday morning, all three friends felt the worse for wear. Bookie was distressed on Beth's behalf, Beth was fretting over the letters from 'Naia Onde'. And Mattie? Well, Mattie wasn't sure whether she had been awake or dreaming when she took off her necklace. So it was in a sober mood that she said good-bye to Bookie and greeted Beth. Mattie and Beth looked at each other, flushed from sun and sand, but hollow-eyed.

"We should either go to the beach more often, or not go at all," Beth said. "No offence, Mattie, but you look a wreck."

"We make a good pair then, Beth, for so do you!"

Mild enough banter to cheer up the day, but it worked. Both women had changed considerably in the last four months. Caught in the maelstrom of Anna's personality, each had good cause to search for their own truths, to wrestle with their own problems, to establish their own balance.

Beth's night had been full of struggle as she argued with herself.

*I have always relied on Alec. First, because he was so much older, I thought him so much wiser. But I don't know. I valued his experience, but now? Some of his experiences I don't value at all. Do I want those days back? No, not any longer. I shall always remember them, always treasure them, always love him, but – yes, there is a 'but'. I am moving on. There is still life out there.*

Feeling both younger, and much older, she had at last fallen asleep.

Mattie's difficulties were both more complex and more palpable.

*Who is Anna? What is she expecting from me? What have I got to give that she seems to need? Is Kurma to become another strand in the web? Who, after all, am I?*

At last, thinking of her time with Beryl and Foster Harrington, her mind cleared.

*I am still who I am, whoever I may be, and whatever the future holds, I can handle it.*

Mattie didn't feel younger, at all.

Bookie's thoughts were very straightforward.

*I am going to look after Beth, whether or not we get together, I'm going to look after Beth.*

Bookie felt surer of himself than he ever had. Perhaps the dormant seeds of gallantry suggested by his name, Horatio, had at last found the right conditions to come to life. Audrey Bean had been right about her son after all. For all three, work had become a haven. In their leisure time, they were beset by their own daemons. Plans, questions, fears, hopes, skittered around in their heads, giving them no rest. Each morning, they fled gratefully to the humdrum of their daily lives. The healing power of tedium should never be underestimated. Beth looked round for some diversion, rather than spend another evening alone.

"I wonder whether you would like to come round to the house sometime, Mattie? Perhaps Bookie would like to come, as well. My old plum tree is covered with fruit this year, which isn't always the case. If you could help me with the picking, I'll put them in the freezer and keep you supplied all winter.

Mattie jumped at the chance. "Tonight! Oh! Good. Yes, I'd far rather stew in plum juice than my own! I'm brooding too much."

Beth's shoulders were slumped with weariness.

"So am I. You know, Mattie, I'm sick of real estate."

Mattie's heart sank. Would she be out of a job?

"Do you want to talk about it, Beth?" she asked quietly.

"It's just such a struggle! Look at all the big players – they have offices all over the country. I've never wanted that. I've really accomplished all I set out to do, that is build Alec's business. I don't feel the need to do that any longer."

That was one result of reading the letters.

"Would you sell out, Beth?"

"Hard to say at this point, but it is a consideration. Then there's you. Would you want to be in a big office?"

"I'm very happy with you, Beth, just as we are."

Beth heard the despondent note behind the reassurance.

"Now, don't you worry. It's just a passing thought. What would I do, retire? I'm too young for that. Oh, come on, let's get Bookie and go pick some plums!"

*One more ball to juggle*, thought Mattie. *I'm going to stay here, one way or another, but I'm certainly not ready to take on the business myself.*

The three of them spent two hilarious hours picking the plums, fending off the hungry wasps, blissful physical weariness keeping all other things at bay.

"We'll just wash them, bag them, and freeze them. Maybe make jam later," said Beth. "They are wonderful stewed, in pies, sweet and sour sauce

– I love plums any way at all. Now who wants what to drink?"

They ended up with hot chocolate as usual, relaxing companionably into a contemplative silence. Then Bookie's wandering gaze happened on the calendar, hanging by the fireplace. "September, 1999," he read. "That's three months! Only three more after this!"

"Is the world coming to an end, at last, Bookie?" Beth asked, lazily. "Do you have inside information?"

"Have we all forgotten?" He cried again. "It'll be the new millennium! Everyone goes on about it so much, it just rolls off me. I admit it had slipped my mind entirely."

Neither Mattie nor Beth answered him. Into the mind of each flashed a signal.

"I must sort this out by the end of the year, one way or another."

Beth gathered up the mugs.

"On that note of startling revelation, I propose to retire for the night. Don't forget your plums."

Which of them would fall asleep first, that night, putting unsolved riddles aside?

Meanwhile, Kurma had decided to leave for Nova Scotia earlier than planned. Arriving at Halifax airport late on September 8$^{th}$, the Wednesday after Labour Day, he decided to spend the night at the Hilton, rent a car and drive out to Calderford the next day. Playing tourist, he took the shore road, relishing in the flashes of sun and sea, the remembered sound of the gulls.

*I was right the first time I came here. This is where I belong. What a fool I was agreeing to sell that property! I had to go halfway round the world to come to my senses.*

Stopping in Peggy's Cove for old times' sake, he lunched, looked wryly at the souvenirs – made in the Mystic Orient – and stood on the bare rocks, marvelling at the power of the waves.

*Yes*, he thought. *Inland, a town is just a point on a map. Here, I feel I have arrived.*

As he drove idly along the South Shore, he came to another decision.

*Before I go to Calderford, I will call on Miss Waters. It would be good to sort out that furniture business before meeting Mattie. I really should stop teasing the poor girl, too. God knows why I do it, but I feel I've known her for years.*

It would be an interesting meeting.

Kurma's first impulse, on drawing up at The Old Mill, was to inspect the dam, then run a critical eye over the buildings. It was he who had restored the old place.

*Holding up well,* was his verdict.

"And what, may I ask, are you doing on my property?"

The voice, materialising from nowhere, startled Kurma. He spun round, and there stood Anna, her expression ominous, her voice intimidating. Both Mattie and Beth would have understood Kurma's feeling of foreboding as Anna's presence loomed, shifting and enlarging, casting cold, menacing darkness wherever it fell.

*So this is the Water Witch*, thought Kurma, *I'd better do a bit of looming on my own behalf.*

Drawing himself up to his not inconsiderable height of 6'3", and wisely not extending his hand, he spoke easily.

"Miss Waters? I'm delighted to meet you at last. I'm Kurma Watson." The effect on Anna was extraordinary. She shrank in on herself, her face paling, showing both hope and fear.

"Kurma." It was a statement, not a question. "So, you have come, as I feared you might."

"As you see." Kurma, puzzled, spread his hands. "There is no need to be upset about the furniture, Miss Waters. I shall be very happy to recompense you for your inconvenience."

"The furniture?" said Anna dully. "Oh, yes, the furniture."

Kurma waited.

"Do you feel all right, Miss Waters? May I get you a drink of some sort? Shall we go inside and sit down?"

Anna turned zombie-like to the door, shoulders slumped, feet dragging. Kurma put out a hand to steady her.

"No," she said thickly, drawing away, cringing almost. "No."

By now regretting his decision to come, Kurma began to understand Mattie's reservations about this woman. As they entered from the porch, he was further astonished by the metamorphosis of The Old Mill's plain living room into something so exotic and theatrical.

Anna sat in her Great Chair, leaving Kurma to fend for himself.

"May I get you some water? I know my way around, of course." He experimented with a small conciliatory smile.

Wordlessly, Anna indicated her goblet. Kurma, running appreciative fingers over its surface, filled it with water in the kitchen. Finding Anna standing by the hearth, he silently handed her the filled goblet. She immediately raised it in her right hand, raising the left in a sweeping gesture.

"Now, Ahriman, now, Ormazd," she intoned softly to the glowing embers. After a minute or so of contemplation, she resumed her seat in the Great Chair. Uninvited, Kurma drew up one of the wrought iron dining chairs, and there they sat, gazing into each other's faces, until Anna broke the silence.

"Is it then to be punishment or salvation?" she whispered.

"Pardon me?"

"I know you were here before."

"Of course, Miss Waters. I restored the place," said Kurma patiently. "I sold it to you, remember? Through my agent."

"Buying, selling. What have we immortals to do with that?" Receiving no reply, she went on, "Are you here to thwart me? Are you here to take Matsya away? Or are you here in all your might as Preserver, to help, to guide?"

Kurma began to gauge the distance between himself and the door.

"I assure you, Miss Waters, I came by to discuss the furniture, you see–"

Anna's bitter laugh interrupted him.

"Say then, are you here to take away this house?"

"Certainly, if you wish to sell it back to me."

"Yes, you would take away the house," Anna muttered. "You would take away my hope! Am I not Daeva of Water? Might I not be even venerated still in India? You, Oh! Vishnu, you could make these things come to be."

"Well, anything I can do to help," said Kurma, nervously. "Anything within reason, of course."

"Reason?" cried Anna. "Reason? It is the heart, Kurma, the soul."

Dramatically, she smote herself on the breast.

He looked at her enquiringly, speechless.

"Matsya, I called her. Am I not entitled?" she pleaded. "Why Mithras, why he? Is not water more powerful, more necessary?"

"Oh, I'm sure you are right – oh yes, quite sure," was the placating reply. "Very powerful indeed – couldn't do without water."

"So advise me then. Do I take her, willing or not, invest her with immortality, to do my duties? Free myself? If I become mortal, would I not be set free by death? Could I not join Ormazd?"

Kurma was growing ever more desperate.

"It seems very reasonable to me, Miss Waters," he assured her. "No need to – ah – take her at all. I'm sure of that. No! No! Quite unnecessary."

"Then how – without her – may I shed my immortality?"

Kurma, searching frantically for some answer that might satisfy her, idiotically quoted the first thing that came into his head – "Be good, sweet maid, and let who will be clever."

"Virtue." Anna nodded. "Reject Ahriman."

"Oh! Every time, Miss Waters, Yes, I should if I were you."

"But then, Kurma, Vishnu the Preserver, what of the woman who took my love? The love I had left behind?"

"Oh, I would just forget about her. Yes, that's the idea, forget it! Just concentrate on the Virtue thing, I should."

Anna nodded dreamily.

"Forget her, yes, a foolish woman, but always will I remember my little Matsya, never will I let her go. Perhaps I will surrender my immortality to her."

Kurma, standing, was inspired by desperation.

"Surrender it now, then join with the Great Spirit for ever more!" he cried, making for the door, and safety. "Surrender!" he cried.

"Ormazd," whispered Anna.

"Oh, absolutely. That would be best," Kurma answered her, escaping through the porch.

Outside, he took out a linen handkerchief and mopped his forehead. He hadn't a clue what had been going on, recognising only the name Matsya.

"And she is not going back there, if I have anything to say about it!" he said. Suddenly remembering, he added. "Mattie told me Anna appeared to be unnerved by my name. If she thinks for one moment that I am some sort of anthropomorphic thingummy, she must be a very disturbed woman indeed. Now let's see what Mattie Peters is like."

Whistling cheerfully, he set off for Calderford and Oxner's Real Estate office, where he found Beth but no sign of Mattie. Beth welcomed him into the office.

"I'm very glad to meet you at last, Mr. Watson. All my contacts have been through your agent so far. If you remember, he had the key and showed you over The Old Mill years ago."

"Oh, certainly. It's a pleasure to meet you in person. Is Miss Peters around, Mrs. Oxner? I need to sort out this business of the furniture. I called in to see Miss Waters on my way."

Beth's look was sardonic.

"That would be an experience worth remembering," she said dryly.

"It was, believe me! I couldn't get any sense out of her regarding the furniture. We seemed to be talking through a smoke screen of metaphysics. She speaks in riddles, like the Oracle at Delphi."

"Got it in one, Mr. Watson! A hard woman to pin down. Oh! here comes Mattie now."

"Beth, I think I may have sold it, at last," said Mattie, coming through the door, "such a nice young couple, and they are going to restore – oh, good afternoon, I do apologise. I'm Mattie Peters."

"Matsya!" said Kurma, immediately attracted to her. "Matsya Peters! I'm your superseder Mattie, Kurma Watson, second Avatar of Vishnu."

"Oh, you're Froggy! I'm sorry, that just slipped out."

They shared a laugh, Beth watching them benignly.

"I thought we might get together this evening, Mattie, and discuss all this antique thing. I have tried my best with Miss Waters, but…."

Ruefully he spread his hands.

"You too, Kurma? You've been to see her?"

She and Beth laughed.

"Then, tomorrow, Mrs. Oxner–"

"Beth."

"Tomorrow, Beth, we could discuss your intentions regarding this place, if that would be convenient?"

Beth was only too happy to agree.

"I'll tell Bookie, Mattie, that you won't be coming. He and I mean to tackle the photographs tonight. You go off and clear up this furniture business for once and for all – if that's possible. If you are agreeable, Mr. Watson, we will meet here tomorrow morning."

"Beth, I am the most agreeable person in the world! Come on, Mattie, come and elucidate some mysteries for me. First, I need to find a motel, and then we will go to dinner, OK?"

"That's a good idea," said Beth firmly. "The River Restaurant is very good. See you both tomorrow."

Matsya and Kurma, those two Avatars, went off to find out what else, if anything, they might have in common.

# CHAPTER 19

After Kurma had left, Anna sat motionless, contemplating what she regarded as 'the visitation'.

"Virtue," she murmured. "What is that? Does it not come from the Latin for 'man'? How should I then be virtuous? 'Good,' he said, 'be good, sweet maid.' *Maid*! Her laugh was low in her throat. "How should I be good? I am what I am!"

Time slipped by into the dusk of evening, and still she sat, staring at the tranquil glow of the fire. Was the warmth speaking to her? A soft insistence in her head repeated. "You know what is meant. You know what is meant."

"And if I know," she whispered into the darkening room. "Does that mean I am able to act on what I know?"

"It is for you alone to have the will. It is for you alone!"

She waited in the gathering shadows, livened only by the fading fire, but there was nothing further. Rising, she wandered around, the darkness suiting her mood. Opening the carved chest, she looked at the contents with lack-lustre eyes.

"Even these were not desired. Not these, not my jewels. Matsya wished for none of it, none of me."

The lid dropped heavily as she turned away.

"So where is there help for me? The time is here, I must decide."

Long into the night she sat in her Great Chair, troubled, indecisive, striving to do something she had never done, temper impulse with reason.

The same thread of indecision was running through the time Beth spent with Bookie, though they started the evening full of good intentions.

"There aren't too many of these, Bookie, considering the years they cover." Beth was blowing dust off the two boxes of photographs. "Why is it that snapshots are such fun to take, and pore over at first, yet such a deadly bore to sort out and store away?"

"Are they dated?" asked Bookie.

"Oh, they are dated all right! Downright antiques, some of them."

"No. I meant, has he written a date on them?"

"Dream on, Bookie. Who ever remembers to do that? Well, some may be dated. Shall I just throw the lot of them out? I don't know these people, most of them anyway."

"You knew Alec," Bookie said gently, wondering at his own altruism. Was this any way to draw Beth's attention away from Alec to himself? "I tell you what, Beth, let's find all the childhood pictures first. They may have been labelled by his parents."

His guess proved correct. One box was filled with snapshots of Alec's family, dating back to before 1940. Alec alone, a chubby baby, Alec with his parents.

"Oh, look, his dad was in the navy! Alec was like him, wasn't he? Oh, look at this one! This must have been taken for his Dad to take to war with him. Wasn't Alec cute, Bookie, in his little sailor suit?"

"Adorable," agreed Bookie grimly. How could he compete with this? "Let's press on, shall we?"

But for a while, Beth continued to look at the chubby 3-year-old. "Alec waves his Daddy off to war", said the caption. Sighing, she put it aside.

There were not very many photographs over the next few years.

"Film was probably scarce, or expensive, during the war," suggested Bookie. Such photographs as there were, were mainly of Alec alone.

The saddest was a professional photograph of Alec with his mother. Both dressed in black, they were posing on either side of a portrait of Alec's father. The caption was "Lost in Action". His mother, not looking into the camera, gazed sadly and wistfully at her son.

"Alec must have been five then," said Beth softly. "How sad they look! So he grew up without a father – better that than growing up with mine," she added bitterly. "I shall keep these, of course. I'm not enjoying this a bit, are you, Bookie?"

"It's – interesting!" Bookie managed, non-committally.

"Well, let's stop for a snack, at least, and then decide whether to go on with it tonight."

Beth returned the photographs carefully to the box, smoothing her hand regretful over the lid, as though saying good-bye to someone she had just met.

"I'll bet he became Mummy's darling after that, Bookie. It explains all the extravagances with clothes, and his giddy way with girlfriends, doesn't it? That dreadful hussy 'Naia Onde' really made a man of him after all," she said, smacking the lid down firmly. "That's his boyhood taken care of. I'm going to make a snack, and then we can decide whether to embark on the next lot, when he becomes a lad about town."

"That should be an eye-opener!" he said, rising to join Beth in the kitchen, "judging by all those hats and sweaters."

"Look how dark it's getting already. Let's not bother with the other box tonight, Bookie. I feel more like thinking about the future than the past."

He found this a hopeful sign as they carried their gingerbread, and the inevitable hot chocolate, back into Beth's cosy living room.

"Now, Beth, what is it you have on your mind about the future? I've known for ages that something was bothering you. Is it the renovations?"

"That comes into it, but it is not the whole story. The truth is, I'm sick and tired of the office. There! I feel better for telling someone! You see, I have always felt that I owed it to Alec, that it was a trust for me. I have always felt that I was still working for him, as I was before he was killed in that crash."

"And now?"

"It was reading those letters. I feel quite different. To me, Alec had always been someone who knew what he was doing. Knew better than I knew how things should be done, and why."

"You think less of him, Beth? They are only foolish letters!"

"Not less of him exactly. They just made him look more – fallible, more – human. Now I think I have done all I need, and would be happy to sell out to one of the big players, but–"

"You are considering Mattie. That is so like you, Beth! You are trapping yourself between two generations."

"It's quite true, but there it is. I've come to think of Mattie as more or less a daughter to me. I wouldn't like to see her hurt, you see."

There was a reflective pause, as they examined their own thoughts. At last, Bookie spoke up.

"I think, Beth, that it's high time you thought about what is the best for you to do for yourself, and if I can be part of that decision, I shall be very happy."

"Oh, I shall need you around, Bookie, believe me! Anyway, I may be worrying unnecessarily. What I am really *hoping,* you see–"

"Is that Mattie and Kurma," interrupted Bookie, "decide that the best way to solve the problem of the furniture is to share it.!"

They laughed in complete understanding, and Bookie drove Boanerges home that night, in a very upbeat frame of mind.

Fleetingly, this solution to the "furniture problem" crossed Kurma's mind, too. He was enjoying Mattie's company enormously. Their conversation had not, as yet, become personal. They both veered away from letting the Water Witch dominate the evening, finding other common interests to discuss.

"Do you enjoy selling real estate, Mattie?"

"That's really hard to say. I do enjoy finding just the right home for people, you see...." She cut herself off hurriedly, not wishing to get into the story of her life.

"Yes?"

"You see, I like old houses, old landscapes, old communities. I really love to see them restored, made liveable. I like to see old communities become viable again, and – oh, I'm sorry! This is my hobby horse I'm riding now."

"That's fascinating, Mattie, because that is what motivates me! What I would like would be to pick up pieces from old building sites, and–"

"Salvage them!" Mattie interjected excitedly. "Sell them to home owners for restoration, or to harmonise new buildings in to the community! There's a building I have my eye on, if I can ever manage it."

"A company," enthused Kurma. "Three parts – planning, salvage, construction. Imagine it!"

"I have," said Mattie happily. She went on to explain her business degree, her study of social housing, her love of the local architecture.

"Is the salmon not to your liking?" enquired a solicitous waitress, hovering over them.

"Oh, delicious, thank you. We are just talking too much," Kurma apologised, with a disarming smile.

"That poor girl would really like us to finish, Kurma. I know how that is! I have done my stint waitressing, too. She needs the tips."

"Can we go on somewhere else?"

"Out here? Not a chance. You can come back to my place, if you like, for a short while. This is so interesting. As long as you understand I'm not inviting you up to see my etchings – if you know what I mean?"

"Understood, of course. It's very kind of you. Now, no nonsense about going Dutch."

Mattie's apartment seemed too small for all that excess of youth and hope and energy as they settled down with their coffee.

"Do you intend to start such an enterprise in Ontario, Kurma?"

"That's not likely. There's money there, of course, but it is all on too large a scale for my taste."

"There are some very pretty places though, not too large, lovely old stone houses. I grew up in Atterbury, south of Ottawa, you see."

"Tell me about it. Is your family still there?

There was a pause before Mattie answered.

"Not tonight, Kurma. That's a long story. Too long for now."

"But you will tell me?"

"Sometime, yes, if the occasion arises."

Kurma nodded agreeably.

"My family, you see, is in Etobicoke, as you know," he said. "But they have no intention of remaining there when they retire, and I thought," he leered craftily, "where could they retire better than here? You see, I am laying plans!"

"What about brothers or sisters, would they mind?"

"You know the old teaser? 'Brothers and sisters have I none. But that man's father is my father's son.' Well, that's me. I'm an only child. No son as yet though, so the rhyme doesn't make sense – yet."

"It's very lonely being an only child, Kurma."

"True, but it ain't all bad either, I had two mothers."

*"Two mothers?"*

"Well, I only remember Migs – my second mother. My 'real' mum broke her neck in a skiing accident, the winter after I was born. I suppose Dad married on the rebound, but it worked out well and we are all very happy together. It was Mum's father who left me a little money – very good of him really, because I hardly knew him."

"Lucky you." Mattie's tone was dry.

"Why, Mattie, I never thought! What about your family. Are you an only child too?"

"As far as I know."

"Mysteriouser and mysteriouser! Do you feel like elaborating?"

"Nope. Tell me about your encounter with Anna. That must have been an eye-opener."

"Mattie, the mind boggles!"

Kurma, trying to report the meeting lucidly, shook his head in bewilderment.

"She gave every indication of believing me to be some sort of immortal being! Not only that, but to have some sort of undefined power to advise and to help her. I've heard people talk to Dad that way, trying to get him to influence admission to some club or other. I mean, she really believes this. It was very–"

"Overpowering? Convincing?" asked Mattie softly. *"Terrifying?"*

"Oh, all of that. Of course it is all complete nonsense! Why? What?" Mattie was shaking her head. "You know I am none of those things, Mattie! But she really believes herself to be some sort of demigoddess, or immortal! I mean, come on, Mattie, get real."

"Kurma, I have been dealing with Anna for weeks now. Let me tell you some of the oddities."

Without mentioning the signet ring, she told him about the mind reading, the blackfly, the apparent rising fully clothed from the lake, and on and on she went. She described the ceremony of the lustral goblet, the robes, the powerful impact of her storytelling, her knowledge of ancient history, her hypnotic gaze. At last she fell silent. It was only to herself she whispered, "I am afraid she is my mother."

"Mattie," said Kurma firmly. "You must not go there again, certainly not alone. These are all your own perceptions. A hypnotist, she may well be, I can accept that! But all this other? No! No!"

"I feel," Mattie said in a small voice, 'I truly feel she has powers above the normal."

Kurma studied her face. Leaning forward, took both her hands in his.

"Now listen, listen to me carefully. No, don't turn away! Let's see if *my* hypnotic gaze works! Just hear me out. It's some 2,500 years since Xenophanes ridiculed the idea of a lot of gods and goddesses running around looking like people, behaving in ways that would shame the worst of us! Even way back then rational minds, at least some of them – at least his – rejected beliefs such as Anna's. That suggests to me that without credulous minds, they would not have been possible in the first place, let alone now."

"That's what Foster Harrington said," murmured Mattie, "I'm an idiot."

"Oh no, Mattie – never that."

They sat in silence for a moment, then Kurma continued.

"He rejected polytheism completely, saying that all is the One, and the One is God, all mind, all eye, all ear, eternal and motionless, ruling by thought alone. All things come from the earth and return to it all water from the sea. All is the One, even the heavens."

"You believe that too, don't you, Kurma?"

"Ah, but you see, as to that, Xenophanes thought that no one knew all the answers, that everything is a matter of opinion."

"And in your opinion he was right?"

"In my opinion he was a very wise man. Also, in my opinion, it is high time I left you in peace to get some sleep. I shall see you tomorrow though?"

"Yes, of course! We are all going to meet. Good night then. Be careful going down those stairs, they are rather steep."

As she prepared for bed, Mattie thought over all the events of the evening.

"'Everything is a matter of opinion,'" she quoted exultantly. "Yes! Oh yes! I really am going to enjoy knowing Kurma,"

Happy and heartened she settled down to sleep, but her dreams were full of Anna's whirling stars, the spin of the earth, and of dark waters overspreading the land.

Next morning, Kurma arrived bright and early at Oxner's Real Estate, just as they were opening for the day. Beth was standing at her desk and Mattie at the filing cabinet.

"I have asked a good friend of mine to join us for this discussion, Mr. Watson," said Beth.

"Kurma, please."

"Kurma. He's been most helpful with his suggestions – even that I undertake the work at all, in fact. Here he comes, now."

As she introduced him, Bookie explained that he had simply closed shop.

"Of course, it took me some time to pacify the stampeding mob of customers, but," he shrugged, "they finally took off for a large book chain in Lower Calder."

Together, the four of them trooped through the building, Beth looking anxiously at Kurma.

"Hmm, yes, well – as far as I can see, it is all very structurally sound, but it has been messed about with quite a bit, over the years."

Beth nodded in agreement. "That's what I need to sort out, you see. What is viable to restore and what is not?"

Briefly, she outlined the situation; how the larger companies were cornering the market. How she was afraid of being left with only mobile homes and write-offs to sell. Mattie listened to her despondently. So much for her hopes of buying in, in a few years time.

"So the question for all of us in this room," Kurma summed up, "is where does our future lie?"

"It hardly includes you, does it, Kurma?" Beth asked with some asperity. "My little project here is not very likely to affect your future, one way or another."

Kurma studied the faces of the other three in the room.

"Well," he said mildly, " maybe it could."

Into the silence following this pronouncement, Sid Heddle erupted.

"Hi!" he said. "What's the occasion? A prayer meeting? I never saw such a set of solemn faces."

"Oh, Sid, don't imagine things. What brings you here?" asked Beth, irritably.

"I got news – or maybe you know already?" he enquired cryptically. They waited patiently. "It's that woman of yours," he said, addressing Mattie. "Packed up and leaving!"

"What!" cried a startled Beth.

"Well, I maybe getting ahead of myself – but I'm off to pick up those two big chests of hers."

"And her furniture, too?"

"No." Sid lost a little of his self-importance. "Well, no, just those two big chests. I've gotta get Danny from school to give me a hand. They're some heavy."

"Oh yes," remembered Mattie, "she said she would be away for the winter, at least. Thank you, Sid."

Disappointment at having caused less of a stir than he thought, Sid left mumbling about "great heavy chests" and "enough to give you a hernia." He was thoroughly aggrieved by the whole thing.

"Beth, if she's leaving, I would like to put in an offer for her house. I told her so myself," said Kurma, frowning. "She asked me had I come to 'take her house away', I remember that. She does seem to be a woman of whims and fancies."

"Amen," muttered Beth.

"About all this restoration, I have an idea that might work out – or might not, and which could include all four of us. If you three are willing to close shop for today, let's adjourn somewhere to discuss it."

"My place," said Beth. "We will spend the afternoon on it. Let's grab a quick lunch of soup at Tim Horton's first. To save time."

And that was when the idea of 'Re-Versions' was hatched.

# CHAPTER 20

Long into the night, until that bleak hour just before the dawn, when will fails and resolution ebbs, Anna sat, rocking backwards and forwards, cradling herself as if she were her own child. A storm of unfamiliar emotions shook her ancient and deeply rooted convictions.

"He came," she whispered. "Vishnu! He of the Triad. Vishnu, he whose name I used."

All through the long night she had struggled to understand what was required of her, that she might become one with the Great Spirit.

"Brahma – Ormazd – are they one?"

Fearfully she stared at the fire as she spoke, but the hot coals glowed serenely back at her. All was well.

"'Be good,' he said, but what is virtue? What must I do?"

Thoughts, slippery as little fishes, slithered and slid through a mind unpractised, a mind unwilling to snare them. What were these elusive qualities? She filled her lustral goblet, raising it to the hearth.

"Ormazd," she whispered. "All-seeing eye! What must I do? Where is the hand of Ahuro Mazdao?"

Unwinking, the glowing fire drew the gaze of her remarkable eyes into its heart. Again there was the insistent voice within her head.

"You know what is meant."

Anna shook her head from side to side in negation.

"I cannot," she muttered.

"Ah! You will it not! But the truth is to be valued above all."

"I try! I shall order my mind! See what I shall do. I shall leave! I shall leave them in peace."

With sudden resolve, she rose. Carefully she packed away all the contents of the great chest other than her goblet. Inserting the slender key in the ornate lock, she hesitated before turning it decisively. Still with determination, she hurried up the wide staircase.

"My robes, all my robes must go."

As she opened the cupboard doors, the brilliance of the garments shimmered into the room like a shaft of sunlight.

"My beautiful raiment," she muttered, running her hands over the bright silks, agleam with threads of gold and silver. "I shall keep one – just one. Surely I may do that? Here, this one, the umber and orange, the red and rust, the gold of Fall, the ripeness of Autumn."

Thrusting it far to one side of the cupboard, as though by so doing the act would be negated, she closed the doors, standing for a moment with her back to them, arms protectively out-spread. With increasing reluctance, she laid her robes in their chest, slowly and unwillingly locking them away.

"You have not finished," whispered the inner voice. "All is not finished."

Anna whirled, as though to confront another presence, then sullenly turned back to her task.

"First the labels."

Down she went, down the wide stairs, stepping more slowly now, to the table where the labels lay. She wrote in bold script, "Theatrical Props". smiling satirically at this abandonment of truth so soon after her vow.

"All is not finished. There is more," echoed the voice.

Flouncing to the 'phone, Anna called Sid Heddle, telling him to come for a delivery.

"So," she said, "these treasures shall be back where they belong. This will I manage. They shall be 'found', some here, some there, over many years. This much I can do."

"But not the jewels." Then she looked furtively about her. "No! not those." Up the stairs once more, with hastening feet she sped, to hold, to gloat, to guard. "These I will keep. Who knows? Perhaps even now it is not too late. Perhaps Mattie can be cajoled."

Shivering with a delicious anticipation, her resolve already weakening, she opened her chest of jewels. There they were, winking seductively, priceless gems from an ancient past. Anna's face changed. Eyes narrowing, mouth twisting into a cunning smile, she reached out both hands, clutching the cascading gems.

"She will never resist them! It may still be possible! Even the opal."

She swung the pretty thing, which she considered to be of ill omen, from her finger, back and forth, back and forth.

"It has the power," she muttered, her voice thickening. Hastening from The Old Mill, glancing nervously over her shoulders, she roamed once more through the woods, her hair wild, her clothes disarrayed. And that is where, with considerable difficulty, Sid Heddle found her by following her trail. Here was another story for the family fireside. He winked at Danny.

"She's a wild one all right! But don't you forget now, young Daniel! It's only between you, me and your Mum. Mind now."

They smiled in perfect understanding, fully expecting a generous tip.

In Beth's pleasant living room, Kurma surveyed the faces of his three companions. Superficially so ill assorted, they had nevertheless an affinity, just as things randomly and lovingly collected over the years have harmony of their own. It was obvious to him that they were an extremely congenial group with which it would be easy to work.

Beth broke the astonished silence. "Whatever are you on about, Kurma?"

"'Re-Versions'. It's just a name! Well, it's more than that, it is a proposal I wish to make. Look at yourself, Beth, look at this room. You are a woman who enjoys keeping the past alive. You have done wonders with this house."

"So far, I agree. Yes, we worked hard on this place, Alec and I."

"Not everyone has the knowledge or the skill to do it, you know, though a great many wish they could. Now Mattie," the look he gave her was almost proprietary, his smile warm, "Mattie has told me how much she would enjoy salvaging, restoring, and preserving old houses and communities."

Beth, noting Kurma's expression, shot a glance at Bookie, daring him to interrupt.

"From my own point of view, I have wanted to do this for ages," Kurma finished.

"Hah!" Bookie objected. "You aren't old enough to have spent ages on anything."

"I'm thirty-two. That's old enough to know a few things about myself, if nothing else, Horatio."

Everyone, except Kurma, giggled. "Do call him Bookie," Beth begged.

"And don't forget that Kurma is an architect," Mattie reproved him.

"All right! All right! No need to team up on me."

Unnoticed, he winked slyly at Beth. "All I have been thinking is that ideas like this often end up being very expensive," he said.

"Point taken, but I would like you to consider it. Now you, Bookie, know a great deal about old books. You can't fool me, Mattie showed me your shop last night."

Mattie flushed. "We talked a lot last night," she said hastily, "and had coffee."

Surreptitiously Beth kicked Bookie, mouthing, "Don't say it."

"So there you have it," Kurma concluded, looking around the circle of faces. "We share a great many interests, and we all want to make a living out of it, if possible."

"I'm beginning to see," Beth said slowly. "You mean pool our ideas and resources, and start some sort of an enterprise along those lines?"

"Exactly, Beth. Let's make a list of the things we know about, to one degree or another."

Bookie produced a pencil, Beth a pad.

"I'll start you off," she said.

"Old houses, property values, local by-laws, water supplies, sanitary requirements, the things we learn selling houses. Some knowledge of local antiques, what the market is, where to find them."

"Heavens, Beth. You don't need *us* at all. Let me add my bit. I'm an architect – I understand building codes, engineering, design, drafting, drawing up contracts, all those practical matters. I too, know quite a bit about antiques, furniture making, types of wood, materials finishes. I am not yet familiar with local markets, but I have restored one property here, The Old Mill."

"I've studied heritage housing restoration," said Mattie shyly. "I don't know as much as the rest of you, but I do have a business degree, and do know a little about antiques."

Bookie shrugged, "I'm not much help. I know a lot about old books, of course, but also old maps, settlements, local history, conditions. I too know a little about restoration, having done quite a bit to my old place. You learn a lot about by-laws doing that."

"Well, there you are then! What else do we need?"

"To do what exactly?" Beth asked, practically.

"For a start, we salvage old buildings that are being wrecked, for one reason or another. We buy the old doors, windows, mouldings, bath tubs, cupboards, you name it. We clean them up and sell them."

"Also we buy, on our own behalf or for a client, rundown properties – such as you were speaking of, Beth. Restored, maybe moved to a new site or foundation, they would be very marketable. We could also design compatible housing, using as much old material as we can. The possibilities are endless! Bookie, with his knowledge of local history, land grants, maps and so on, would be an enormous help. He would be our archivist! "

Bookie's face glazed with delight. "I have plenty of room, you see! I could do that!"

"We could buy old furniture and fittings, hinges, knobs," put in Beth, "fabrics, needle-point! Oh, what fun it would be!"

"I could keep track of everything," Mattie contributed. "I am really good at that! Well, I am," she insisted, as they all laughed. "I know a bit about these other things, but I am a whiz at organising money."

There was a pause, as they all looked at each other beatifically.

"But–" It was Beth.

"Oh, dear! The inevitable 'but'," Kurma groaned.

"But," repeated Beth, inexorably, "there is the little matter of money."

"Ahh – there's always that!" sighed Bookie.

"I have a little – a very little though," said Mattie.

"Well, I have quite a bit, but I can't afford to lose it," Beth said. "I'm not young anymore."

"Same here," echoed Bookie. "I have the property – thanks to Mum and Dad – and I have the stock, plus a small investment, but I am no spring chicken either."

"I may be of some help there. After all, I'm young, and I need to build for the future – just as you did, Beth. Kurma Deulkar has been urging me to do something of the sort ever since Anna Waters' offer came. I was amazed. He signed over the company to me, plus what he called a 'little working capital', which I hope to pay back. That, plus a small legacy from my grandfather should help to get us started. I'm more than willing to take the chance. Don't you agree, Mattie?"

She flushed, uneasily.

"I can offer my wits and my determination, Kurma. Nothing more."

There was a thoughtful pause as they studied each other's faces, then Kurma took up the thread again.

"I see this as a very viable proposition. We make this an area that will attract people from all over the place. This used to be quite a gathering place at one time. We will do for Calderford what L.L.Bean did for Freeport, in Maine! I'm quite serious about this and I'm willing to take the risk."

"We might even start a school, to teach the skills."

"We could train the local people, who are all so creative and capable."

"There are good builders – Garnet Romberg, for one."

Of course practicalities were bound to surface and curb their eagerness, but there and then, they were full of enthusiasm.

Leaving Bookie behind with Beth to finish sorting the photographs, Mattie and Kurma set off together.

"Are you going to offer me a coffee, Mattie?"

"Oh, better than that! I will make you an omelette and salad. That much I am able to cook. Wouldn't it be wonderful if it works/"

"We will make it work, Mattie," cried Kurma, seizing her hands, "it has to."

Mattie made the omelette, while Kurma made the salad. Once they had cleared the meal away, they talked about the afternoon, both aware that they were stalling.

"Tell me about it, Mattie. What is it that you are trying not to say?"

"Is it that obvious? Well, it's true. I said I would tell you about my family, but now, I don't want to go into it at all, it's so bizarre – but here goes."

What started out as a bald outline of the facts gradually expanded. Reluctantly she took out her necklace, saying, "Here it is, you see, with the note and the box." Kurma whistled.

"That's incredible!" he said. "It is certainly no reproduction. Mattie, it looks very old, and is very beautiful. So that is why you are called Matsya! Your mother must have been familiar with the name. Why, whatever is the matter, do you feel all right?"

"Not really, Kurma. Far from wanting to know who my mother is, I now dread finding out."

"This is bad, Mattie. Why?"

Haltingly at first, she told him the rest of the story, the part even Beth had not heard. She had told him about the signet ring, and how she had grown comfortable about that, but it was only after he had coaxed her out of her silence, that she completed the tale.

"It was when she was re-enacting the story of how I came to be left in the porch of St.Peter's."

"But didn't you say she was an actress?"

"I thought she might be, and that is why it seemed so real, but now? I can't convince myself. I'm sure I hadn't quoted the words of the note, Kurma! And she repeated them, word for word. How did she know?"

"Are you saying that you think she knew your mother? Wouldn't that help you?"

"What I am saying, is that I am afraid she *is* my mother."

They both sat quietly, thinking about this.

"What do you know about her, Mattie?"

"I know that she is very knowledgeable, knowing a great deal about stars and the ancient world."

"Is that so bad?"

"Sometimes, in dark moments, I believe that she was *there* at the time."

Kurma's laugh was so infectious, and she found herself joining in.

"Like the man in Gilbert and Sullivan, whose top half, being fairy, could get through a key hole, while his legs, being mortal, were left sticking out behind!" he said when he could control himself. "Oh Mattie, what a wonderful cockeyed idea! Let's see, you would be 25% immortal! Or maybe not? I don't know how these things work. Oh My Lord, this is amazing! Now what else do you know – and I mean *really know*?"

"She is very volatile, sometimes malicious. Imperious, yes, she is that too. She is amazingly fascinating, and I wouldn't want to be like her at all."

"Oh, a lot of people feel that way about their parents, don't they?"

"I wish I could convince myself, Kurma, that this is all just that – ordinary, commonplace. I really wish I could." She held the amber necklace out to him. "See the little insect trapped in there? Sometimes, I think it is like me, at other times it is the unreachable secret of my past."

"Mattie, you know what I think? I think you have been on your own too much, and for far too long, brooding about this. Now I think I shall have to do something about that. Will I see you again tomorrow?"

"Tomorrow I go to see Anna."

"Not on your own, Mattie."

"Yes, Kurma, on my own. I can handle this alone. I must handle this alone, so I can live with myself."

"And would you then be able to live with someone else?"

"I haven't thought it through that far, Kurma. At the moment this is enough for me. Yes, I'd like to meet you again, later in the day, perhaps?"

And so that is what they agreed.

Mattie stared after him, reflectively, as he left. What was it he said?

"Then you would be 25% immortal! Or maybe not? I don't know how these things work out."

*Nor I*, she thought grimly, as she went back up to her apartment. *While Kurma was here, I thought it was funny, too. But now?*

Like Anna's, her night was restless. She tried to recall what she had read about the death of cells in the body. Weren't they trying to use this death of cells against cancer? Did cancer, refusing to die, simply proliferate?

"Why didn't I read it more carefully?" she sighed. "I'm full of half digested information. Then there is mutation. Suppose the body mutates, and just refuses to die?" She shuddered. "Perhaps immortality is gender-linked! Mother to son – or is it mother to daughter? Here I go, over-tired, and over-fanciful again. At least I can't be a clone – we are not at all alike! Maybe I have discovered something different, a new mutation 'Annamattie', and none of my children, till the world's end, will ever die! I will bring forth a Mightier Mitochondria!" By now she was giggling foolishly. "A world of Annamatsyas!"

And it was with a vision of fish-headed women with hypnotic eyes, flooding the earth with water that Mattie at last drifted groggily off to sleep.

In contrast, Beth's evening with Bookie was placid to the extreme. At least, that is how it started out. They discussed Kurma's proposition, seeing it from a different perspective.

"They are so young, Bookie! So confident! I myself am a little uncertain about the risk."

"Mmm, yes. Think of it this way, though. We would essentially still be doing the same as we are now, but with more scope."

"Yes, I can see that, but my investment in 'Re-Versions' – a great name, isn't it? – would have to be limited. How about you?"

"Agreed. But things are very slack, Beth, just now. I would be very happy with the role planned for me. I have never wanted to be very rich."

"It would work, I suppose. Mattie has a good head on her shoulders, and from a business point of view probably understands more about business than the two of us put together – no offence, Bookie."

"That wouldn't be hard in my case, Beth. Now where are the rest of those photographs?"

The second box was like a quick run-through of fashions for the young from the late fifties. It soon became apparent that Alec avoided all the fashion extremes, but there was the long hair, the wide-bottomed pants, the inevitable leather vest – the girls. Short ones, tall ones, the full spectrum of hair colour, natural or not. There were miniskirts, and dresses sweeping the floor, blue jeans, blazers. Alec had cut quite a swath.

"Humph," said Beth. "He never went to college, you know, but that didn't slow him down! Look at that car!"

For there was Alec leaning on a flash Corvette.

"My, oh my! Whatever became of all his money?"

"Beth, be charitable – maybe he gave it to his mother."

"He was quite something though, Bookie, wasn't he? I wonder what quietened him down."

"His mother dying?"

"Mothers aren't the answer to everything, Bookie! Whatever has happened to free will? Thank God, here's the last package."

Then Beth became very quiet, her face pale, In her hand she held a large sealed envelope, expensive paper, probably handmade. They recognised it at once.

"Naia Onde," she whispered. "See! That is Alec's writing."

"Aren't you going to open it?' Bookie asked. Beth held it out wordlessly. "Shall I open it, Beth? Or would you rather just – chuck away?"

"No! No! Bookie – open it for me. See? My hands are trembling"

Bookie took the fruit knife from the fruit bowl on the table, and carefully opened the seal, fearful of damaging whatever lay within.

There it was, a photograph of the anonymous Naia Onde.

Jaws slack, they looked at it wordlessly. It was unmistakable. The rippling hair, cascading loose, the compelling eyes, the imperious look.

"Anna," breathed Beth, softly. "Anna."

# CHAPTER 21

Saturday morning dawned bright and clear, a beautiful September morning. Trees flared and glowed their fall colours against the blue Nova Scotian skies. In the flowerbeds, the hardier plants continued to bloom; fruit and vegetables stands were loaded with the harvest. It was the kind of perfection that couldn't last.

"Don't be fooled by the blue skies," the CBC weatherman said cheerfully. "A rapidly moving stream of warm moist air from the South is on a collision course with a cold front moving in from the North. It could mean trouble!" He was annoyingly happy about it.

Kurma, still asleep, missed the forecast entirely, Mattie wasn't listening. Beth had grumpily switched it off. Bookie looked at the clear sky, shaking his head disbelievingly.

*They must be wrong*, he thought, pleased to have a focus for his discontent.

None of the prospective partners in 'Re-Versions' had passed a tranquil night, each of them, for one reason or another, feeling anxious and restless far into the early hours. Each waking resolute in the light of morning – Joan of Arc or Sir Galahad perhaps – to "sort things out once and for all" There was a dangerous amount of nervous energy flowing between the four of them, chafing and ill controlled, ready to spark a fine old emotional storm, and the centre of the turbulence, the hub, the navel, the omphala, was Anna.

Anna, herself, was well aware that the escalating emotions within her were becoming uncontainable. This tension between her wish for virtue and her will to evil, was a thing no longer possible to escape by fleeing. A choice must be made, and the time was imminent.

"Today, while Mattie is here, I will try once more, for she must take my place. Let the burden of immortality rest on her shoulders, as it should! First I will try to reason with her," she paused, aware of her weakness. "But should reason not succeed, I will cajole, entice," here she smiled with grim amusement. "These never fail me"

Remembering Mattie's gift of the rosy cranberry glass jug, of Mattie listening to the story of her own abandonment, of her glaring at Anna, eye to eye, as equals, Anna paused, her expression softening for a fleeting moment, then once more hardening.

"If those fail me – there are other ways, old ways, tried ways. Yes, I will use those."

This decided, she took up her lustral goblet, polishing it with a silken cloth. Glancing briefly at the hearth, she left The Old Mill, walking swiftly to the barn. The strips of amanita long since dried, stood in a jar of dark glass on a shelf below the table, alongside a mortar and pestle. Humming contentedly, Anna pounded the strips to dust, pouring the fine powder with great care into the jar.

"I only need to use enough – as I have before. Not too much or she will die."

In a dream of content, she returned to The Old Mill, to await the arrival of Mattie.

Beth, looking all of her fifty-three years, sat at her kitchen table. In front of her she had arranged the photographs. First Alec by himself, on his face a foolish smile of infatuation, then Anna alone, beguiling, sensual, spread indolently on a rug, smiling upwards at the camera.

"Oh, Alec! How could you? She is so – so blatant."

Disturbed by Anna's transfixing power, she set these two aside, turning her attention to the six remaining. In these last six, Anna and Alec were together. It had obviously taken a couple of tries to set the camera, but the last two had succeeded only too well for Beth.

"Alec never kissed me with such passion," she reflected sadly. "I feel as though I am spying on him, like some sleazy paparazzi."

It was with relief that she heard the door bell, "Oh, Bookie," she said dully, "come in."

Gently, he took the photographs from her hands.

"I've come to make you some breakfast, Beth. Have you been to bed?"

"To bed, but not really to sleep, Bookie. I mean, look at these things!" She essayed a smile. "They look like stills from some porn movie!"

"Oh, come on, Beth. Don't exaggerate. It looks like Purple Passion, but they may have been acting for the camera, you know, hamming it up."

"I don't think I knew Alec at all, Bookie."

"Nonsense!" Bookie said robustly. "You knew the real Alec, Beth, the true Alec! This has the look of infatuation to me, as you say, a B movie."

"No. There's something more between them, I just know it."

"Here – eat some breakfast – go on! I insist. I want to look at these again. Where are they, do you think?"

"Oh, up at The Old Mill, undoubtedly, before it was restored. See the head-pond is overspilling the dam, and in this you can see how decrepit the barn is."

"This must be inside, Beth, don't you think? What a shambles. It certainly needed restoring. Some love nest."

"I'm sure they made it cosy enough," said Beth bitterly. "It looks like summer. I just hope the blackfly were biting."

"They wouldn't dare! Come on, Beth, laugh!" Bookie looked at the photographs again. "You know, I don't believe she ever came into town. You don't need to feel her presence in the apartment at all!"

"Why, that's true!" said Beth, perking up. "Good heavens, look at the time! I have a client to see at eleven! Out of my way, Bookie my love." She gave him a resounding kiss. "I must go and put on my war paint!"

"I don't know why you bother, Beth, you are much prettier as you are."

Beth's heart was almost light as she went upstairs to change, but after Bookie and Boanerges had left, she went back to the kitchen, and stuffing the photographs into their envelope, she slipped them, along with the letter, into her purse, planning to copy them in the office. Her intentions beyond that were unclear.

Kurma, who after all had been very busy since his long trip from India, lazed away the morning, planning to go out later for brunch. Clever and hard working, his energy had been focused largely on his own ambition. He was a young man on whom fortune had smiled. Healthy, loved, clever, good to look at – that already would be enough. Then the generosity of his uncle and the money left to him by his grandfather overwhelmed him,

*I need something to challenge me, I need to pay something back, and now there is another consideration.* He shook his head as though re-ordering his thoughts.

*I can't understand myself, at all. I've only known the girl for two minutes! But she's amazing! No money, no family, and look what she has managed to do! It hasn't made her bitter or sorry for herself. She just gets on with things. It doesn't hurt that she's attractive. What a smile!*

These pleasant thoughts stayed with him throughout an early lunch – not brunch, after all – and accompanied him on a run down to the coast, taking the road through Lower Calder.

*Might as well see the sights while I wait for her to come back from The Old Mill.*

At the thought, he drew to the side of the road, and sat drumming his fingers on the steering wheel.

*I don't like it. She shouldn't have gone there on her own. That woman is capable of absolutely anything. If I go there she will think I am interfering, but no, I don't like it.*

Finding a convenient place to turn, he headed back the way he had come, Stopping in Lower Calder, he found a flower shop, deciding to take Anna a peace offering.

"I would like a really nice bunch," he told the florist, feeling flustered in this unaccustomed environment. "It's to be a peace offering, you see."

The florist smiled knowingly.

"Ah! For a young lady? I would suggest long-stemmed red roses and a nice card."

"Oh no! It's not that at all," blurted Kurma, red and embarrassed. "These are for quite an elderly lady."

"Your mother, perhaps," hinted the florist, "we have such nice cards for mothers too. Maybe some carnations?"

Kurma began to feel desperate.

"Pink roses. Just bunch them. No, not my mother! Just something pretty – no card. I will deliver them myself."

*Well, I made a balls-up of that!* he reflected, driving back to Calderford, *and I don't know why I should apologise – I don't really see what I did wrong! I know, I'll offer to buy The Old Mill back again. She is assuming that is why I went to see her, I think. Oh, who knows? She's just weird, and Mattie shouldn't be there alone with her.*

As he drove he noticed that to the south the sky was dark and threatening.

*Wherever has that sprung from? I'd better switch the radio on. I haven't heard a single weather forecast today.*

"Better make for the high ground," said the local station chattily. " We're going to be dumped on. There'll be a lot of rain and high wind, so if you are at the beach, better make tracks! Now for a rainy day, stay tuned for 'Stormy Weather', a remake by the Bedlam Boys. See if you recognise it!"

*It must be very tiring being so hearty all the time*, thought Kurma. *I wonder how it pays.*

He drove steadily in the direction of Calderford and The Old Mill.

Bookie fussed around in Once read Books, watching nervously for Beth's Elantra.

*I'm getting to know her so well, I wouldn't put it past her to go right out there, and confront Anna with those photographs. It's such a waste of time! It all happened long before she met Alec. Maybe she's still off with her client somewhere, but the weather's changing, it's getting quite dark. If I don't hear from her, maybe I'll run over to The Old Mill, just to see if her car is there.*

This decided, he turned to help the one or two customers in the store.

Mattie's dreams fled with the daylight but, like Kurma, she had overslept.

"Damn!" she muttered. "I wanted an early start. And it is already eight thirty."

By Mattie's standards, this was late indeed, but she too had missed the weather forecast. As a result she rejoiced in the clear blue sky and bright sunshine.

*Good! Just the sort of day I hoped for, no clouds, no rain. I need all the help I can get. Today, I'm going to confront Anna, try to get some answers. before she leaves for the winter. I'm not quite sure how to set about it, but now is the time, before all this shake up at work, and – other things. I just can't endure all the overspill of emotional energy every time Anna feels like it. I will just talk to her. After all, we are both rational beings.*

Even as the thought ran through her head, she denied it. Rational? Anna?

"I shall wear Peri. If anything can charm the truth from her, he can."

It was Bookie who christened the little creature in the amber pendant 'Peri'.

"Peri is Persian for spirit or fairy, you see, Mattie. And how about 'periapt', an amulet? You wear it round your neck, don't you? Oh yes, that little guy should be called Peri," and Peri it had been ever since.

Mattie pondered strategy as she prepared breakfast.

*I must be direct – but not too direct. Forceful – but not rude. I need an ice breaker.*

This preoccupied her as she ate her cereal, then her face cleared.

*I know, I'll take lunch. Something to cook on her barbecue. Salmon. I'll wrap it in foil, with lemon and black pepper. Rolls, a salad. I wonder whether she has charcoal briquettes? Cranberry juice would be good. I don't fancy a mixture of Anna and wine! There will be volatile spirits enough, without that.*

She lingered over her shopping in the Save Easy, stalling for time, carefully selecting local pears, apples, tomatoes, lettuce. The planning helped to ease her tension over the confrontation that was bound to happen.

*It will be like playing with matches near a gas leak*, she thought morosely. *One wrong word, and poof! It's always much safer just to listen, and then play echo. Well, not this time!* Still she dawdled. *I'd better take some butter for the rolls, and salad dressing of course. Oh, good Heavens, look at the time.*

Full of the guilty feeling Anna so often inspired, she hurried out to the car, resolving not to apologise, reassuring herself, *My time is my own, after all.*

As she drove up to The Old Mill. She saw Anna waiting for her in the doorway, her expression unreadable, her stance rigid, uncompromising, her voice icy, accusing. Wearing her fall robe, aglow with gold and all the colours of autumn, she was an imposing figure.

"So you have at last decided to favour me with your presence!"

"Yes, here I am, complete with lunch. Isn't it a lovely day? I thought how nice it would be to use your barbecue. See? Salmon, fruit, rolls, salad, juice! Oh good, you have garden chairs!"

Surprised, Anna stepped aside, allowing Mattie entry into the house. Hands busy, it was easier to talk to an outmanoeuvred and uncommunicative Anna.

"May I use your kitchen? I have charcoal and everything we need. I know you have matches." Mattie glanced at Anna's forbidding face.

"Sid Heddle came in to see us the other day, you see, and he told us that some of your things had gone, so I supposed you were off for the winter."

"Gossip," spluttered Anna angrily, " you have been gossiping with that man! About me!"

"Not at all, Anna, but I wouldn't want you to leave without my wishing you a good trip. Where are the matches? May I use this tray? First, I will start the barbecue. I'm not very good at this, are you? I'll leave the tray here for now."

Chattering nervously to fill the silence, Mattie went out to the barbecue, managing at last to get the briquettes going. Back in the kitchen, she rinsed off her hands.

"There. The barbecue will soon be hot, I'll just prepare the fish and salad, then let's sit down together and talk. There are some things I would like to understand before you leave."

"My! My! Aren't you in a managing mood today? Yes, by all means, let us talk. There are a good many things you fail to understand."

Touching the lustrous black opal nestling duskily at the base of her throat, Anna smiled in tolerant amusement. Understand? The child understood nothing.

"Come, my dear, we will sit in the garden. Bring the tray."

Mattie followed her, hoping that the delicious little lunch would make things easier.

"Now, my child, what is it that you need to know? I'm sure there are many things."

Dismayed by Anna's sardonic smile, Mattie drew a deep breath.

"I have been asking myself how you knew about Matsya, the fish?"

"That's all? My dear child, who doesn't know *that*?"

"Most people, in my opinion, Anna. But lay that aside for now. What I really want to know is, why me? What is it you require of me? I know there is something."

"All the big fuss is about that?"

"No, not quite, Anna, there is something else. When you told me that wonderful story about my abandonment…."

Anna froze, dropping the opal from her hand. Mattie, watching her steadily, continued.

"You described the leaving of the necklace and the note."

"Very beautifully, I thought." Anna's voice was husky.

"Yes, very beautifully. You repeated the words in the note exactly."

"Of course, Matsya, you told me what was said in it."

"No, no, I did not."

There was a brief silence, before Anna replied.

"How curious that I should choose the exact words – they came quite naturally to me. They were all that were needed, after all," was Anna's bland reply.

"And the note ended, 'I will be back!' Do you remember that?"

"What mother would leave her child, not intending to return?"

"Mine," Mattie replied bitterly. "Mine."

"And how do you know that, Mattie? Could she not have considered you to be happier without her? Might she not indeed have been back? How would you know?"

Mattie's expression was stricken, and her head drooped. How could she ever know that? Then, raising her head once more, her eyes met those of the older woman.

"What I need to know, Anna," she spoke quietly. "Is did you come back? Are you my mother?"

There was no answer.

The two women sat facing each other, in silence. As Mattie waited, behind her, to the south, the darkening sky was full of menace.

# CHAPTER 22

All Anna's plots and schemes lay in tatters about her feet. Never taking the straightforward approach herself, this direct question took her aback. Mattie, nervous no longer, waited patiently for her answer, which, when it came, was no answer at all.

"Whatever reason can you possibly have to consider such a thing possible, you silly child?"

"That is your answer?" said Mattie, angrily. "Another question is your *answer*?"

Indeed, the equivocation should have been answer enough, but Anna waved a dismissive hand.

"My child," she said, playing for time, frantic to turn the situation to her advantage. "Life is full of unanswered questions. Many, in fact, are impossible to answer."

"Not this one, Anna. This is simplicity itself. Either you are in fact my mother, or you are not."

"Come, Mattie, that is a truism, is it not? You ask that of anyone, and it would be true!"

As she spoke, a small flurry of wind picked up the paper napkins from the tray. Years of habit sent Mattie scurrying after them and, for a while, the tension was broken. Anna, glad of the distraction, waved the tray away impatiently.

"Oh, do take that tray back into the house, Mattie, and tidy it away. I will wait for you here."

With unthinking obedience, Mattie took the tray back to the kitchen, noting as she went the dark clouds moving in from the south. It made more sense to clear things up, as she always had. Realisation of what was happening came to her as she hung up the tea towel.

"I'm doing it again!" she cried. "Anna always manages, in one way or another, to put me in this position. She always contrives to be the one calling the shots!"

Closing her eyes, she sought within herself the strength and determination that had brought her out to The Old Mill a couple of hours ago.

"I shall make a vow, as Anna does, a promise to myself."

Eyes now wide open, she made her way to the hearth, where the usual small fire glowed like a watching eye. Opening wide her arms, she intoned as she had heard Anna intone, no mockery in her voice.

"I vow that I will get an answer – I believe in myself. I do not believe Anna has the power to hurt me."

The fire shot up, lighting her face, shining in her eyes. Was it a warning? Was it a blessing? The warmth flooded her veins with courage. Watching it subside, Mattie upbraided herself for her weakness, for her fantasies.

"I do not believe in imaginary powers. Belief feeds on itself, power feeds on credulity. Hasn't Foster Harrington suggested that very thing?"

Holding her hands out to the fire, now glowing sedately, she stood reflectively for a moment, before returning to the garden. Anna was no longer there, After some minutes she emerged from the barn, her self-assurance fully restored, her plans falling into place once more.

"There," she said contentedly. Now, I am willing to indulge your little fancies."

"Oh, come off it, Anna!" said Mattie angrily. "For three months now you have been playing a cat and mouse game with me. You know it, and now so do I. If ever I began to show independence from you, out comes your paw. It has nothing to do with furniture, I realise that now. There is something more, some tie or bond, a connection I recognise now, but that you refuse to acknowledge. That is the only reason for me to be here. Tell me what it is."

Flinging her arms wide, in a gesture such as Anna herself might make, Mattie rose, impelled by a surge of desperate energy. Standing in front of Anna, eyes wide and compelling, face flushed and purposeful, she was transformed from the quiet 'sepia print' Beth first knew. Anna, looking at her in amazement, uncertain of what might come next, sat immobile. The intensity of the moment far exceeded the small confrontation over their gifts. At last, when Anna spoke, she sounded small, petulant.

"You refused my gifts."

"We *exchanged* gifts that day, Anna. What greater gift are you withholding from me, now? What is it you know?" Involuntarily Mattie's hand closed on Peri, her little keeper of secrets, her talisman.

"Alexander," whispered Anna. "Alexander."

"I don't understand you."

"That is how he spoke," Anna's voice faltered. "I knew him, Alexander, your father."

Mattie's heart leapt, before recalling all she had been told by Kendrick Gibson.

"How could you know? No one knew. He didn't know that himself."

Anna laughed contemptuously, her fears evaporating.

"Oh no, you silly child. *I* said that, remember? Was my story so convincing? Is your belief in me so great? If you believe me in this, Mattie, why not believe all I tell you now? Yes, I have the powers you so fear – Yes, I am immortal – Yes, I gave you one life, no matter how, and yes, I can offer you life forever! Do you believe this? Do you know me at all? Did I know your father? Was he Alexander?"

All the time she was speaking, she prowled around Mattie's chair. "Believe in me, Mattie. I can give you such powers as mine, riches beyond your imaginings! I will invest you with my immortality. Now, Mattie, now! Now it is time! Say it! 'I believe you, Anna. Yes, I will follow, you.'"

Halting, she confronted Mattie, her face implacable, her voice compelling.

"Say it, Mattie. See what I offer you in return for your belief."

Now there was no sun in the sky. Heavy clouds lowered threateningly, behind the trees. The water in Kingfisher Creek ran dark.

"No," whispered Mattie, dully. "I don't want to believe any of it. No, I won't. I can't." Her voice trailed away, weakening with each passing moment.

Behind her a car door slammed, breaking the spell that Anna had woven.

"I hope I'm not intruding," called Beth, "but I have something to show you."

# CHAPTER 23

When Kurma reached Calderford, he decided to go first to Mattie's apartment.

*It's no good tooling off to The Old Mill if Mattie's already home*, he reasoned. *Why put the cat among the pigeons?* Adding, as he recalled the time spent with Anna, *Though in this case, which would be cat and which the pigeon?*

At Once Read Books he found Bookie still dodging backwards and forwards to his window, peering this way and that. His greeting to Kurma was warm.

"Well, thank goodness you're here! Maybe you know where Beth and Mattie are?"

"Bookie, I was hoping you could tell me! I know Mattie set off to see that fearsome woman at The Old Mill. Is she a dime or two short of the dollar, Bookie? Anna I mean, of course. I couldn't make head or tail of her."

"I wouldn't worry about it, if I were you, Kurma. Mattie has always come home before! I'm more worried about Beth, truth to tell. We found some photographs of Alec, her late husband, with someone who is unmistakably Anna. I wouldn't put it past her to go rushing down there to find out for certain. Mind you, she may be going quietly about her business somewhere. I certainly don't want to stir anything up by hot footing it out to The Old Mill! No use provoking a storm in a teacup. The weather is bad enough without that."

"What's the latest on that front? No pun intended."

"Oh, let's hope they aren't talking about one of those weather bombs. That's what they call them in the Maritimes."

"A *weather bomb*?"

"A system moves in from the west, then all that warm air, full of piss and vinegar, comes steaming up from the south, then pow! It gets pounded by a cold front from the north and all that energy bursts out in a super storm. Wind, buckets of rain, you name it. Hangs around for a day or two. This probably wont be that bad, but it looks like a doozer."

Kurma joined Bookie on his window watch, concern showing in his troubled expression.

"I'll wait another hour, then I'm going to find Mattie, Bookie, want to join me?"

"You bet. We'll take Boanerges. That old van is used to this sort of thing. Meanwhile, why don't you look around here? You may find this building suitable for your office. There at the back is the Save Easy, but they are planning a bigger store further out. The old store would hold your salvaged material, and be handy to your office, too. Lots of parking space."

Kurma looked at Bookie with growing respect.

"But what would you do with your bookstore, if we decided on that?"

"Move over to Beth's place," said Bookie, promptly. "Take Emily Hiltz's old place, plus the space upstairs for the archival stuff. You know, if this succeeds, we will be creating all sorts of opportunities for the local people. It would just about save this little town."

"We could initiate a course in the local community college! One or two years. Draughtsmen – 'draughts persons', I should say." They giggled conspiratorially, all men together. "You know, why stop there? We could involve landscape gardeners, decorators, craftspeople."

In their enthusiasm, they failed to notice how time was slipping by, until Kurma remarked, "Of course, you have more space upstairs, haven't you?" Suddenly he realised he was talking about Mattie's apartment, but where was Mattie?

"I think it's time we went to look for those two. I'll park my little rental car at the back. Where's Boanerges?"

Bookie, putting up a "Closed " sign, in the window, led the way. Kurma's pink roses lay forgotten on the backseat of his rental car.

At the sound of Beth's voice, Mattie sprang to her feet as though startled from a dream, instantly alert.

"What is it, Beth? Have I forgotten an appointment?"

"Not you, Mattie, I have something to show to Miss Waters."

Going over to the barbecue, Beth put copies of the photographs on to the table, stacking them carefully, then raising her eyes to the older woman. Anna, full of apprehension, did not even glance down at the table, memories of the past flooding her mind.

"Everyone has games to play this afternoon," she said icily. "Everyone, it seems, is full of questions." What power, what trickster, had contrived this moment – Kurma?

She had been so near to bending Mattie to her will, so near to enticing her. Should she lose her self-control now, giving vent to her rage, to her jealousy of this woman, then Mattie would be lost to her. Beth's voice broke into her thoughts.

"Those are photographs of Alec, my late husband. They were taken at a time before I knew him. Look at them closely, Anna, for I am sure that the woman is you. Do you remember them?"

"I really have no wish to see any of these. Of what possible interest could they be to me?"

Seizing the little pile from the table, she threw them into the barbecue, which immediately died down, leaving the photographs unburned. Gingerly, Beth retrieved them.

"I can understand your impulse to do that, Anna, but I have plenty more copies. There are also," she said levelly, "some letters. I have them here in my pocket."

Anna held out her imperious hand, urged by the desire to destroy the photographs, the letters, the woman herself. Two things intervened. Torrential rain started to fall, at the same moment as Bookie and Kurma drove into the driveway.

"Trouble," said Bookie, "I can smell it and I don't just mean the storm. Hello!" he called, raising his voice. "We have come to see if you are all right. The weather is very bad and there may be flooding."

Anna looked at him dismissively, until her eye fell on Kurma. He had come again.

"Perhaps we could go inside, Miss Waters?" Kurma suggested politely. "I had better just check on the dam, first. You go ahead." He added firmly.

Immediately a new scheme formed in Anna's head.

*Let it flood*, she thought, forgetful of her struggle in the creek. *When have I ever been afraid of water? I Anahita, Anaista?*

"Why yes," she said civilly. "By all means let us celebrate this little gathering. I *do* apologise to you, Mrs. Oxner," with heavy sarcasm. "Of course I will be happy to study your little snapshots."

Once inside, in haste before Kurma should return, she took up the lustral goblet.

"Look!" she cried dramatically. "We will have a toast. A loving cup!"

Hurrying to the kitchen, she ran fresh water into the goblet. She took from her pocket the dark jar of dried amanita, tipping a little of the powder into her goblet, she stirred briskly, adding cranberry juice to mask the discolouration. Then, taking off the pendant, she dropped the black opal into the powerful brew, glowing darkly red through the translucency of the lustral cup.

"Let them drink it! Let it flood! What care I? Ormazd has failed me!"

She raised the shining goblet. "To Ahriman," she whispered.

Returning to the living room, she found Beth, Bookie and Mattie, poring over the photographs. Mattie's wide eyes told of her mixed emotions; her amazement, her fear of what it meant to be Anna's child, hope that in Alec she had found her father, that Anna was capable of love. Impulsively she put an arm around Beth's shoulders, drawing her close. Anna, seeing all this with growing dismay, unwillingly put down the goblet, to join the group at the table. As she studied the pictures, memories of that long-ago summer came flooding back. This, to her mind, was her husband, Beth a usurper.

"Alexander," she murmured huskily. "Alexander."

"Alec," said Beth.

Confused, Anna shook her head in angry denial. "No, not I. You are mistaken."

The two women studied each other, Mattie looking from one to the other.

"That woman gave him what I couldn't give him," said Beth softly.

"And you," said Anna unwillingly, "healed where there was hurt. We should all drink to that!"

At that moment, Kurma came in soaking wet.

"It's like a monsoon! I'm not sure the dam will hold. The creek is washing away the upper structure, Miss Waters, I think we should leave.

"But before we do, a toast!" said Anna. "To old friends rediscovered."

She held the goblet out to the fire, which flared angrily. Turning to Mattie, she added softly, so that only Mattie could hear.

"To my daughter, Matsya."

Unprepared for the look of joy, of a love so undeserved, on Mattie's face, Anna's will faltered. Was this at last the test she had so often imagined?

"No," she said, "Mattie and I will stem the flood. Come!"

Horrified, Bookie, Kurma and Beth, all took a step forward, hands outstretched. But as Mattie had seen before, all movement was arrested. There was no sun to dazzle her eyes now. All, except Anna, Mattie herself, and the leaping fire, remained still. Mesmerised, she held out her hand to this woman who claimed to be her mother. Anna, holding aloft the goblet, clasped Mattie's outstretched hand, and together they went out into the storm.

# CHAPTER 24

Time had collapsed on itself, sucking in all movement, all sound. Only Anna, bearing the goblet, and Mattie, whose hand she held, had any presence. They were following a path between walls of glistening droplets, rainbow arched, opening before them without motion, motionlessly closing behind. All they could hear were their own soft footfalls on the grass, their own hushed breathing, no purling of running water, no rustle of leaves. Approaching the barbecue, they could see that it, too, burned cheerily with a liveliness unnatural to charcoal. Anna turned her face towards the creek, releasing Mattie's hand. She raised both arms, holding the goblet aloft.

"Oh Alkuon! Little Halcyon Bird from the ancient days! Come, come to our waters! Make your nest of fish bones, set it afloat! Charm the winds and waves into calm! It is I who summon you! I, Anahita Anaista, Daeva of Water!" Like a figure on an antique urn she stood, waiting.

"See! He comes!" she cried, joyfully

But Mattie could see nothing but the flaring coals. Anna set the goblet on the table by the fire.

"Now, we shall talk," she said. "But first, if you are to hear and understand what I have to say, you must take one small sip from the cup, one very small sip, as shall I."

Dazed, Mattie sank into a chair, reaching for the goblet, gazing trustfully into the eyes of her newfound mother.

"Wait," cried Anna, surrendering all hope of using Mattie for her own freedom. "Wait! What need have we of this, you and I?"

Snatching back the goblet, spilling some of the contents, she set it down on the table. Carefully she lifted out the pendant, which hung there like a dark eye, weeping tears of blood.

"Help me, Ormazd! Mithras, help me!" cried Anna.

Gently she swung the pendant to and fro over the hot coals, flame leaping up to lick greedily around it, burning away the ominous drops.

"Purified," murmured Anna, removing it from the flames, continuing to swing it back and forth before Mattie's dazzled eyes. Cooling in the mist of rainbow light, the dark opal glowed with a radiant sheen, full of promise, of hope. Smiling serenely, Anna clasped it round Mattie's throat.

"Now, Matsya, it is filled only with the good omens of love," she said gently, "and we are ready, at last. Listen well, for we speak only from my mind to yours, and yours to mine."

"What if I fail to understand?"

"You will hear all of it, understand some of it, and thereafter bury it deep in your primal brain, where much will be lost. First, we must journey together."

Time meaningless and space negated, they journeyed back to the infant Earth, tumultuous, cloud-covered. They saw the whirling particles as it took shape, the thick atmosphere, erupting volcanoes, heavy clouds, deluges of rain. They saw into the depths of the flooding waters, where life was beginning, Archia, Methagens. They watched as the land mass emerged, split asunder and drifted apart. Slow tides of ice, growing and shrinking, around the poles. Mighty currents and floods washed out new landscapes shifting, changing – forests, deserts, plains, water, forming new patterns, a new mosaic.

Mattie, exhilarated, terrified, exhausted, quite literally in no time at all, viewed the history of the Earth.

"We shall move closer yet, Matsya."

"Now I see creatures, Anna, animals. Strange, wonderful creatures, long since dead."

As she watched, entranced, the whole scene was obliterated. A monstrous asteroid impacted the Earth's surface. Clouds of particles filled the air, obscured the sun. Could any life survive?"

"It must," gasped Mattie, "for we are here."

Anna smiled.

"Let us move a little closer," said Anna.

Now Mattie could see small, ant-like figures, scurrying wherever there was water, busily building little structures, tilling the land.

"People," sighed Mattie. "People at last."

"Ah, such people, Matsya! Such people, when the world was young! They thought, as people always think, that the world they knew would last forever. But watch."

"Oh no!" cried Mattie, horrified as the waters of the Atlantic broke through the mountain barrier into the inland plain, sweeping away all in its path, until a vast sea lay in the heart of the land.

"All those people drowned?"

"Their homes, their places of worship, their farms, Matsya. Salt in my clear fresh springs!"

"*You* were there?" asked Mattie, wonderingly.

"I am wherever water is, wherever streams flow, wherever I wish to be. Do you believe it? Do you believe I was there, Matsya?"

Closer they went, as though falling, falling, until they drew near to the old land at the far eastern end of the Mediterranean Sea.

"But this is not as it is now!"

"No, Matsya, it is not as it is now. See!"

A mighty explosion rocked the Earth's surface, shattering the land, inundating it with seawater. Where there had been mountains and fields, there were now scattered islands.

"Santorini, Matsya, the volcano that reshaped the old world, ending the Cretan Empire, threatening my shrines, defiling my clear water with salt."

Anna's eyes flashed angrily.

"Then the people turned to me more reverently, to me, Anahita Anaista, Daeva of Water! Soon, our journey will be over."

Now Mattie could see the people clearly. She could see the shrines, the temples. She could see Anna.

The people knelt to her, they decorated her with garlands of flowers, sang songs, danced, performing elaborate rituals. Anna sat in a great chair, her lustral goblet in her hand, rewarding, punishing, laughing, careless. Generation after generation, came and went. Gradually the ceremonies grew less, the garlands shrivelled, the songs were forgotten. Now it was the people who were laughing, pointing, reviling, until Anna, neglected and bitter, grew unforgiving.

"They fouled the streams, cut the trees, grazed the land. See, Mattie, how the beautiful lakes dry, the streams silt up; the green earth turns to desert! My anger made me harsh."

The vision ended

Anna spoke aloud.

"Once, Matsya, they brought their pleas to me. I was revered. But there were so many, for thousands of years, until I grew weary of their constant demands. Even so, I was Daeva of Water. I still had the power to help had they but heeded me. Even here, where the world is new, the priceless gift of lakes and streams are squandered, and I am weary."

She paused. Mattie remaining silent. Anna continued, her voice burdened with melancholy

"Their belief was placed elsewhere. There was only Ormazd, the All-Seeing eye. The One Spirit, the Great light. Mithras he kept, the God of Fire, adding that light to his own."

"And you?" asked Mattie softly.

"A petty little Goddess," said Anna bitterly. "Reviled as evil, a mere instrument of the adversary, Ahriman."

"And then?"

"I came to the New World, where there is still hope, where water is still, in some few places, clear and pure. And here I met Alexander."

"My father."

"Yes, your father. In my heart he was my husband. Strong, good, gentle. I felt a passion I had never known." She fell silent, then added bitterly, "I, the great Anahita! I visited on him all my anger and grief, and still he loved me. And I? My lesson only half learned, I left him. He never knew I bore his child, the child I would need, and I have always felt ill will towards the woman who might take my place."

"And so, what of that child?" asked Mattie sadly.

"What knew I of life, I who could never die? I left you as I have told you, as you know, to be raised for me."

"But I have never known the day of my birth, Anna, never."

Anna, her voice filled with regret, whispered sorrowfully.

"It was the sixteenth day of February, the year 1976. A cold day, as unforgiving as my heart."

Mattie, studying her mother's face, asked stoically, "And what was it you expected from me, Anna?"

"That you would take my place! Free me from the endless ages!" Her voice broke. "To be human, Matsya, to die."

As Mattie shrank away from her, Anna smiled at her, her face transformed.

"Don't be afraid, Matsya, for you have completed the lesson Alexander began. You could still free me, but you yourself must find the way. Hold my hand, Matsya. Do you believe?"

Unwillingly at first, Mattie grasped Anna's hands. Between them flowed a message, this time not from the mind but from the heart. Slowly Mattie shook her head.

"Not as those ancient people believed, as you believed, no. That time is past. Perhaps you need to surrender your own belief, but we must each of us decide for ourselves what is to be believed, what is true."

Anna's hands tightened as though in pain. Mattie looked steadily into her eyes.

"Don't you see, Anna, that we can only free ourselves?" said Mattie softly. "We each have our own imaginings to explain the world we live in, and they have as wide a spectrum as the rainbow around us, and as little substance."

Here she paused, pressing her mother's hands warmly.

"But Anna, insofar as to believe means to cherish and to trust, then yes, Anna, I believe you. You are beloved."

"Then come with me to the water's edge, Matsya, my little fish."

Together they stood by Kingfisher Creek.

"A libation," said Anna, pouring most of the dark red draft into the water, like sacrificial blood.

Immediately the spell was broken.

Mattie gasped, for the storm had gone.

"Look, Anna, the sky is clearing, the rain has stopped. Whatever can have happened? See! There is a kingfisher skimming over the water."

Anna watched the blue and white of the kingfisher flashing in the sunlight.

"Thank you, Alkuon, little halcyon bird. Thank you," she said.

Together, Anna's arm around Mattie's shoulders, they walked slowly back to The Old Mill

# CHAPTER 25

Following Anna into the room, Mattie stopped in dismay.

"Oh no!" she breathed. "My friends! What have we done?"

She saw their reaching hands, the consternation on their faces, their helplessness, and took a step towards them.

"Wait," Anna said calmly. "All will be well!"

"Bookie? Beth?"

Anna nodded.

"And Kurma – what about Kurma?"

"Oh!," said her mother slowly, searching her daughter's face. "Yes, Kurma is quite unaware."

"Of what? He isn't who – or what – you think he is," Mattie insisted. "He doesn't understand you, Anna. Kurma Deulkar is only his father's *friend*, not his brother. They are not blood-related at all."

They confronted each other as they had before, each staring the other in the eye.

"A very close friend indeed Mattie – and of his friend's wife too, a very close friend."

Waiting, in vain, for some reaction from Mattie, she shrugged.

"As I said, he is quite unaware. Come! We will welcome your friends back."

Moving over to the hearth, she raised her goblet as a pledge, then dropped it to the floor, spilling the rest of the crimson contents on the rug.

"There!" she cried gaily to the silent room. "It did not break! No harm done. No need for such concern. And see!" she went on while the others looked about them, in confusion. "There's sunshine coming through the window. The storm has passed as suddenly as it came! Now, do let me look at those photographs again, more carefully. I am so sorry for being ungracious before."

Anna actually apologising drew everyone's attention, and they collected their scattered wits. Briefly her eyes fastened on Kurma, drawing his gaze deep into her own. Seeing there a fleeting consciousness, a sudden recognition, she turned away, satisfied.

"Why not collect them up, Kurma, and we will all study them."

Unwillingly he picked them up, passing them slowly from his hands to Anna's, feeling like a conspirator as she took them from him, thanking him extravagantly.

"Come," she said, spreading them once more on the table.

*Like a conjurer*, thought Mattie, uneasily.

Gathering round the table they looked repeatedly from the photographs to Anna's non-committal face

"How odd," said Bookie at last. "I don't think this is Anna, after all. The eyes look different. The cheek bones not so high."

They looked repeatedly from the photographs to Anna's non-committal face, and back to the photographs. Incredulous, Beth checked again and again, but it was true, there was a strong resemblance, but no more than that.

"It's as though they have changed," she gasped, taking the originals from her pocket, looking them over carefully. "Tell me, Anna, truthfully, is this woman you?"

Anna looked away, deliberating, her supple mind considering the repercussions of her reply. To her the woman in the photographs was dead. What was now the truth? Were truth, faith and loyalty not rooted in the same soil? Mattie held her breath.

Anna turned to Beth, smiling ruefully.

"I will answer you faithfully, Beth, as you deserve. I recognise the resemblance, which is of no surprise to me, for the blood that ran in her veins runs in mine."

"You say ran. Is this your sister? Is she dead?"

"It is because of her death that I am here. Undine – or Onde – is dead. Blood ties are very strong, and for far too long I tolerated her capriciousness and cruelty – for far, far, too long."

Her voice trailed away, the truth, as she saw it, intact. Then she turned to Mattie, her face transfigured.

"But for all that, Matsya, she never forgot you, never! I can assure you of that."

"So why have you come here now?" Beth persisted. "What are your intentions?"

"My last act on Undine's behalf. I have come to find her child, to give her a blessing and to be sure she receives her legacy."

Spreading her hands as though asking for forgiveness, she turned from one to the other.

"I needed proof – and proof I have found. Now I can complete my task."

Beth looked at her doubtfully.

"We thought–" she said haltingly, "that is, Mattie thought, she feared–"

Kurma broke in.

"You have caused us all a great deal of anxiety," he said angrily. "We thought you were Mattie's mother, and that you were treating her shamefully."

"Does it matter?" Mattie asked them. "I know now that Alec was my father. Does the rest of it matter now?"

Anna was watching Kurma.

"And you, Kurma," she asked silkily. "What do you believe?"

Her bland smile was tinged with mockery, and she saw his expression change from anger to confusion.

"Shall I tell you, Kurma, what I believe of you? Oh! the games we play with ourselves! But let me get on with my business."

From a deep pocket in her splendid robe, she took out the deed to The Old Mill.

"I am empowered," she smiled ruefully at her choice of word, "to hand over the property to Mattie before I leave. I hope you will, all of you, bear witness."

Signing it with her customary flourish, she passed the document from hand to hand, giving it at last to a stupefied Mattie.

"There is no need to buy The Old Mill back now, is there, Kurma?" said Anna, enjoying his discomfiture. "I won't be disturbing you anymore."

As each in turn signed – Bookie reading it through carefully first – she gave them a brief hug.

"Thank you. Now I must ask you to excuse me for I am leaving very soon – as no doubt the redoubtable Sid Heddle has already told you. I still have a great deal to do."

Reconciled but unappeased, Beth gathered up the photographs warily. Once again she felt as though, somehow, she had been outmanoeuvred.

"Well, Anna," she said, striving for graciousness. "You have at least made our lives very interesting. I wish you well for your journey – coming, Bookie?"

As they made for the door, Kurma lingered uncertainly.

"Mattie?" he asked, diffidently.

"Later," she said firmly. "I would like to help Anna with the packing. But I will see you out to Boanerges."

As she led the way to the door, Kurma lagged behind, giving Anna a curious half-salute, an acknowledgement of something as yet beyond his understanding.

She watched them leave, then sank, exhausted, into her Great Chair.

Feeling as though released from a great restriction, she was near to sleep.

*Why!* she thought happily, *I feel – old.*

Shaking off her lassitude, she rose as Mattie came back to her.

"Come," she said. "Now you are able to accept my gifts, the ones I bought for you."

Upstairs, standing by the jewel case, Mattie raised her hands in protest.

"I wish for nothing further, Anna."

"Just the pendants, Matsya, and the signet ring. In accepting the amber you chose well. It is considered protection from witchcraft – even from the Water Witch." she added slyly. "Now, here is the amethyst, your birth stone, symbol of sobriety, my levelheaded child, then the peridot, just because I thought you would like it. The opal you wear, now brings only hope."

"So I was right, Anna. These are not as old as the other jewellery, and I do like them very much."

"Now the signet ring to go with the pendant I left to guard you, all those years ago."

She slipped the signet ring on Mattie's finger, saying softly, "My little fish, use it wisely."

"Why is my name *Matsya*, Anna? Why did you call me that?

"Come with me to the fireplace, Matsya. We will sit there together for a while."

Anna sat in her Great Chair, Mattie on the stained rug. The small fire burned serenely.

"In a way I can see why you would choose to call me 'a little fish', you, Daeva of Water; I, your daughter."

As Mattie said this so matter-of-factly, with no hesitation, Anna's wonderful eyes shone with happiness.

"Until you freed me, Matsya, by your love, I feared I would live forever, disrespected, unloved, and with diminishing powers. But there in Brahma's world, the world of Vishnu, I thought a Daeva might have a place. I sought his protection, I called you Matsya."

"Protection for me, Anna?"

"Matsya, I thought only of myself. I planned to use you, as I have said. Vishnu the preserver could protect me through you. I deserved no respect, as you can see."

"And now?"

"I need no other protection, my child, than your love, a love so ill deserved."

"Oh Anna," Mattie laughed gleefully, "see what has happened? Because of you, I met Kurma! And Kurma is–"

Anna interrupted, "Quite unaware of the part he has played! And yet – there is a pattern."

In silence they stared into the heart of the fire.

"Then it is done," said Anna. "I will not offer you the robe, though it would suit you so well. Why burden you? The ancient jewels, the silver, the lustral cup, I will disperse. Let them be discovered after my death, some here, some there. Treasure Trove."

"Shall you keep the cranberry glass jug?"

"Oh yes, My Very Dear, until I die."

She laid her hand on Mattie's shoulder.

"Must you go?" asked Mattie sadly.

"I must."

"Will I see you again?"

"No, Matsya, no, my dear."

"But–"

"No, Matsya, my dear, dear, child, but this I promise you. You shall stay in my heart, and I in yours. I like your new family, Bookie, Beth. She, after all, knew Alexander's love, and he knew hers." This she said quite without rancour. "You will be happy with them. And through the years, perhaps you will forget."

"I never, never could forget you, Anna."

Their embrace had a finality recognised by both.

On the way back to Calderford, Mattie drew to the side of the road, exhausted by the conflicting emotions of the long day.

*I can't meet the others just yet. It's too soon. I'm not ready. I need – I need–.*

Uncertain what that might be, she leaned on the iron struts of the bridge over Kingfisher Creek.

"Little Halcyon Bird," she murmured. "I need you to calm me."

She watched the turbulent water, swollen by the storm, tumbling to join the Calder's rush to the sea.

*Round and round,* she thought dreamily. *The river, the sea, the clouds, the rain, the river, the sea....*

Turning, she looked upstream to The Old Mill, where her mother was preparing to leave.

"Belefan – believed, belieben – beloved," she whispered, taking out the pendants, swinging them in the sunlight.

"What is left to me of *you,* Anna, when you are gone? What are these and The Old Mill, after all?"

Listlessly, she turned the signet ring on her finger, thinking of her mother, mesmerised by the flow of water.

"Anahita," she murmured. "Anaista, Water Witch, Mother."

All at once her pulses quickened, as though the powerful surge of the creek ran in her veins, a vitality straightening her back and brightening her eyes, as her mother's reassurance streamed down to her, bringing a last blessing of strength and love and understanding.

"Yes!" cried Mattie, suddenly full of hope. "Yes, I'm ready now, whatever happens! Perhaps Kurma's 'uncle' *is* his father. Maybe he will have his own dilemma, his own choices to make."

Going slowly to her car, she sat for a while, her expression enigmatic, her eyes full of an ancient wisdom.

"Such children as we will have!" she thought exultantly. "Such possibilities."

This last thought filling her with happiness, she started to hum, and then to sing.

Soon, as Anna had foreseen, memories of the time they had spent together throughout the summer would dim. Revisited frequently, their edges would be smoothed, the patina of long usage making them comfortable and familiar. But her mother's blood flowed steadily through her, and wherever there was water, Mattie always felt the presence of the strange woman she had come to know as mother, illusive and illusory as the water itself.

# GLOSSARY

**Ahriman** – The embodiment of Evil in Zarathustraism.

**Ahuru Mazdao (Ahura the Wise, also called Ormazd)** – The embodiment of Good in Zarathustraism, acting by rules rather than by caprice.

**Alkuon, the Halcyon bird** – When Ceyx drowned on his way to an oracle, his wife Alcyone threw herself into the sea. The Gods changed them into birds. Their nest of bones is on the sea, and while the eggs are hatching, there will be calm weather – halcyon days. The kingfisher is associated with the Halcyon bird.

**Aryan religion** – Anciently followed in the region that became Persia, it was polytheistic and anthropomorphic – i.e. there were many half-mortal Gods and Goddesses (Daevas).

**Avatar** – The manifestation of a God or released soul in Hindu mythology

**Brahma** – In Hindu mythology, the Creator, Brahma, Vishnu the Preserver, and Siva the Destroyer form the Hindu Triad.

**Daeva** – Aryan demi-god or demi-goddess.

**Ki-din-nu (In Greek, Cidenas)** – 343 BC. Babylonian astronomer. He recorded the longitude of the stars.

**Heliocentric** – Centred by the sun.

**Hipparchus** – 146-127 BC. Greek astronomer. Extended the work of Ki-din-nu, forming the theory of the precession of the stars.

**Lustral** – Adjective, meaning used in a purification ceremony. From lustrum, Roman purification ceremony after 5-yearly census.

**Mithras (or Mitra)** – Aryan God of fire and light.

**Mitochondria** – Specialised structure found in cells containing genetic material

**Spiracle** – External breathing opening in insects, whales and some fish.

**Stigma** – In addition to being a distinguishing mark, often of disgrace, it is also an insect's spiracle.

**Xenophanes** – 6th century BC. Founder of the Eleatic school of philosophy, later refined by Parminedes. He taught that there is one unifying principle.

**Zarathustra (in Old Persian Zardeshi, in Greek Zoroaster)** – Founder of the wisdom of the Magi (See above Ahriman and Ahura). He relegated all Daevas to the evil Ahriman, except for Mithras, whose light he added to his own. During life the power of Ormazd is limited by Ahriman, but after death everyone is judged by Ormazd.